PRIDE AND THE PENALTY BOX

A HOCKEY ROMANCE

PHEBE POWERS

For Philip, who only wins when I let him.
And for me.

CHAPTER 1
HOOKED

A PUCK SHOT across the ice in a blur, narrowly missing the tip of Ally's blade. She swiveled around. "Are you *trying* to hit me?"

Another puck followed the first, this one flying through the air. There was a dull thud as the second puck connected with her shin guard. "Ow!"

"Get your head out of the clouds, Bryant." Ally's captain, Lauren 'Wren' Johnson, pulled a third puck out of the small pile beside her. She dragged it back and forth across the ice, taking aim. "Besides, I heard that hit plastic. Can't have hurt that much."

Ally rolled her eyes but took off toward the rest of the team, who were skating warm up laps around the face-off circles in the defensive end. Wren had already completed her cardio and was continuing to prep their goalie, Matt, now that Ally had removed herself from the line of fire.

Shaking her head at her captain's unorthodox but effective tactics, Ally slid into formation beside her fellow wing, Madison. They'd been two of the first on the team when Wren took it over a couple years back and their friendship had been fairly quick to form: they'd gone from exchanging text messages about practice times to binging adaptations of classic novels together on Ally's couch in a matter of weeks.

Madison watched those movies for the men in tight breeches, but Ally actually cared about the accuracy of the adaptation. What could she say? She was that kind of a nerd. It had started with her first library card, aged six, and continued all the way through high school, after which she'd found herself happily ensconced in the undergraduate English department at Boston University.

"How's your leg?" Madison slowed slightly to accommodate Ally, who was still warming up.

"What?"

Madison laughed. "Wren was right. Clearly it can't have hurt that badly, if you've already forgotten about it."

Ally grimaced, glancing down at her unscathed shin. It sort of hurt—if she thought about it. "Wren's wristshot is like the speed of light."

"Yeah, but her slapshot's faster."

"I'm surprised there aren't more physicists at our games," Ally grumbled, still thinking about her shin. "Seriously, that was mean."

"It was earned and I seriously doubt it still hurts," Madison countered. "Besides, you were literally in the crease. How is anyone supposed to get a shot past you when you're as deep in the net as the other team's goalie?"

Ally scoffed. "It's my job to be aggressive. They call us the offensive line for a reason."

"Yeah, yeah. But when Wren's got five minutes to warm up Matt?"

"I was helping!"

"Sure. And when you're so deep in the crease, their D starts a fight?"

"That's half the fun!"

"Maybe, but you know where it leads."

"To victory?"

"To yet another penalty." Madison had never been quite so hot on the chase as Ally, but then again, she never got so angry when thwarted, either. Madison was a peacemaker, whereas Ally had a temper.

Sighing, Ally switched the subject. "How's Hardit?" Madison's boyfriend watched most of their games, one of many demonstrations of his devotion to her.

Madison smiled as they crossed the hash marks for the umpteenth time, happy to let go of their little argument. "He's swell."

Ally laughed. "What is this, the 19th century? 'Swell?'"

"You're the one who's obsessed with old books, babe. I'm surprised you don't talk like an Austen character."

"I'm more of a Brontë *babe*, myself," Ally retorted. Then she pouted. "I thought you knew that about me."

"I know too much about you," Madison sighed fondly over the sound of their skates cutting up the ice. "Any word on the new guy joining us tonight?"

Ally cocked her head even as she shook it. "New guy? This is the first I've heard of him." Wren was supposed to tell her stuff like this, seeing as Ally was her assistant captain. She frowned. "Why is he jumping in on a game day? Why not wait until practice, so we can see how he plays?"

"It's not like we can say no to him. You know Wren's rule: if you can pay, you can play." The fees weren't much and went toward custom jerseys, matching socks, and ice time. Any leftovers were used for a scholarship fund, for those who could play but not pay. "Plus, according to Skye he already took the concussion baseline test. So he's cleared."

"Still, wouldn't it have made more sense to wait? What if he sucks?"

Madison chuckled as they made a tight turn. "Oh, he doesn't suck. No way Wren would have let him on tonight's line up if he weren't golden. Besides, cap says he played in college. Like you."

"Club level?"

"Nah," Madison answered, pulling ahead to close another circuit. "The real deal."

Ally scoffed, projecting so Madison could still hear her. "Well, first of all, screw you. Club hockey is just as legitimate as D1 or whatever. It's far more fun, second of all. And third, as I've just pointed out, I didn't play on the school team, I skated club, so clearly he didn't play in college 'just like me.'"

Madison groaned. "I didn't say '*just* like you,' I said '*like* you.' As in, kind of like you. Not half so sensitive about his college hockey career, however, if I had to guess."

"Whatever." Ally forced herself to let it go, lest she make a mountain out of a mole hill. As was her wont. She was an argumentative person by nature, although nurture had had a look in—her parents weren't the most peaceful pair. "Where's he coming from?"

"Up north."

"Like, Connecticut? Massachusetts? Or further?"

"I dunno," Madison huffed, sounding slightly winded. She slowed so that she was level with Ally. "Isn't the Northeast pretty much all the same?"

"As a former Bostonian myself," Ally began, "I strenuously object to your—"

Madison's laughter drowned out Ally's protest. "You were a 'Bostonian' for four years, Ally. Before that, you were just another kid from the suburbs."

"Long Island is *not* the suburbs. Westchester, on the other hand..." They'd both grown up about forty-five minutes outside of New York City, in somewhat opposite directions. It could have been the basis for a regional rivalry, if Ally hadn't immediately liked Madison as much as she did.

Ignoring the argument Ally was attempting to start, Madison added, "I do think Wren said Boston, however."

"Boston?" Ally twisted her lips thoughtfully. "And he played in college? God, I hope he isn't—"

"Look! I think that's him." Madison stuck out her arm as she stopped skating, forcing her teammate to come to sudden halt.

Catching her balance, Ally squinted in the direction Madison was pointing. A tall skater in a maroon jersey decorated with a large 'H' had stepped smoothly onto the ice, hitting his stride without hesitation.

"—just another asshole who went to Harvard," Ally finished dryly.

Ted pushed off the thick sheets of plastic, leaving the boards behind. As he cut a path across the ice in the direction of the home bench, he inhaled two lungfuls of icy air. It carried the scent of countless drops of sweat that had dried into his gear over the years.

Sure, he stank a little, but right now the familiar smell soothed him. And he didn't want his new teammates to see how nervous he was, especially not since his first day happened to be a game day. He'd been eager to get out there, and his new captain had been impressed by his extensive experience, despite his recent drought.

Ted's right skate dug into the ice, and then his left, as he increased his speed. It felt good to be back in a rink after a year without so much as a free skate—he'd been unable to play during his second year of business school because he'd been working in addition to his studies.

"You must be the new center," a tall, broad shouldered woman called out to him. She was skating over from the far blue line, where she'd evidently been warming up the goalie.

He noted the C-shaped patch stitched to her jersey and, as she drew closer, the tips of her cropped hair, spiking out from under her helmet. A pale but unapologetic pink. "You must be my captain."

She removed one glove. "And coach."

They had been exchanging emails for a few days, but it felt good to put a face to an email signature. "Lauren?"

"Call me Wren. Like the bird."

They shook hands. "Because you fly across the ice?"

She grinned. "Something like that."

Ted was increasingly aware of the other skaters' eyes on him. He could practically feel their stares, boring into his skin. He took a steadying breath and projected self-confidence. "So, how's this going to work?"

"I figure we'll warm you up with the rest, start you on second shift, and see how it goes from there." She slid her hand back into her glove. "Any objections?"

"No, sir."

She shook her head, smiling. "Go skate some circles."

"Yes, sir." He gave a jaunty little salute, because she didn't seem to mind the honorific, and took off in the direction of the rest of the team. Half of them were clustered around a white-board propped up on the boards near the blue line. The other half were still skating laps.

Ted picked up a puck from the dwindling pile at center ice and joined the latter group.

The Manhattan Monsters were friendly enough and quick to introduce themselves. He caught a flurry of names and smiles as they did crossovers around the face off circles. All except one woman, who kept to herself. When he skated toward her, she sped up. When he caught up to her, she broke away from the group and headed for the folks clustered round the whiteboard. Another, friendlier one of his new teammates, who'd introduced herself as Madison, watched the whole thing with an amused but apologetic smile.

"Don't mind her, she can be prickly. Didn't you have another jersey?"

Ted looked down at his practice jersey, a relic of his Harvard days. "No, not one that I could find." He wasn't going to drive up to Massachusetts and root through his parents' garage just to please a teammate who wouldn't even let him introduce himself to her.

"Well, I suppose maroon is close enough to red. The other team's blue, so it's not like anyone will get confused."

With an acquiescent shrug, Ted kept skating. He didn't really care if he stuck out like a sore thumb in a slightly darker hue. He was more worried about the woman who was actively avoiding him. He tried to pay her no mind, but when he glanced over at the group by the boards, he caught her staring at him.

Quickly, she glanced away. But not before he saw her baleful glare. Like a grizzly bear. A beautiful grizzly bear, he couldn't help but notice, with long brown hair in an intricate braid and lips that looked lush and full, even when she frowned...

"Listen up, folks." Wren's echoing words recaptured Ted's errant attention. Immediately, everyone stopped. With the way the rink reverberated, sound bouncing off the boards, their captain-slash-coach needed no megaphone. "The enemy has arrived."

"He certainly has," someone muttered. Ted looked around and found that woman glaring at him again. What the hell was her deal?

"Oy, shut up."

They all snapped to attention again. Wren's presence was imposing.

But Ted couldn't help but glance over at the mystery chick every couple of seconds. She seemed to be studiously avoiding meeting his gaze. Did she know him from somewhere? Surely he'd remember if he'd been rude to her before—unless he hadn't even realized what he was doing.

"As I was saying, the enemy has arrived." Wren shook her head in the direction of the team that now occupied the other side of the ice. "Let's not let Brooklyn kick our asses again. It's embarrassing to be beaten by my home borough."

"I thought you moved to Tribeca," someone said.

"I did, but I grew up in Greenpoint."

"Isn't that where they filmed—"

"Once again, kindly shut up." Wren's tone was fond but frustrated. "We've been over the strategy already. Wings, I want you to weave. D, don't be afraid to get in on the action. As usual, protect Matt at all costs. And don't let those fuckers in the crease. Capisce?"

Wren's players nodded enthusiastically.

"Now pick up those pucks—I've gotta go talk to the refs."

Wren skated off towards center ice. Ted did his part, picking up a couple of pucks and depositing them in a bag on the boards. As he turned, someone skated into him. Ted caught himself against the glass.

"Watch where you're going, Harvard." Apparently, she was no longer ignoring him.

"Hey!" Ted called out to his new teammate, who turned back with one brow raised. "Why do you hate me?"

She flicked her fishtail braid back from where it had been lying over her shoulder, revealing a patch shaped like the letter 'A.' Fine behavior for an assistant captain. "Who said I hated you?"

"Your eyes did, when they shot daggers at me. What did I ever do to you?" He narrowed his own eyes, thinking about Madison's remark regarding his jersey. "Don't tell me—are you a Yalie or something?"

That had been a miscalculation. If looks could kill...

Still, she was pretty beneath her full grill. So pretty, he didn't see her stick snake out to hook his skate. In fact, the only thing Ted saw was the gleam in her hazel eyes, before he was flat on his ass, staring up at the bright bands of light that stretched across the rink's high ceiling.

Harvard yelped as he fell. Ally bit down on her mouthguard so as not to laugh. "Oh my god, are you okay?" She offered him her hand—and a smile so fake it felt like Botox.

He stared up at her, flat on his back, his baby blue eyes wide. Shock? Outrage. "Are you serious?" That accent again. It grated on her ears. Boston blended with the BBC, like a goddamn Kennedy.

Ally shrugged. "Fine! Pull yourself up by your bootstraps! There's a first time for everything." As she spoke, he pushed to his feet.

"You know that idiom is ironic, right?" He loomed over her, and for the first time she got a good look at his face.

He was handsome, in a boring way. Dark hair, light eyes. A straight nose—goody-two-shoes, probably never been in a real fight. And a muscle ticking in his clenched, but still chiseled, jaw. Ally swallowed, suddenly feeling a little...

Anyway.

"It's physically impossible to pull yourself up by your bootstraps. That and the Puritan work ethic—they're both bullshit."

Ally leveled him a look. "If you're done mansplaining the New England psyche to me, I've got a game to play." Without waiting for his response, she skated away.

Roughly an hour later, the clock ran out and the buzzer did what it did best. Matt raised his stick in the air and Wren performed her victory celly. Madison turned to Ally and they exchanged an elated glove-bump. Ally then glanced to the stands, amused to see their four fans cheering like they'd secured the Stanley. Understandably.

Because they hadn't just won. The Manhattan Monsters had, finally—after so many losses that it was honestly less embarrassing to stop counting and start calling them innumerable—defeated their arch-nemeses. Ally wasn't sure how, but they had actually done it.

Scratch that—she knew exactly how they'd done it, but she wasn't willing to admit it. She wasn't willing to credit Harvard with their historic win.

Ally shook her head and skated towards the center line. One by one, she high-fived the players on the other team, too happy to rub it in with any real mockery. Then she followed Madison to the exit.

"Bryant!" Wren called her name. She sounded pissed.

Swallowing hard, Ally skated over to her irate captain.

"Another penalty? Roughing? Really? We talked about this."

"I'm sorry, cap. I don't know what came over me."

Wren raised her eyebrows. She'd taken off her helmet and her mullet was a sweaty mess of pink. "Same thing that came over you during warm ups, when you hooked one of your own teammates?"

"I didn't mean to—"

"Bullshit, Ally. You have the temper of a professional player. But this is practically a pick-up league. No one's paying you to get into fights!"

"I'm sorry, Wren. I'll do bett—"

"I'm not finished. I'm stripping you of assistant captain status until you demonstrate that you can keep your temper in check. Consistently. No more of this bullshit."

Shame and mortification burned in Ally's cheeks as her captain's decision sunk in. Out of the corner of her eye, through a film of angry and embarrassed tears, which she refused to let fall, she caught sight of a maroon jersey.

Damn him. This was all his fault. She wouldn't have been in such a temper if he hadn't showed up and gotten under her skin. If she wanted to keep playing, she'd have to stay away from him.

Ally blinked hard and cleared her throat. "Understood."

"Good." Wren sighed. "Now, go home and take a cold shower. You need to cool off and you smell like the inside of a teenager's skate." Wren patted Ally on the shoulder, just above the 'A' she could no longer claim. Ally was dismissed.

The locker room was abuzz as Ally thudded into it: her teammates were passing around a thirty rack of Natty, Wren's postgame playlist was blasting out of Matt's portable speaker, and the new guy was having a hard time removing his shoulder pads because he kept having to answer high-fives and return exploding fist-bumps.

Ally supposed he *had* scored half of their goals. She hadn't scored any, hadn't got so much as an assist. Her game was off. And she knew whom to blame.

"Hey!" Madison was breathless with excitement. "Why the long face? We won!"

Ally forced a smile. "Yeah, we did. Good job, Mads." She went to her spot on the bench and started stripping. Harvard's eyes followed her. "This isn't a peep show, pervert."

He raised his hands. "Whoa. Relax. I was just waiting for the right moment to congratulate you."

"The right moment doesn't exist. I didn't contribute to that victory."

His eyebrows lifted. "Every player counts."

She snorted. "Somehow I doubt that's what they teach you in Cambridge."

"What *is* your problem? I can't help where I went to school."

Ally threw her shin guard into her bag. "*You* are my problem. Not everything is about you!"

Matt swaggered past in his massive pads, grabbing a fresh beer from the box beside Ally. "Nice work, new guy." He punctuated his compliment by cracking open the beer and raising it to his new teammate before taking a sip, then shuffled back to the bench on the other side of the room.

Harvard waited to answer Ally until Matt was out of earshot. "That's a contradiction, if I ever heard one."

She rolled her eyes. "A polite person would have pretended not to notice."

"And you expect me to be polite, when you're being so very impolite?"

Ally groaned. "Just go away. I'm about to take my shirt off and unless you're paying…"

"Message received," he muttered, returning his attention to his bag.

Meanwhile, for all her protests about peep shows, privacy, and politeness, Ally couldn't help but stare as the new guy stripped his sweaty shirt from his torso. The man had abs like a washboard. Ally counted six. Six! Who even had a six pack, in this day and age?

It was ridiculous. *He* was ridiculous.

Ally shoved the remainder of her gear into her bag, hoisted it over her shoulder, and abandoned the locker room. Belatedly, she realized she hadn't said goodbye to anyone. Whatever. They were busy with their beers and besides, they were used to her icy-hot temper. One of these days she would clean up her act, but at the moment she couldn't be bothered.

Splurging on a cab, Ally rode home in silence. As the car approached her apartment, she tried to let the lights of the East Village fill her with cheer. She loved her neighborhood, with its never-ending noise and its historic character and its constantly proliferating graffiti. But love wasn't enough, sometimes. Neither was winning.

Sometimes, a girl needed a whole bottle of wine and a half season of reality television. She'd have a headache in the morning, but who cared? It was going to be awful anyway; tomorrow was a Monday.

CHAPTER 2
PERSONAL DEVIL

ALLY SLAMMED her hand down on the alarm clock, possibly shattering the plastic screen in the process, but at the very least shutting it up. The last thing she needed was public radio at this hour. It was five-thirty and she felt like she was going to puke.

But she was going for a run, because she always went for a run. Well, not *always*. But most days. And once a week, Madison tagged along—because Wren thought it was good team-building and Wren was usually right. Except about *him*. Why couldn't her captain see that letting Harvard on the team was, point blank, a bad idea? Ally felt like a canary in a coal mine, and not for the first time.

Grumbling to her cat, Heathcliff, who had been awake for the better part of the night, Ally clambered out of bed. She pulled off her pajamas—a grubby white t-shirt and red flannel boxers embroidered with the Boston University logo and a pair of hockey sticks—and fumbled for a sports bra and some leggings. When she was sufficiently attired, Ally slid on her sneakers and tied them with a double knot. Then she grabbed her keys, promised Heathcliff she would feed him when she got back, and locked the door on her way out.

Ally stopped on the street to detangle her headphones

before hitting play on the Maroon 5 playlist she'd been listening to since high school. She turned the volume up just loud enough for her to be able to listen to the lyrics and still hear the sounds of the East Village awakening: the burgeoning traffic, an overpriced coffee shop blasting a bad radio station, and the occasional friendly shout as the guy who owned the bodega on the corner greeted his regulars.

Lord, Ally felt sick. Nope, take that back—she was going to *be* sick.

Ally ducked into the alley next to that building where she'd heard Trotsky had once worked and emptied the contents of her stomach with alacrity. Wiping her mouth on the back of her hand, Ally decided that was enough running for one day.

Walking home, she watched the sun slowly rise above the skyline. It was a beautiful morning, beyond the boundaries of a certain alleyway, but that was not a sufficient balm for her bad mood.

Once returned to her shoebox of a one-bedroom, paid for in part by her parents, she fed Heathcliff, who had been waiting by the door. Then she dragged herself into the shower, where she brushed her teeth and washed her hair.

Naked, with her wet hair up in a towel, she wandered back into her bedroom to the overstuffed closet, from which she pulled a dress at random. She didn't particularly care what she wore. It wasn't like she had anyone to impress.

Ally scrambled three eggs for breakfast, figuring she should consume some extra protein to compensate for whatever she'd lost by puking in an alleyway. God, that had been embarrassing. She hoped she hadn't ruined anyone's day—or, worse, their living space. Muttering a curse on the head of the mayor, who seemed intent on making the housing crisis worse, Ally poured coffee grounds into an instant press.

"It's a good thing you're quiet, Heathcliff."

Sometimes Ally talked to her cat, but he never talked back.

Rarely so much as meowed, which was good because, per her lease, she wasn't supposed to have pets. The quieter Heathcliff was, the less likely her landlord would find out about him.

"You like being a secret, don't you?"

Heathcliff stared unblinkingly up at her. There was something deeply melodramatic about the haunted look in his little eyes. Haunted, her ass. Spoiled was a more accurate adjective.

"God, you're so brooding. At least your name suits you."

Flicking his tail, Heathcliff jumped up on top of the counter and started to circle her half-drunk coffee.

"Hey! I didn't say you could get up there!" She scooped him up and carried him away from the kitchen, although she couldn't go far. Her apartment wasn't exactly big.

Ally set Heathcliff down on the arm of the small sofa, which was one of his favorite places to sit—hence the cat hair that had accumulated there. Ally shook her head. She needed a new lint roller. Or ten.

Checking the time, she gathered her bag and water bottle, tossed back her antidepressants, and slipped into a pair of sneakers that looked vaguely like flats. Since her run had been cut short, she had made the executive decision to walk part of the way to work today. Besides, it was nice out. An early October morning.

Tucking her errant waves into a loose bun, Ally threw on some mascara and a dash of tinted lip balm. Then she scratched behind Heathcliff's ears and put on WNYC, so he wouldn't be lonely.

Ted sang loudly and unabashedly into the second shower head while the first doused him with water from above. Today was his first day at his new job and he needed all the positivity Katrina and the Waves could lend him, plus his daily core workout tended to energize him.

After a couple more classics, he subjected himself to a final, freezing cold rinse. His little sister had once told him that doing so closed the pores and besides, it woke him up more than coffee. Ted was more of a tea person, anyway.

Toweling off, he donned a kimono-style robe and boxers, letting the robe flap open as he strode in the direction of the kitchen. An alarm went off on his phone, which he'd left in the pocket he'd hand-sewn haphazardly into the kimono.

The sound of the alarm soothed him—it meant he'd finished his shower on time. Turning it off, he set the device face down on the kitchen counter, which was a dark green marble—as was the backsplash—contrasting the sunset-orange of the walls. He hadn't been the one to choose the colors, but he appreciated the decorator's whimsical touches.

Humming one of Wham!'s greatest hits, because the point of this particular playlist was to relish the relics, Ted set to work slicing up fresh fruit and vegetables. Ever since he'd made the Harvard hockey team, Ted had taken to drinking a fresh smoothie in the morning. He figured it improved his play.

Besides, Ted liked to cook. He supposed it ran in his family—his late aunt, the woman who had left him this amazing apartment, had been something of a chef herself. To put it mildly. And she'd taught Ted everything he knew. Well, almost. This recipe was Ted's own creation. Lots of leafy greens, berries, seeds, and a couple of spoonfuls of peanut butter—for protein. While he might have the musical taste of an 80s club-goer, Ted wasn't a powder guy.

His phone buzzed, although he almost didn't hear it because the blender was going. Ted finished making his smoothie before checking his notifications.

Have a great first day, Teddy!

He smiled and sipped his smoothie.

Meanwhile, his little sister started typing again: *Hope you don't fuck this up!*

Ted frowned and set down his glass to send back a stern yet playful response: *Thank you for your unwavering support, Belle.* She replied with a string of emojis that he could barely decipher. Still, he was fairly certain she was wishing him well...

Taking another sip of his smoothie, he wondered what Belle was doing up so early. It was six-forty-five, after all. Maybe she was getting in a workout before class?

Belle was a sophomore at Northeastern, studying marine biology. She was the smarter of the two of them and, aside from their parents and an aging golden retriever named Max, it was just the two of them.

Another alarm went off on Ted's phone, prompting him to chug his smoothie. It was time to get dressed.

Ted always allowed himself a leisurely fifteen minutes to get dressed. He timed it, like he did the rest of his morning routine. It made him feel calm and in control of himself, better able to appreciate the beauty and the chaos of the outside world.

Sliding his glass into the dishwasher, he strode in the direction of his bedroom, his feet bare against the cool hardwood floor. Already, he was debating what to wear today. His new job was at a tech company, so he could go for something cool and casual. But he had been hired into a senior management position, and he was new, so maybe something classic, something slightly more formal, would be more appropriate.

Opening the cherrywood wardrobe, he removed a dark grey suit. Thumbing through his shirts, he settled on a pale blue that would compliment his eyes—Ted wasn't above a little vanity. Setting his kimono aside, Ted threw on an undershirt and a pair of magenta dress socks—he wasn't above having a little fun, either. Then he donned the trousers, shirt, and suit jacket. He finished off the outfit with a pink Liberty print handkerchief, folded neatly and tucked deep into his breast pocket, so that it was scarcely visible.

Ted preened in front of the mirror for a few minutes, practicing his introductions, then went to the bathroom to brush his teeth. It wouldn't do to have bad breath on his first day at a new job. Ted put stock in first impressions. Which was why he still harbored a lingering unease at his interaction with that woman on the hockey team. She'd hated him, for some reason. Well, not for some reason. Because he'd gone to Harvard, apparently.

Ted understood why people hated Harvard alums. He hated a lot of Harvard alums. Not that he considered himself a particularly hateful person. But he got it. The power, the privilege, the pretensions. It was nauseating, at times. And it was why he'd left his social club, once he'd realized it was a bastion of white male mediocrity, even if the move had cost him all his so-called friends. But was the name brand of a person's higher education really what everyone else ought to judge their character by?

He frowned and flicked off the alarm that had just come on. It was time to head out. Time to focus on the fresh day ahead, not the stale night before, or the crushing loneliness that always accompanied him out the door.

Ted took the stairs down to the first floor, said good morning to the daytime doorman, Albert, and hurried on his way to the subway. He took the 6 downtown and the L crosstown, then walked the rest of the way. GreenLight, the tech company that employed him as of today, had recently acquired new offices in Chelsea.

Coming to a standstill before the building's entrance, he stared up at the glassy facade with its pre-war architecture. The space had once been the site of garment factory, or something, but now housed a company with a hundred million dollar annual profit. Ted tried not to be intimidated. He tapped into his Boston-bred arrogance, his slight but slightly problematic sense of entitlement, and projected a casual confidence. Then, he pretty much walked into the glass door.

"Psst."

Ally glanced up from the email blast she'd been drafting.

Vanessa was pointing with a pencil at the elevator, which had just opened with a ding.

Harold, their boss, had stepped out and was standing to one side. Behind him, a tall man with cropped dark hair was exiting the open doors.

"Fresh meat."

Ally had heard about the new hire. Brought in to manage the new partnerships. He was a Harvard graduate, apparently—undergrad *and* a recent MBA. As a Boston University alumna herself, Ally had no time for Harvard men. Besides, she was deeply skeptical of Ivies.

The new hire had recently moved to Manhattan, according to Jane in Accounting, who'd spilled all the deets over boba on Thursday afternoon. Jane said that Miles from HR had interviewed him and swore that he was a certified hottie. Ally couldn't remember his name, because she was bad with names and Jane had only said it the once, but she remembered its sounding vaguely presidential. God, he'd better not be some kind of Hyannis Port snob.

Ally squinted at the new hire from across the room, trying to make out his features. He and Harold walked over to the first cluster of desks and, presumably, Harold made some introductions. Ally saw several handshakes before the duo moved on to the next cluster. As he got closer and closer, Ally thought the man looked familiar.

Her computer pinged. An email had come in. She looked down at the screen, but it was just spam. Well, not actually.

But it wasn't something she particularly cared to read. She looked up again.

He was standing over by the snack bar, admiring the offerings. Admittedly, they were admirable—everything was free, from upscale Icelandic yogurt cups to tiny ginger juice shots. GreenLight was on a bit of a health kick, with the exception of Keg Fridays—a beloved tradition that could be traced back to the company's start-up days.

Ally refocused. She could see his profile in some detail from this angle. He had a long, straight nose that was more hook than button. A strong, angular chin and a sharp, clean-shaven jawline. Broad, muscular shoulders that were just a little bit tense. He looked like he belonged on a coin. Or playing the part of the land-owning lord in a BBC miniseries. And then it hit her.

He was the asshole from last night.

"*Shit.*"

"What is it?" Vanessa peered at Ally curiously over her cat-eye glasses.

Realizing she'd spoken aloud, Ally scrambled to make up an excuse for her expletive. "Oh, nothing. Just realized I forgot my water bottle."

Vanessa rolled her dark eyes indulgently. "Ally, that's your water bottle. Right there, on your desk. Be careful—the lid is off. Wouldn't want to knock that over on a work computer."

Ally forced a smile. "Right. Of course. Silly me! I guess this morning's dose of caffeine hasn't passed my blood-brain barrier yet."

Vanessa laughed and went back to ogling the new hire.

What had his name been? Ally struggled to recall her conversation with Jane. Certainly, he hadn't introduced himself during last night's game.

"Ooh, he's coming over here next!"

Ally swiveled around to find that, indeed, the asshole and

her boss (also a bit of an asshole) were approaching. She scowled. He caught her eye and, his own eyes widening with recognition, smiled. It was a wicked smile, the kind the devil wore when he invented a new type of torture.

Harold pointed to Vanessa. "This is Vanessa Chen, one of our copywriters."

"A pleasure," the asshole murmured, directing his light blue gaze—like a cloudless summer sky, Ally noted with displeasure—at Ally's favorite coworker.

Vanessa beamed.

"And this is—"

The asshole turned the full force of his smile on Ally. "The girl who tripped me."

Ally glared up at him. She refused to stand and offer that man her hand. "That was an accident, and I strenuously object to being called a 'girl.'"

"I am woman," he murmured, "hear me roar."

God, she wished she could trip him again. Deliberately, this time. If only to wipe that wicked smirk off his annoyingly attractive face.

Ally froze. She wasn't attracted to him. She was just... observant. Like all good copywriters.

Harold cleared his throat and Ally snapped to attention. "...Allegra Bryant, another copywriter. Ms. Bryant, this is Theodore Lewis, our new Senior Product Partnerships Manager."

"Allegra, is it?" They hadn't exactly exchanged names the night before, just searing looks.

"Everyone calls me Ally," she confessed, uncertain as to why she was sharing this information with him. Certainly, they would never have occasion to call each other by nicknames.

He shrugged. "Everyone calls me Ted. Except my mother."

"And what does she call you?" Ally had no idea why she

was asking, except that he'd dangled the piece of information out in front of her like bait. What game was he playing?

He flashed a boyish grin and Ally suddenly found it hard to hate him. "Teddy-bear."

"Fascinating as that is, Mr. Lewis, we have another three floors to cover." Harold called everyone by their last names, for some stick-up-his-ass reason. Really, for the Vice President of Marketing at a relatively new tech company, he was remarkably uncool.

"Of course, sir." Ted appeared chastened. 'Appeared' being the operative word, because he winked at Ally as soon as Harold turned his back on them. Her stomach very nearly flipped. A remnant of this morning's alleyway embarrassment, no doubt.

"You may carry on working, Ms. Bryant," Harold called over his shoulder, walking away. Ted went with him.

Ally answered Harold absentmindedly but in the affirmative, staring at her new teammate and coworker's retreating form. What was his deal? Had he been sent here by God to torment her for her sins? What sins had she committed, to deserve her own personal devil? Ally frowned, and rattled off a few choice misbehaviors mentally. Perhaps it was time to show up to confession.

CHAPTER 3
THE SKELETON

TED FOUND himself sitting alone at lunch, like it was the middle school cafeteria all over again. He'd been a late bloomer and hadn't found a good group of friends until boarding school, which had been its own miscellany of pain and privilege. But at least he'd had friends, with whom to grow and endure and occasionally break curfew.

Then had come college, and his boarding school friends scattered to the wind. One or two of them had gone with him to Harvard only to disappear in the crowd, but most had charted their own courses. They hadn't really kept in touch, not that Ted hadn't tried. Desperately.

He'd made friends in college, sure. But after a couple years, Ted called it quits on them and their social club. He couldn't stomach their casual misogyny, their toxic masculinity, their elitism and entitlement. Ted had fucked up, he'd realized, and fallen in with the wrong crowd. They'd sought him out, a fellow prep school kid, and made him feel at home on the basis of similar backgrounds. Until, gradually, one by one, they'd shown their true colors.

When Ted had finally spoken up, it was too late. Those few years had witnessed the death of his friend group's collective capacity for empathy by a thousand self-inflicted cuts. Ted still sometimes felt like he'd failed his so-called friends, but maybe they'd been the ones to fail him, in the end.

Upon graduation, Ted once again found himself alone. He'd gotten a job at a financial firm because it seemed like the thing to do, only to realize that he hated what they were doing to the world—not to mention, he never got any sleep. So, he enrolled in business school and stayed busy by working throughout his degree.

Of course, even if he'd had time to join any clubs or otherwise socialize, his peers weren't interested in watching movies or talking about their favorite books or cooking together, just for the fun of it. They already had friends; now, they were looking to network. After two years of classes that alleged to teach entrepreneurship and Excel-based exams, Ted left home and Harvard for good, taking the first job he was offered in New York City.

And that was how he'd ended up here.

Ted sighed, glancing around the glorified cafeteria as if its layout could stem the flow of unwanted memories. He knew he wasn't a bad person. And he was capable of being a good friend. He just... Well, whatever. Maybe this time, right?

The cafeteria was spacious and well-lit, and the food looked good, for company grub. Well, technically it wasn't company grub. According to Harold, who had given him a particularly dull tour of the building and its amenities, the company outsourced to local restaurants, maintaining a variety of options and changing them up every few months. Tech companies knew how to treat their employees. At least, on the food front. He'd just have to wait and see about company culture.

Determined not to waste a perfectly good meal on sour memories and self-pity, Ted stood and picked up his platter. Glancing around the cafeteria, he spied his new teammate and coworker—Allegra Bryant—and her desk buddy—

Vanessa, was it?—sitting outside, next to one of the giant windows. He located the door nearest to them and made for it.

Allegra Bryant might hate him, but at least she knew who he was. That was more than he could say for anyone else in this dolled up food court.

Her head was down and she was shaking with laughter when he approached. Ted was mesmerized for a moment before he shook himself. Her friend was similarly indisposed. Ted took a second to bask in the early autumn air and clear his addled head.

"So then I said to him—"

"I hate to interrupt a hilarious anecdote," he offered, sincerely, "but do you mind if I join you?"

Allegra glared at him—whether for his rudeness in interrupting her story or his audacity in daring to exist in her general proximity, he doubted he would ever know.

Vanessa, however, scooted over. "Sure! Sit here." She sent a wicked look in Allegra's direction. "Ally was just telling me about a bad Flutter date."

Flutter was the newest dating app. Ted had considered giving it a go, himself, given how desperate he was for company.

Allegra turned her glare—quite a fearsome thing—on her friend. "It's nothing," she ground out, then grimaced up at him. "Couldn't find any alums to wine and dine with, Harvard? I'm sure there's a couple inside. Just follow the sound of self-aggrandizement."

Ted was, once again, bewildered by her animosity. He was not, however, put off. Ted liked a challenge. And her surliness was an opportunity for him to be cheery. Fake it till you make it, his mother had always said. "Ah, but I prefer the great outdoors," he said, gesturing to the nearby shrubbery, "where I can have the piss taken out of me by someone I've met twice."

Ally rolled her eyes. "Whatever. Just sit, you're causing a scene."

"I'm not sure he's the one causing a scene, Ally…"

"V! You're supposed to be on my side!"

Vanessa laughed. "I wasn't aware there were sides. We're all on the same team!"

"Literally," murmured Ted, as he took his seat between them. Somehow, his dark mood seemed to be lifting.

Vanessa cocked her head at him. "What do you mean?"

"Ms. Bryant and I are on the same hockey team," he replied, breaking apart his chopsticks.

Vanessa exchanged a look with Allegra. "How nice!" He was fairly certain she was being sincere. "What position do you play?"

Ted swallowed a mouthful of sushi. "Center."

"Naturally…" muttered Allegra.

"I used to play D," he said casually, picking up another piece.

Vanessa giggled. "Don't mind me, I'm just thinking of all the dirty jokes I would make if I *played D*…"

Ted laughed, as did Allegra—reluctantly. "I've heard them all…"

A somewhat stilted silence fell over their table and they all retreated into their meals. Until Allegra, apparently emboldened by Ted's awkwardness, decided to interrogate him.

"So, Ted."

He looked up, immediately suspicious of her use of his given name.

"Where are you from?"

Ted didn't trust the warmth in her tone for a minute. "A little town, west of Boston. It's horse country, mostly. Not a lot of people, houses far apart."

"I see. And where did you say you went to school?"

"Allegra—"

"Ally."

"Ally," he continued, correcting himself, "you've been making fun of me for it for two days now."

She smiled, catlike. "Not college, Harvard. High school."

"Oh." He could suddenly see where this was going. "Essex," he admitted, the back of his neck growing hot with embarrassment. Not that he was embarrassed to have attended the prestigious prep school, just that he knew she would judge him for it. And he cared what Allegra Bryant thought about him. God only knew why. Possibly because he suspected that, beneath her quick-to-judge exterior, she had a rather discerning eye.

Ally's tone had grown glacial. "I see," she repeated, but she didn't, not really.

"Look, my grandfather went to Essex, my father went to Essex, it was what was expected of me—"

"Oh, don't make a fuss, preppy. I'm just getting to know you." She smiled wickedly, warmth returning.

Ted's breath caught in his chest. He doubted he could withstand the full force of her real smile, if she turned it on him genuinely.

"Fine," he said when he could breathe again. "Where did you go to—"

"Not your turn, Harvard." She wagged a finger at him.

Vanessa watched, amused but maybe a little alarmed, judging by the slight widening of her eyes.

"One last question and then you can shoot your shot." Had she intended the double entendre? "What was your major?"

Ted cleared his throat. "Art history."

Ally's eyes went wide with surprise.

Vanessa looked at him appraisingly. "Oooh, you'll have to tell us all about that," she said, nudging Ted. She appeared genuinely interested.

But Ted was too pleased with Ally's response to offer Vanessa anything more than a polite smile.

Ally's eyebrows knit. She looked like she was doing a complex calculation in her head, but really Ted knew she was just confused. Art history wasn't a typical major for businessmen—or "bros." And both groups had let him know.

Recovering, Ally stood and beckoned to Vanessa to do the same.

Ted wasn't even half-finished with the food on his tray. He looked up at Ally with dismay. "What about my turn—"

"It's time we copywriters got back to our keyboards," she said, looking pleased with herself. "But to answer your question," she continued acidly, picking up her tray, "I went to public school."

Ally started to walk away. Vanessa shrugged apologetically.

"What about college?" Ted called out.

"Oh, she went to BU," Vanessa offered with an air of apology, before following Ally indoors.

And with that last scrap of information, another piece of the puzzle that was Allegra Bryant clicked into place.

Ally wasn't sure why she had scheduled her next appointment for a Monday. She also would have preferred to do the session via video call. Nevertheless, after work, she dragged herself to her therapist's office, a nondescript building in midtown Manhattan with a glass exterior and a man at the front desk. Not the same man as the last few times, she noted as he checked her ID.

"Seventh floor, elevators on your right as you walk down the hall," he said, dismissing her with a wave as he returned to his novel. A romance novel, Ally realized, if its bodice-ripping cover was anything to tell by. Huh. She hadn't read that one. Making a mental note to add it to her TBR, Ally walked down the hall and pressed the button for the elevator. A few minutes later, she entered her therapist's suite.

Linda Boyd was an experienced psychotherapist with pale blonde hair that Ally was pretty sure had been dyed to hide the grey. She was neat and tidy, whereas Ally was messy and mildly chaotic; she spoke in a soothing tone, whereas Ally's voice went up and down with her emotions. They had an interesting and effective partnership, employing DBT and CBT and occasionally a bit of Jungian analysis—when they were feeling frisky—but mostly they stuck to a psychodynamic approach.

And they both liked the Brontës, which mattered to Ally. She remembered their first meeting—she'd seen the collection on the therapist's shelf and immediately quizzed Linda (or Dr. Boyd, as she'd called her at first) on which Brontë book was the best: the one with the abusive employer, the one with the abusive husband, or the one with the abusive childhood crush. Linda had chosen *Jane Eyre*, which didn't surprise Ally, because she reminded her of Jane. Determined, quiet, persuasive, punctual. At least, Ally imagined the eponymous Jane Eyre was punctual. Except for that time she arrived to meet Rochester, late.

"Ally." Linda smiled fondly. "Welcome. Do come in."

Linda's greeting never changed. Ally's differed, depending.

Today, Ally met her therapist with a vexed monosyllable: "Hey." Then she crossed the room and threw herself down onto the couch. It was a royal blue velvet, and the room's accents were all soft shades of yellow and blue. "I think there's something wrong with me," she announced as she flopped into a more comfortable position.

Linda sat, crossing her ankles. "What do you mean?"

Ally frowned, crossing her arms. "I'm just so grumpy all the time."

Linda watched her impassively. "Maybe grumpy is a part of your personality. Are you depressed?"

"Honestly?" Ally sighed. "No, the meds are working. And the exercise. But it would be easier to explain it if I were."

"Easier to explain what?"

"The grumpiness!"

"Hmm. Are you sure there isn't anything that's bothering you? Anything new in your life?"

Harvard flickered in Ally's consciousness, but she pushed the image of him (shirtless, of course) out of her head. Ally then thought reluctantly about how lonely she was, how lonely she had been, for so very long. And how angry she still was, at *him*, for how *he'd* treated her all those years ago. "No."

"Ally…"

"There's nothing new, it's just the same old skeleton in my closet," she huffed.

Linda folded her hands in her lap. "Ah. Everett."

"I can think of a couple other names for him…"

"Oh?" Linda appeared curious and a little amused.

Ally shook her head. "They're not fit for polite company, as my mother would say. Although, she's called him one or two of those names publicly."

"And how do you feel about the nature of that break-up?"

"Nope." Ally made a show of sealing her lips. "We're not doing this today."

Linda nodded, but Ally wondered if she was annoyed under the surface. Ally would be. But maybe therapists didn't get annoyed. Maybe they had special, therapist-only emotions. Drilled into them in therapist school…

"Ally? You're disappearing on me."

"Oh." Linda's voice anchored Ally in the present. "Sorry."

"You don't have to apologize," Linda said gently. "Where did you go?"

Ally smirked. "I was just thinking about therapy. Therapists, rather."

"You're not going to distract me that easily, Ally." Linda's expression was polite, but her gaze was piercing. "We haven't spoken about Everett in months. Why the sudden return to the past? Did something happen?"

Ally laughed, but it was without humor. She supposed there was no point in keeping a secret from her therapist. "Some*one*, more like it."

"This new person... what are they like?" Linda asked, cocking her head slightly to one side. "What did or didn't they do?"

"He's a new coworker. He works on the business side of things."

"At GreenLight?"

"Yeah. But he's *slightly* more senior than I, a mere copy-writer, could ever hope to be." Ally rolled her eyes. "*And* he's a teammate, as if pillaging one area of my life wasn't enough."

"On your ice hockey team?"

Ally shot her therapist a look. "Linda, you can just call it 'hockey.' It's field hockey that's weird and needs a modifier."

Linda chuckled. "I think my nephew, who plays field hockey in Ireland, would take offense at that pronouncement."

Ally sat up. "I didn't know you had a nephew in Ireland."

"That's because you're the client and I'm the therapist," Linda answered pertly but with good humor. "Come on, tell me about this man."

"Who said it was a man?"

Linda looked confused. "I'm sorry—I shouldn't have assumed. It's just, your use of masculine pronouns..."

"Oh, right. No, he is a man. It just sounded like you were saying he was *a man* and not, like, you know, a man."

Linda, keeping up admirably, asked, "And which is he?"

"Well," Ally scoffed, "he's certainly not *a man*. I wouldn't sleep with him if you paid me. I mean, fine. Maybe. But that's not the point!"

"And what is the point?" Linda leaned in.

"The point is, I'm not interested!"

"Why not?"

"Because he's an arrogant, entitled, narcissistic boor! With two 'o's!"

Linda looked fascinated. "How do you know?"

"He went to Harvard, Linda."

She shrugged. "I went to Yale." She pointed at a framed diploma.

"Yes, and that's tragic, but that's not the point. He went to *Harvard*. Not only is Harvard my alma mater's one true rival, it means that he's just like *him*."

"Who?"

Damn Linda, she was just trying to get Ally to say Everett's name. Well, she could try. "The skeleton in my closet, duh."

"And how do you know that this man...?" She trailed off, waiting for a name.

"Theodore. Ted," Ally uttered his nickname with not insignificant malice.

"How do you know that Ted is just like Everett? And, more importantly, even if he is just like Everett, why does it matter? You've already sworn off sleeping with him." Linda cocked her head again in an excellent impression of innocent confusion.

Ally groaned, flipping over onto her stomach and burying her face in a needlepoint pillow. Therapists. They always won.

Ted took the steps out of the 77th Street subway station two at a time before walking north on Lex. He pulled his phone out of his pocket and swiped through to Favorites, then he held the device up to his ear. After a few seconds, the ringing ceased and the bright voice of Ted's little sister sounded through the speaker.

"Teddy! To what do I owe the pleasure?"

"Hey, Belle. You free to chat?"

"Sure! I've got a kegger in a couple hours, but apart from that my afternoon's all clear."

Ted frowned. "A keg party? On a Monday? What about homework?"

Belle laughed. "It's already done, duh."

"Good." Ted could feel himself slipping into a sterner tone. "Because the parents don't pay for you to party."

He could practically hear her rolling her eyes. "All work and no play makes Jack a dull boy."

Ted sighed. She was right.

"If you're just going to sermonize…"

"I'm not sermonizing," he protested weakly, but she had a point.

"Besides, you weren't exactly a saint during your college days."

Ted crossed over to Park Avenue. "No, but—"

"No 'buts!' Hypocrites suck. And former frat bros suck even harder."

"Hey! I've reformed. Besides, I think my history uniquely qualifies me to look out for my baby sister."

"Relax, Ted. I don't need looking out for. You, on the other hand…"

Ted stopped still. "What's that supposed to mean?"

In lieu of an answer, Belle laughed again. "Why'd you call, tiger?"

Ted shrugged. Then he remembered she couldn't see him. "I don't know, I just wanted to chat."

"You could've texted," she said, but she didn't sound like she was complaining.

Ted started walking again. "I've been staring at a screen all day."

"Fair. So what's up? How was work?"

Ted thought about this. "It wasn't bad for a first day. You'd hate my boss; he's as dull as a lead pipe." He glanced about him, feeling mildly guilty for saying this out loud.

Belle smirked—again, he could practically hear her lips quirk. "Lead pipes have their uses."

"Please don't tell me you've ever hit someone over the head with one…"

She laughed outright. "No, but in the shows I watch…"

"And here I thought you were still watching *Winx Club*."

Her tone turned wry. "Like those girls weren't kicking ass on the regular."

Ted smiled. "Fair point."

"So, what else? Aside from your new boss whom I'd absolutely detest anyway because he's your boss and I don't approve of such hierarchical power structures?"

He sighed. His little sister, the radical of the family. "The amenities are nice—we've got free organic snacks and a private theater for demos."

"Do you have to work in tiny cubicles? I can't see you fitting into in one of those. It'd be like something out of *The Incredibles*."

"Lucky, then, that I'm not actually a superhero and that this is a SaaS company—"

"Sass? What does that mean?"

He spelled it out for her before explaining, "Software as a Service, like the big search engines. They all compete for the most creative office plan."

"Like, officially?"

"No," he admitted, "but it'd be nice if someone wrote up a piece about our 'industry-changing' desk layout for *The Pacific*."

"You know what I think would be 'industry-changing?'"

Ted silently resigned himself to one of her rants. Which were, admittedly, usually on target.

"Paid parental leave, equal—*actually* equal—pay, a robust union, and, oh, I don't know… a worker's revolution?"

"Yes, well, you'll have to wait on the latter, comrade. For now, though, GreenLight's got the first two covered, at least compared to our competitors."

Belle snorted. "Okay."

"You know I wouldn't have signed on to lead a team if I didn't have some faith in the company or its mission!"

"Yeah, yeah. But tell me, what's really bothering you? You wouldn't have called if there weren't *something*."

Ted sighed. He couldn't avoid it forever, however much he enjoyed sibling banter.

Belle heard his quiet exhale and ran with it. "Aha! So there is something, after all! I was mostly just bluffing, but you've as good as confessed! What is it? An office romance? Love at first sight?"

"No, although that would be nice." It was lonely, here in the big city. Ted needed to make some friends. That was why he had joined the hockey team, wasn't it? Of course, that train of thought just led him straight back to her… All roads to Rome, or whatever.

"I met a girl," he confessed.

"A woman, I hope," Belle teased.

Ted huffed out a laugh. "Funnily enough, she corrected me on that, too. I think you'd get along well."

"But you don't."

Impressed but not surprised by his sister's omniscience, Ted asked, "How'd you know?"

"Because you said "I met a girl" like it was a problem and not a reason for the parents to throw a party."

"You are a wise one, Bluebell," he said, using his childhood nickname for her. They'd come up with it when she was five and he was fourteen; he used to amuse her by telling her stories about the flower fairies that lived in their mother's garden at the summer house out on the Cape.

"So, what's the catch? She hate your guts?"

"That she does."

"Oh." Evidently, Belle had been half-kidding when she suggested hostility. Ted, too, was confused as to the source of Allegra's animosity. Well, he had been. But Vanessa's comment, and Ally's running commentary, had rather cleared things up. Somewhat.

"She hates me because I went to Harvard, whereas she went to Boston University. She sees me as a rival." But even after he said it, he remained confused. No one cared about college rivalries that much, especially not six or seven years out of school, which surely she must be. No one who was well-adjusted, or who hadn't been a rabid frat bro. No one like Ally. So what was her deal?

Belle didn't sound convinced, either. "Are you sure you didn't say something to piss her off?"

"Nothing, other than ask if she were a Yalie—but that was before I knew about BU."

Belle blew out her breath. "I don't know what to tell you, brother. I also don't know why you care. If she's a rotten apple, leave her beneath the tree."

Ted didn't know how to articulate his feelings for Allegra Bryant, which were not nonexistent. He was attracted to her. He wanted to impress her. He liked her slapshot and the sound of her laughter. "Yeah, we'll see."

CHAPTER 4
BAD ATTITUDE

"How'd you like them apples?" Ally laughed, bumping fists with Madison. Her teammate had just scored and Ally had given her the assist. It was only practice and the net was empty, but it felt good to be so in sync with her friend. Took her mind off the depressing reality of her being stripped of AC status.

Ally's laughter died as Harvard skated up, fresh out of the locker room. His chin strap was still hanging loose. "Nice flick," he offered Madison, referring to her wristshot technique. Then he addressed Ally. "Matt says Wren's just texted; she's running late. Says we should start practice without her."

Ally nodded. "I'll set up some cones. We can start with stick-handling drills."

"I did think we were a bit sloppy, on Sunday," Madison concurred.

Ted frowned. "Shouldn't we wait for Matt to make a decision? Wren said he's in charge."

It enraged Ally, to hear him talk about the situation so casually. Like it wasn't gutting. Still, she couldn't correct him. He wasn't wrong. "Fine. We'll waste five minutes as we wait for Matt to finish putting his gear on."

Madison glanced uneasily at Ally. "Ally—"

"No, it's fine." Ally was clutching at straws, trying to keep her temper in check. She gave Harvard a scathing look. "Oh, and Theodore? Your chin strap's loose."

"Thanks, Allegra." His smile, bravely weathering the storm of her anger, did strange things to her stomach. Or maybe it wasn't his smile, maybe it was his courage. He wouldn't back down just because she frowned.

Ally shook herself. What was she thinking? He was the worst. His smile was smug and that wasn't courage, that was arrogance. He thought he was better than she was, just because he'd scored more goals than she had. Just because his position at GreenLight was more senior than hers. Well, she'd show him. It wasn't all about scoring goals, and making money, and having perfectly white teeth. Teamwork and trust —they were more than enough.

Matt stepped onto the ice, sidling through the doorway so as to fit his gigantic goalie's pads. "Alright, alright, alright. Ally, Mads, grab some cones." Ally shot a triumphant look at Ted. "We're starting with a Half-Peanut."

Ally and Madison hurried to retrieve four cones from the boards, then place them in the correct positions: one on either side of the crease, at the hashmarks, and two just outside the blue line by the face off spots. The rest of the team started to line up in the corner with pucks.

"Wren would want to see snow on those cones," continued Matt, skating over to the net. "That's how close you should be cutting it when you make your turns. And don't take it easy on me, either. I'm wearing pads for a reason."

"Yeah, the reason being, we can't aim for shit," joked Skye, one of their team's newer members. They had a point. Only a handful of players—Ally, Madison, Wren, and Ted (Ally was forced by recent reality to admit)—ever scored. And not for lack of opportunity or because some people hogged the puck. Ally's team was alright, but they weren't good. That was part of why Ted's sudden addition stung so much. It was like Wren cared more about winning than she did training the team.

Ally kicked at the boards where she waited in line for her turn. It wasn't fair to think such things about Wren. She was a good captain. And they were improving, all of them. Ally smiled wryly, remembering her first season with the team. They'd lost every single game. That was before Madison and Skye and Nikki and some of the other players joined. Back when Matt, Ally, and Wren had been the only ones on the team who knew how to skate.

"Bryant, you're up." Wren's voice cut through Ally's musings, sharper than a blade fresh off the grindstone. Ally jumped to attention at the sudden arrival of her captain, picking up a puck and skating through the course she'd helped construct, finishing with a close-range wristshot. Matt caught the puck in his glove, but barely. He grinned.

"Nice one, Ally."

She skated back to the corner, slightly breathless, and turned to watch the person behind her. Harvard, naturally. How could he not be, in that hideous jersey? And he scored. Bully for him.

Ted skated up to Ally, grinning and not the least bit out of breath. "I love drills like that."

"Why? Because you can show off your skills without worrying about any of us interrupting your moment of glory?"

He frowned. "Is that what you think of me?" The question hung in the air, contributing to its frost. Ally found herself frozen in a sea of icy blue—Ted's stare. Hurt, as much as it was accusatory.

A whistle blew. "Bryant!" Wren sounded irritated.

Ally grabbed a puck and started moving. She got halfway around the course before she realized Matt wasn't in the net. Ally stopped, spraying snow all over a nearby cone.

"Where is your head?" Evidently, the question was rhetorical, because Wren kept talking, projecting her voice across the rink. "If you were listening, you would have heard me the first time. Stack those cones. You all seem sufficiently warmed up."

Ted watched Ally—his teammate, his coworker, the woman who seemed determined to hate him no matter what he did—collect cones while the rest of the team skated over to the face off circle at center ice.

"Lewis, get your head out of the clouds," Wren called to him. "You're needed here. You too, Bryant. I wanna see some hustle."

Ted glanced over his shoulder as he joined the rest of the team; Ally had returned the cones to the bench and was headed in their direction. She didn't look happy. No, her happiness was reserved for his absence, he had quickly come to understand.

"Cheer up, Bryant. I've got a surprise in store for you."

Ally groaned, stopping short with a spray of shaved ice. "Oh, god. Tell me we're not doing wind sprints."

"You know we don't have the equipment budget for that," Madison whispered, then stood to attention. Ally, too, perked up at the promise that they wouldn't be doing any speed or acceleration training today.

"No, it's not wind sprints." Wren sounded dejected, until her tone took a mischievous turn. "But it does involve running."

"Are we doing a team 5k?" Ted asked, confused. He'd tried and failed to organize several charity-benefiting team 5ks in his college days.

"Jesus, Harvard. Don't give her any ideas."

Ted turned to Ally. "It could be a good bonding exercise."

She scoffed. "The only one who needs to bond here is you."

"But that's just the thing, Bryant, isn't it?" Wren's brown eyes narrowed, but her lips curved. "Poor Lewis doesn't have a workout partner."

They all turned their attention to Ted, who would have been unnerved by it if he hadn't been so intent on watching Ally toss her long, brown braid over her shoulder. Her hair was glossy and dark, the color of candied walnuts. The scent of it wafted over to Ted as Allegra moved, faint but sweet. What shampoo did she use? He liked it.

"That's his problem," Ally announced.

"No, Ally, it's yours."

A silence fell, an eager hush, as everyone watched Ally, waited for her to react. They were rewarded a nanosecond later, when she demanded, "What?!"

Wren's smile was slow and wicked. "I want you to take Teddy here under your wing."

"But I already have a running partner! Madison—"

"Has agreed to work out with Matt."

Ally turned to Madison, her eyes full of fury and not a small amount of hurt. "Judas," she hissed.

Madison raised her eyebrows. "That's a little grandiose, Ally, even for you. Besides, Matt lives near me."

"And Ted and I are, what, roommates by comparison?" Ally turned back to Wren, her tone taking on a desperate tinge.

Wren snorted. "I can't imagine him wanting to shack up with you, after the way you've treated him."

Ally stiffened. "Then why the hell are you telling me to take him running?"

It was a good question. Ted wasn't sure he wanted to spend that much time with Ally, either.

Oh, who was he kidding. He liked her. Even if she hated him. Probably partly because she hated him. He liked her passion, her aggression, the way she stood her ground. Even if he didn't understand her in the least, he was certain there was something else there, some explanation. And maybe, if they were workout partners, he would get to hear it.

"I didn't say you had to run." Wren smothered another smile. "You could rent bikes. You can do whatever—and I do mean whatever—you like," she added, her tone just a little bit suggestive, "so long as you get some good cardio in. You know how I feel about cardio."

Ally glared at their captain. "Why are you doing this, Wren?"

Wren shrugged. "I felt like causing a scene? There's not enough drama on this team."

Ted couldn't help it; he laughed. And then, meeting Matt's wide eyes, realized his mistake.

Ted could have sworn Ally's voice had previously gone up an octave, but it came back down double when she twisted to face him and said, in an accusatory tone, "*You* did this."

"What?" It was Ted's turn with the monosyllable. "What are you talking about? Wren did this."

"Well, she's gonna have to undo this."

Wren, who had already pulled a small white board out from behind the boards, snorted. "Do you hear the way she talks about me, Lewis? I might have to invest in the equipment for wind sprints, if only to communicate to Bryant that I am, still, the captain of this team and, therefore, I remain in charge." She began marking X's in the corner of the board. "Well, Lewis? Thoughts on this recent development?"

"Uh, no comment?"

Wren laughed, turning to face them again. "Sheath your sword, Bryant. You can't fight your way out of this one. And it's only the once, anyways, unless you continue to piss me off." She glanced at Ted. "Besides, he doesn't seem that bothered by it. Tell me, Lewis, were you secretly hoping for something like this?"

Ted's jaw dropped. He scrambled for an answer that would satisfy both Wren and Ally—but maybe not honesty. "I, uh—no." He watched Allegra, who now appeared affronted. "I mean, I'm not upset—Ally's a great player, and I'm sure we have a lot we could learn from each other, and—"

"Relax, Lewis, you're not on trial for murder." Wren's lips twitched. "Yet."

"If anyone kills someone, it'll be me." Ally announced. "Seriously, Wren? First AC, now this?"

"Wait, what do you mean, 'first AC?'" Ted asked, confused.

Wren grimaced. "Do you want to tell him, Bryant, or should I?"

Ally sighed and rolled her eyes. She mumbled something unintelligible.

"What?" Ted hadn't been able to make out a word of what she said.

"I *said*," Ally continued in a significantly louder voice that carried across the ice and captured the whole team's attention. "That she stripped me off my status as assistant captain on account of my pugilistic tendencies and bad attitude."

The team stared. Ted stared. Ally glared. She turned to Wren. "Please, please reconsider, Wren. I promise, I'll be perfect!"

"You'll be perfect together," Wren refused her gently.

"Wren—"

"Till death do you part," she added, cheekily. "Now, take a look at this drill. I'm worried the corners will be a clusterfuck."

❄

Ally shoved her left elbow pad into her beat-up duffle bag then zipped it closed. Standing, she swung it over her shoulder, staggering slightly under its weight but soon finding her balance. She refused to give Harvard any reason to doubt her ability to carry her own weight.

He already had reason to doubt her ability to play hockey.

Ally's game had been off all night, following the announcement. Wren had effectively, silently, given her a choice: suck it up, or quit the team. And she was not losing custody of the Manhattan Monsters to Theodore "Harvard" Lewis, the second-worst asshole to walk into her world. He probably played with a monogrammed maroon mouthguard.

Okay, it couldn't be maroon because she'd seen him spit it out and it was royal blue. But it might still have a monogram! And, like, an unreasonably long one at that. Five letters and a numeral. He'd been a legacy admission at Essex, after all. Ally might have gone to a public school on Long Island, but she knew about boarding school boys. They were the worst.

Everett had been a boarding school boy. Not Essex—he wasn't smart enough to get into Essex, despite being from the right kind of family. But he'd attended prep school alright, to prepare him for Harvard. And, during the two and a half years that they were dating, Ally had overlooked this. She hadn't thought much about it. But now she knew it was a stain on his soul. His soul, which must have looked like Dorian Gray's portrait to make up for the fact that his face recalled Guillaume Geefs' infamous angel. An angel who wore needlepoint belts made custom for him by his mother—and who enjoyed inflicting emotional abuse.

Ally bet Ted was just like Everett, a Harvard man with no conscience and a cold heart. The only difference was his dark hair and good manners. A decoy, the latter quality. He probably got away with murder.

Speaking of murder...

Ally caught up to her captain and *former* friend. "Wren, I'm going to kill you."

Wren turned as she exited the rink. "Still not over it, Ally?"

"It's not fair! You did this deliberately."

Wren grinned, but then her expression sobered. "I did. But I didn't do it to mess with you." She zipped up her leather jacket. Ally hadn't worn a coat, so she just shivered in her sheen of still-drying sweat. "Ally, listen to me. You were the second best non-goalie player on this team, aside from me. Now, you have competition."

Ally rolled her eyes. "Just because he scores a lot of goals—"

"A fact with which you can't seem to cope."

Ally stopped in her tracks. "That's not true! I'm coping."

Wren stopped, too. "Oh really? By racking up penalties and threatening to off your captain-slash-coach?"

Ally sighed. "Alright, fine. Maybe I have been a bit wound up…"

Wren raised her thin, frosted pink brows.

"But it has nothing to do with the idea that he's better than I am. My pride is not so colossal that I can't handle a bit of competition!"

"Then what's going on, Ally? Why the hostility?"

"He…" Ally took a deep breath and exhaled on a plaintive whisper. "My ex went to Harvard, too."

Wren groaned. "Ally, you can't judge a book by its college!"

Ally scuffed her soles against the pavement. "You can when it's *that* college."

"No," Wren insisted, "I can't believe I'm saying this, but you can't. Besides, how different from Harvard really is BU?"

Ally started walking again, toward the subway. "I'm not going to argue with you."

"That'd be a first," Wren muttered, following her.

Ignoring her friend, Ally continued. "Just tell me why you stuck me with him. Was it really to torment me? Is this some kind of punishment? Because I promise you, losing assistant captain was enough!"

Wren sighed. "This isn't punishment, Ally. I wish you would see that. I put you two together because I truly believe you could learn the most from him—more than from anyone else on the team—and he could learn a lot from you."

Ally suppressed a slight smile at the compliment. She was still frustrated with her friend. "It's just one run, Wren. That's what you said. We have to work out together, once. I'm not going to learn anything from one run. And neither is he."

"It might not be just one run," Wren offered ominously. "You might end up enjoying your new partner…"

Ally shook her head. "Nope, you'll see. Nothing will come of this."

Wren laughed. "We'll see. Besides all the skill-sharing the two of you could get up to, if you decide to continue to work out together, I really think there are some valuable lessons you could learn from each other in terms of demeanor and attitude."

"Just because he's never gotten a penalty—in the *one* game we've played with him—doesn't mean that he's any less deserving of one than I—"

"Ally. Be realistic. You are a firecracker, a wrecking ball! You *cause* trouble. Ted? He's chill. Too chill. He doesn't get riled up by anything—except, maybe, by you."

Ally huffed. "So you're saying you want us to what, swap personalities?"

"No," Wren countered, smiling wickedly. "Just rub off on each other. Maybe rub each other off."

Her jaw dropped momentarily before she found her voice again. "You want me to *sleep* with him?! Jesus, Wren, that's diabolical and *highly* unethical!"

Wren put her hands up, adjusting the bag that hung over

her shoulder. "Hey, hey. I didn't say you had to. Just focus on working out, then. Go for a run—or a ride. Talk strategy and technique while you're at it. You two could teach each other a ton."

"But—"

"You may not be done arguing, but I am." They had reached the station. "Come talk to me again when you've gone on your 'one and done' run. But otherwise, quit complaining. I've done you a favor, Bryant, whether or not you can see it for what it is. I expect you to make the most of this."

Ally sighed and swiped into the subway behind her captain and friend.

Theodore Lewis was going to be the death of her. If he didn't drive her insane first.

CHAPTER 5
FLUTTER

TED LAY on his king-sized bed and stared up at the glowing screen of his phone. He was in the app store, looking at the various dating apps. *Why not?* He thought, and downloaded the one in question—the one about which he'd heard so much. It was a Friday night. He was lonely and bored and he had nothing better to do with his time. Why not look for love? It wasn't like he was going find it.

Ted worried his lip as he read the rules of Flutter. No underage users, no inappropriate images, a zero tolerance policy for harassment and abuse. That all sounded good. Plus, they wouldn't sell his information. Nice.

The set up was simple: you created a profile, complete with a photo of yourself and a brief bio that included your age, your age-range, your gender, your sexuality, and your sun sign. *Huh.* He wondered whether Ally was into astrology. It didn't *seem* like it, but…

Whatever, this wasn't about Ally.

Ted refocused on the screen, which was prompting him to choose a photo from his library. He selected a few that were recent enough and, by his estimation, attractive enough. It took him a couple minutes to find several that weren't selfies or filled with family. He didn't want random strangers knowing what his loved ones looked like.

Next, you listed some interests. Ted typed and suggestions popped up. Hockey (ice), hiking, Katharine Hepburn movies, contemporary romantic fiction, New England, ghosts, cat cafes, cooking, lacrosse, sailing, reading, history, dinosaurs, travel, 00's rom-coms. Somewhat satisfied with that eclectic list of interests, and confident that he would eventually remember more that he could add later, Ted clicked through to the next step.

In the next step, you answered a few questions—which you had to update regularly because they changed monthly, the app warned him. Was Ted a cat person or a dog person? Both. Wait, why wasn't there an option for both?

Ted shook his head at the creators of the app, who were clearly trying to create discord for the sake of engagement.

What was Ted's favorite brand of coffee? Ted was more of a tea-drinker, but he supposed when forced he preferred Wild Goose, a Pennsylvanian brand whose stores doubled as delis. Where was Ted's favorite view? That was a good question, honestly. He would sound like a prick if he put "off the balcony of my parents' summer house" so instead he typed "Quai de la Tournelle"—because Paris was romantic, wasn't it? He wondered whether Allegra had ever been.

Shaking his head to clear it of inconvenient emotional clutter, Ted finished designing his profile. When he was decently satisfied, he screenshotted it and sent the images to Matt along with a text that read:

Hey, man. I'm thinking of getting into online dating—Is this a good profile?

Ted scrunched the pillow behind his head, struggling to get comfortable. Hopefully the dating would merely start online, but soon continue in person. Hopefully there would be dating, and not just swiping. Except that Flutter ran on clicks, not swipes. Ted scrolled back to the rules and read.

Click to view profile, double-click to delete profile from dating pool, click and hold to keep profile in dating pool—or "prioritize" that person. It was different from the system of swipes that had been all the rage the last time he signed up for a dating app. He supposed he would get the hang of it eventually, however. Click, double-click, click and hold.

A notification popped up, blocking the top of Ted's screen. Matt had texted back his approval as well as a vote of confidence, on the condition that Ted removed the "lacrosse" tag because that "sounded douchey." It did, didn't it? *Whew*. Good thing Matt caught that.

Ted returned to Flutter's interface and fixed up his profile a bit. He agreed to the rules of conduct and the privacy notice. And then he was good to go. Ted clicked through to his "dating pool."

It was empty.

Apparently, though, it was supposed to fill as the app found nearby profiles with shared interests or similar answers. Sure enough, within thirty seconds, the app refreshed and a stack of profiles landed on Ted's screen. He started clicking through them, one by one. Interestingly, the app showed their profiles first and their names and pictures second.

This woman hated animals, so that was a no-go. This one liked rom-coms, so maybe they could bond over Katherine Heigl. But she thought all athletes were "assholes" so Ted had a feeling that wouldn't work. This person loved dinosaurs and their favorite view was from the Eiffel Tower *and* they looked cute in their profile picture—but they were looking for a fourth for their polycule, and Ted was a one-at-a-time kind of guy. He sighed. And then he saw the next profile.

A woman, 28, interested in men. Scorpio with a "fire moon," whatever that meant. She loved Wild Goose, too, *and* she played ice hockey. Her interests included Katharine Hepburn movies, travel, cat cafes, reading, and ghosts. Ted's eyebrows rose. Had he met his match? Already? He clicked through to the picture.

Allegra.

Ted stared at his screen for a long moment before starting to swipe through her pictures, telling himself he was just curious. She looked lovely in the first image, which was a bathroom selfie pretending not to be. She looked sweaty, in a good way, in the second—which had clearly been taken after a game, because she was waving her stick and wearing a Monsters jersey. She took his breath away in the third.

It had to have been taken professionally, or at least by a very skilled amateur photographer. She was mid-air, mid-jump, hovering above a pile of red and gold leaves. There were leaves in the air and in her hands; her fists were forever half-furled. Her hair bounced around her, a hint of curl, burnished bronze through the warm autumnal filter. Her smile, however, warmed him like the summer sun refusing to fade on a late September day.

He blinked and it broke his fascination long enough for him to toss his phone away. Then he scrambled after it, to make sure it hadn't accidentally clicked to prioritize her profile. He'd never hear the end of it, if he accidentally held onto her.

Ted sighed, sinking into the squashed pillow. After a long minute in which he struggled to stay the course of his thoughts, he stood up, switched on a light, and set off for the kitchen. It was dinner time. He'd had enough of online dating for one night.

"Fuck him." Vanessa sipped her frozen piña colada through a black paper straw.

Ally nodded. "Exactly."

"No, I mean, *fuck* him."

Ally stared blankly at her friend, who had set aside her drink and was now staring at her expectantly. "Are we not saying the exact same—"

"No! We are most certainly not!"

Ally cocked her head. "Then what exactly—"

"Oh my god, I cannot *believe* you are making me spell this out for you. You should have sex with him!" Vanessa punctuated each word in the last sentence with a clap.

Ally recoiled, not quite instantly. "What? No!" Why was everyone saying she should have sex with Ted? First Wren, now Vanessa?

"Why not? Hate sex is always the hottest." Vanessa went back to sipping her drink, giving Ally an amused side eye.

"V, I am not having sex with him. Not now, not ever." Ally took a swig of her sour. It was bracingly bitter, like her. Or so Everett had once told her.

Vanessa sighed. "Okay, whatever you say. But the sexual tension in the office has skyrocketed since he arrived and, I hate to break it to you, it's all you."

"Don't be ridiculous. I can't be the only one." Ted was tall and handsome. "Other people are bound to have noticed—"

"Aha!" Vanessa pounced, her eyes wide behind her cat-eyes. "So you admit that you *are* attracted to him."

Ally flushed. "I admit nothing! But even if I were, who wouldn't be?"

"Uh, me?"

Ally rolled her eyes. "You don't count, you're spoken for. Super spoken for." Vanessa and her boyfriend were wildly, passionately, publicly in love.

"But if I weren't, Ted would be my type." Vanessa signaled for a refill. "A tall glass of ice water. Single, single-minded…"

"What do you mean, 'single-minded?' And how do you know that he's single?"

Vanessa laughed. "I did some snooping after lunch the other day. His socials all list him as single."

Ally shook her head, savoring the sour's cruel cranberry flavor. "That could just mean he never updates."

Vanessa whipped out her phone. "No, check this. Two posts in the last week."

Ally reluctantly looked at the screen. Vanessa was right. He was active.

"And he hasn't posted a photo of himself with a girl since 2016. Well, a girl that's not his sister or his mother." Vanessa switched to a different app and scrolled for Ally's benefit.

"So he's a private person! He probably still has some chick he met at his parents' country club on the side."

Vanessa tsked. "Don't be such a reverse snob, Ally. Your parents are hardly poor."

Ally gulped her drink. Maybe she was playing up Ted's socio-economic status symbols so that she didn't have to think too deeply about him as a person. "Fine, whatever. I'm just saying. He could be secretly dating a Kennedy, for all we know." She thought about it. "I mean, if he *were* dating a Kennedy, he'd *have* to keep it a secret. Look at what happened to Taylor Swift!"

"People judged her," Vanessa nodded, sagely. "Like you're judging Ted."

"I am doing no such thing!"

"Look, Ally. I'm not your therapist. I'm not your mom. I am your friend. And as your friend, I am obligated to tell you when you are being a bitch."

Ally's jaw dropped. "V!"

Vanessa held up her hands, then extended one to accept her second drink. She thanked the bartender, who was sweet on her, with a smile. "Don't look at me like that, Ally. You are. You have been all week. And did I hear you *tripped* him at the game on Sunday? A member of your own team?"

Ally scoffed. "Oh, so he's spreading that sob story."

"No! You muttered something about doing it again under your breath the other day when he beat you to the copier! Jesus, Ally. Get a grip."

Ally blew out her breath, feeling her cheeks heat. "I'm sorry," she muttered.

"Don't tell *me* that," Vanessa replied pertly. Then her tone softened. "Look, is this about your evil ex?"

"*Don't* say his name," Ally warned her.

"I didn't!" Vanessa put a hand on Ally's forearm. "Ally, I know it's hard. But he's not him."

"He just walks like him, talks like him, and went to the same college has him."

"So, maybe you have a type!" Vanessa shrugged. "Besides, I do not believe for an instant that Evelyn, or whatever that other dude's name is, was half so polite or charming or pleasant as Ted."

Ally sent her friend a skeptical look. "Oh, so now you're his best friend *and* PR firm? What, is he paying you to say this stuff about him?"

Vanessa laughed. "Not even he could afford my fees." Then she leaned in. "Tell me about Evelyn."

Ally shook her head. "Everett, and no thanks."

"Come on, what else are Keg Fridays for if not exorcising your evil ex?"

"V, Keg Friday is over. We left the office an hour ago. And all the alcohol in the world wouldn't exorcise Everett. Trust me, I've tried."

Vanessa swiveled on her barstool. "I wasn't saying, 'drown your sorrows.' I was suggesting the other oral method." She paused. "Well. The other *other* oral method. Talking!"

Ally shrugged, already uncomfortable. "There's not much to talk about. Everett was perfect, for the first few months. We met during the winter of my freshman year at BU. He was a sophomore at Harvard. By the time summer rolled around, he had evolved into this emotionally abusive asshole. Cheated on me twice—that I know of. Constantly put me down. Made me forget about our fights, somehow? Don't even ask me how that's possible. Manipulated me, frequently.

"At one point, two years in—I know, I should have broken up with him, but—whatever. I loved him. And he made me believe I needed him. So, when he pressured me to move in with him, I did. Because he made me feel like if I didn't, he wouldn't love me. That he would leave me. And what would I have been, without him? I'd already alienated most of my friends *for* him."

Ally shook her head, feeling vaguely ill at the thought of not just the abuse but the years of her life that she had wasted on her abuser. "God, I wish he *had* left me. When I think about the way he used to hold rent payments over my head... Or how he'd leer at freshmen girls in front of me! Or the way he'd come to my games only to yell at me about my 'shit strategy,' when he hadn't even played hockey since he was in high school! And the whole time, everyone thought he was this upscale, classy gentleman. Because he was from Harvard, and Brixley before that."

Brixley was a posh boarding school in Massachusetts, allegedly less academically rigorous than Essex, where Ted had gone, but the same general principle. A place for promising young men. And, she supposed, since the late 80s, women.

Vanessa exhaled slowly. "Jesus, Ally. I had no idea. I mean, I knew he was bad, but... I didn't realize he was abusive. I'm so sorry." She rested her palm on Ally's forearm, and Ally felt a little less sick but no less alone.

"Thanks, V. But—yeah. That's why I'm not having hate sex with Harvard. He's probably an Everett 2.0, an upgrade on the prototype designed to destroy my life." She sighed before she could get too lost in sci-fi analogies. "He is hot, though."

"He *is* hot," Vanessa echoed. A silence fell over them as she watched Ally pensively.

"What?"

Vanessa twisted her lips. "Still… I'm not so sure Ted's the monster you think he is."

Ally sighed. "Do I have to go over it again?"

"No, no—just listen to me. I've spent a bit of time with him this week and honestly I'd recommend his company. He's very thoughtful and pretty sweet. And I think he saved Sally from getting fired the other day." Sally was another copywriter, prone to making mistakes that would have been comedic if they weren't often also disastrous.

"What happened?"

"Harold," Vanessa answered, dryly.

"Well. Acts of alleged heroism aside… Are you sure *you're* not crushing on him?"

"Ally. I am happily taken, as well you know." Vanessa raised her immaculately threaded eyebrows. "All I'm saying is, give him a chance. Not romantically, not even sexually, just… interpersonally. Try. For me."

"Why? What's in it for you?"

Vanessa parodied a winning Miss America smile. "World peace."

Ally and Vanessa each enjoyed their respective fills of eye-watering sours and fruity cocktails, to go with the office gossip. Then they parted ways as Vanessa went off to join her boyfriend, Marcus, at a friend's party in Hell's Kitchen. Ally considered tagging along—Vanessa had invited her, after all —but she wouldn't know anyone and she didn't really like big parties.

She took the subway across town and walked down First

Avenue to her apartment. By the time she turned the key in her door, she had sobered up significantly.

"Heathcliff!" She cried, as her cat jumped up from his perch on the counter to greet her. "Did you miss me, baby?" He rubbed against her shin and started to purr. "You haven't been this affectionate since I gave you a piece of bacon last weekend. What are you up to?"

Just then, Ally's phone started to ring.

"Hang on, one second, I'm coming," she said, to no one in particular. She shut the door behind her and pulled her phone from her tote bag, which was painted to look like the cover of a book. *Wuthering Heights*, to be precise.

She read the display, not recognizing the number. It was probably spam.

Still… It could be one of her friends—kidnapped, her phone stolen by kidnappers, forced to use a payphone now that she'd escaped. Which of her friends would have the kind of change required for a payphone? It wasn't like people walked around with wallets these days. Well, they did. But cash was a rarity—even more so, change. And, besides, did payphones have 508 area codes?

Sighing, Ally answered the call. "Hello?"

"Allegra? Sorry, I mean, Ally?"

She recognized his slight Boston accent instantly. "This is she."

"This is Ted Lewis, from GreenLight. And the Monsters, of course."

Ally laughed. He was such an idiot. "I know who you are, Harvard."

"Right, of course." He exhaled.

Ally found herself attuning to his breathing's rhythm. Weird, but okay. "Well?"

"Well, what?"

"What do you want, Ted?"

"Oh!" He sounded genuinely surprised that he needed a

reason to talk to her, as though he had called just to hear the sound of her voice. "I was calling to ask if you wanted to go on that run."

"Now?!" It was eight o'clock on a Friday night! Didn't he have something better to do? Some*one* better to do? Didn't she?

Sadly...

"No, not now." He laughed nervously. "I meant tomorrow. Between nine and noon, whenever suits."

No, no way. She was not going on a run with the enemy, whatever Wren had said. Ted would probably be in better shape than she was and rub it in her face.

Vanessa's face flickered in her memory. *Try. For me.* Then it was Wren's turn to appear, like the ghost of Christmas whenever. *You two could teach each other a ton.*

Ally sighed. She hated having such wise and conscientious friends. Not that there was any wisdom or justice in this. Reluctantly, Ally returned, "Where?"

She could practically hear him perk up. "So, you'll do it? You'll come for a run with me?"

"Yeah, just... wear a shirt." Oh, god. Why had she felt the need to say that?

"What?"

"Wear a shirt!" Ally repeated, a little shrilly. "No one needs to see that." She remembered his abs, glistening with sweat. Was she body-shaming him for being sexy?

Ally straightened. No, he wasn't sexy. He was condescending, and aloof, and clueless, and rude, but he wasn't sexy. Sexy was reserved for non-assholes. And movie-stars, who were all assholes. Except Heath Ledger, may he rest in peace.

"Okay, I'll wear a shirt. Was planning on it, actually." He sounded confused. Welcome to the club, Harvard! "What about Central Park?"

"It's nice, I guess. Why?"

"I live near there. Would you want to meet at the northern entrance to the zoo?"

"Are we planning on watching the polar bears eat breakfast? Will a small child be in attendance?"

"There are no polar bears at the Central Park Zoo. And no, I don't have any children."

Yet. Ally could just see him, surrounded by children. Dark hair, light eyes. Laughing, screaming, building sandcastles on the Cape…

Something flickered in her, a warmth that she wasn't expecting. She shoved it down, smothered the spark that was threatening.

"Fine, we'll meet at the northern entrance. By the haunted clocktower."

He chuckled. "It's not haunted. Trust me."

"Trust you? What are you, some kind of ghost hunter?" She scoffed.

"No, but I happen to like ghosts. And they like me. If there were any ghosts in that clocktower, they'd have said hi to me."

She wasn't sure if he was kidding or not. Deranged and slightly disturbed, eh? Harvard had more depth than she'd bargained for. "Whatever," she said, shaking her head. "Encircled by dancing animal statues? It's creepy."

He sobered. "Yes. It is creepy."

"So… is that all?"

Ted was silent for a moment. Reluctantly, it seemed, he agreed. "Yeah."

Feeling a strange twinge of disappointment, which she immediately disregarded, Ally said her goodbye. "See you tomorrow, preppy. At ten."

He huffed a little laugh. "See you, Ally."

Ally hung up her phone and tossed it on the sofa. She felt… restless. A little excited, even. She needed to clear her head, which was currently full of Ted's baritone. Determined to settle her nerves the best way she knew how, she went to her bedroom and closed the door. Heathcliff could scratch away, but she wasn't letting him in anytime soon. Ally needed privacy for this.

She went to the overstuffed closet and reached for a box on the top shelf. Some sweaters fell out as she pulled it from its perch. She left them on the floor, promising herself she would pick them up them later. Ally set the box on the bed and started to strip.

Her skin tingled as she slowly removed her blouse, dragging the silky material up over her stomach. Her pants came next, a quick shimmy that left her feeling frisky and free. Remembering the blinds, Ally closed them. Then she crossed the room to the radio, which she turned on—the classical station. Ally didn't know a thing about classical music except that it masked the buzz of her vibrator and made her feel... in touch with herself, as she touched herself. Something about the way the music crescendoed helped her to climax.

Ally lay down on the bed and leisurely removed her bra but not her panties. She let one of her hands trace a delicate path around her nipples and down past her navel. Like a breakaway drill, only there was no puck and the net was empty. And when it came to scoring in this game, she was without a doubt more skilled than Ted.

Ally sighed. She let her fingers circle her clitoris over the cotton of her underwear. The sensation made her squirm slightly. She played with herself through her panties for a minute or two, watching the material darken with moisture. Then she reached for the box, popping open the lid to reveal a small collection of silicone toys. She extracted her trusty old bullet—which needed replacement, as soon as she could afford a nice one—and rotated the base so that it started to rumble.

Shoving aside questions like "what happened to hating

him?" and "is this even ethical?" Ally allowed herself to remember. And then, to imagine.

Ted.

His shirt, wet with sweat, discarded on the bench. His abs, shining in the low light of the locker room. They were alone, and the air smelled sweet like honeysuckle or mead. He hooked a thumb into the waistband of his compression underwear, which left little to the imagination. Still, she was a greedy girl. She wanted to see it all. Ignoring her hatred for him—or, rather, the hatred she was supposed to be feeling, but couldn't for the life of her locate—Ally pulled aside her panties and turned up her vibrator.

One night. One orgasm, even. And then she would be done with this ridiculous, inconvenient attraction. Which was probably just the alcohol's effect, anyway. Ally moaned and reached for a dildo. Licking it up and down until it was lubricated, she then slowly drew it into her cunt. Fuck, it felt good. It felt even better when she closed her eyes and pretended it was him.

No longer caring about her confused feelings, Ally brought herself to orgasm. Again and again. Her body trembled, and her mind went blank. Except for his name, which she called out even as she came.

CHAPTER 6
THE SKELETON, REVISITED

TEN O'CLOCK ON THE DOT.

Ted leaned against the arched base of the creepy clock tower, sensing not a single specter. He'd worn a shirt, as requested, and some running shorts that were perhaps a little short. Not that he was *trying* to show off his thighs, but he did rather think they were an asset.

He checked his smart watch, the tiny screen glowing in the arch's shadow. Two texts from his mother but nothing from Ally. He wondered briefly if she'd missed the subway by a minute, then remembered that it wasn't actually normal to be exactly on time. Ted pulled out his phone and opened his mother's messages. He might as well respond while he waited.

Good morning, Teddy-bear!

Your sister says you met someone. Why didn't you tell me?

Is she smart? Pretty? She is a she, isn't she? Not that it matters to your father or me!

Ted sighed. Thanks for spilling the beans, Belle. He started to type but stopped when someone coughed. Ted jerked his head around.

Ally was leaning against the brick wall beside him,

watching him. She smelled like orange blossoms and she looked... suspicious.

"Who's the girl, Teddy-bear?"

Ted quickly locked his phone. "What?"

Ally shifted against the arch, her hair pulled back into a ponytail that accentuated her high cheekbones, aided by the surrounding shadows. "The one your mother was asking about."

Ted swallowed, trying to focus on Ally's words and not her cheekbones—nor her parted lips. A smile hovered at one corner of her mouth, curving her lips just the tiniest bit while lending the slightest warmth to her words.

Shaking himself, Ted remembered that the last time they'd been this close, Ally had tripped him.

"It's rude to read someone else's texts."

She shrugged. "I'm rude. Horribly rude. Haven't you noticed? Besides, I couldn't help but see. You don't tilt your screen."

Ted was about to protest that he shouldn't have to, but she continued.

"Anyway, you shouldn't read top secret texts when some-one's standing next to you."

"I didn't even know you were there! You snuck up on me."

Ally pushed off the arch and planted her arms akimbo. Ted was helpless to avert his own gaze, which traced the curve of her waist, the swell of her hips. "Your lack of situa-tional awareness is not my problem, Harvard. Unless you intend to bring this kind of cluelessness to the ice."

Ted rolled his eyes at that remark, even though he knew it was intended to provoke. Most of what Ally said was intended to provoke. She was.... provocative. "My guard is usually up during a game. Less so, when I'm in the park waiting for my running partner."

Eyebrows raised, Ally checked her phone. "Ted, it's 10:03.

I'm barely late. Besides, it's not my fault. My train missed me."

"Don't you mean you missed your train?" Ted stood up straight and started walking before his body got other ideas, ideas more in line with his present state of being alone in the shadows with a beautiful woman. A beautiful woman who hated his guts. Or at least, so he had thought. Flustered, he nevertheless gestured for Ally to join him.

After a moment's hesitation, she fell into step beside him. "No. So where do you live, anyway?"

"On 82nd."

"Uptown boy. Exactly as I expected." She looked satisfied, as though he'd fulfilled the stereotype of her choosing. "Why the Central Park Zoo? Wouldn't the Met be a better land-mark? I could have taken the express to 86th Street."

Ted thought about it. "I don't know, I suppose it reminds me of home."

"The zoo?" She laughed, somewhat derisively.

Put on the defensive, Ted clarified. "Not the zoo itself. Just the seals." He wasn't about to tell her about spending summers on the Cape, because she'd hate him more than ever, so instead he searched for a different memory of the animals. "They remind me of the aquarium in Boston. I used to go there with my kid sister when she was little."

Ally lit up. "I love the Boston Aquarium!"

Ted smiled slightly. It was the most enthusiastic he'd ever heard her. "I didn't know they still took students on field trips in undergrad," he teased.

She shot him a look. "They don't. But it's not that far from BU's main campus."

"It's not far from Cambridge, either."

Ally's expression dimmed.

Ted scrambled, cursing himself for having brought up Harvard again. The collegiate chip in Ally's shoulder was as deep as the Mariana Trench. "Hey, have you stretched?"

She shook her head.

Ted slowed. "I haven't either." That wasn't technically true, but it would have to do. "Shall we?"

Ally nodded. "Wren would kill me if you pulled a muscle on my watch. She'd probably accuse me of injuring you deliberately. Something about sabotaging my potential soulmate."

Ted chose to ignore this comment, rather than to ruminate on her word choice or retort with a reminder that she had, in fact, tripped him once before.

As he bent down to touch his toes, Ted glanced at Ally. She looked decidedly glum. Was working out with him once really such a tribulation?

"Why are you determined to dislike me?" He asked quietly.

Ally wobbled on one foot, stretching her right quad. She narrowed her eyes at him. "Why are you so determined to like me?"

Ted shrugged, lowering himself to the ground. As he settled into a butterfly stretch, he answered, "Because you don't like me." And it was almost the truth. Telling Ally that he was attracted to her would only scare her off or make her hate him all the more.

She sighed, switching legs. "That makes no sense."

Ted suppressed a smile. "It's like this, Ally. You're a challenge. One I believe I'm equal to. And besides, I'm not so sure you actually hate me. You did say yes to working out with me."

"It's a run, Ted, not an offer of marriage. Besides, I had to say yes. Wren ordered us to do some cardio together."

He chuckled. "She's our captain, not our commander-in-chief. I would have lied for you," he added, surprising himself. He didn't like to lie, but it was true—he would have lied, if she'd asked it of him.

"Whatever." Ally started to roll her ankles. "Just understand this. I am not some puzzle for you to solve. Nor am I a broken doll."

"What?" He'd understood the first metaphor, but she'd lost him on the second.

"Don't try to fix me, Ted. This isn't a Hallmark movie."

Ted happened to like Hallmark movies, although he wished they had more chemistry, not to mention a mere minute of sexual activity. But he got the message. "I get it. And for the record, I like you just as you are."

She glanced at him sharply.

Ted grinned. "*Bridget Jones' Diary* isn't a Hallmark movie."

"Regardless, I've never seen it."

Ted's jaw nearly dropped. "But it's a classic! Literally, it's an Austen adaptation."

Ally shrugged. "And I'm more of a Brontë girl."

"I thought you said you weren't a girl."

"What?" She squinted down at him.

Ted smirked, leaning back on his palms. "You're a woman, remember?"

She kicked him, gently. "Shut up, preppy."

Ted sprang to his feet. "The attacks continue! I'm telling Wren."

Ally started to jog away. "She hates crybabies. As do I."

Ted caught up with her in a second. "Well, I guess that means we'll never be able to watch *Jane Eyre* together. That whole thing about the invisible string always makes me cry."

"Rochester said that to manipulate her." Ally shook her head in evident disgust.

"I didn't say it was romantic," Ted countered, lengthening his stride.

Ally sped up, eyeing him curiously. "Then why does it make you cry?"

Ted sobered. "Because it makes me think of what his first wife went through. The love he should have showed her, but didn't."

Ally dodged a tourist, keeping her eyes on the path ahead. Eventually, she responded in a cryptic tone. "Bad men aren't a fictional phenomenon, Ted."

"So, you're from the middle of nowhere, Massachusetts, right?"

"Yeah." Ted didn't even sound winded, halfway through their run. Ally supposed she shouldn't be surprised, given his performance on the ice. "I mean, the town has a name. And technically it's not that far from civilization—about halfway between Boston and Worcester."

"Whoa!" Ally let out a surprised laugh.

Ted slowed, turning to her. His cheeks were a little pink from exertion. "What?"

"Your accent!"

Ted's brows knit, sending a rivulet of sweat down his nose. He wiped it away without taking his eyes off of her. "I don't have an accent."

"Umm, yes you do." Ally slowed, too, until they were walking in the shade of the old trees. "You sound like a long lost Kennedy."

Ted's eyebrows skyrocketed. "I do not—"

"But when you said 'Worcester,' it went the way of the dodo and this stereotypical, practically Southie accent took its place."

Ted scoffed, but his curiosity was clearly piqued. "Nonsense. I pronounce Worcester the same way I would any other city's name."

"Woostah's more like it…" She grinned at the look on his face. "I hate to break it to you, Theodore, but you sound like a run-of-the-mill Masshole sometimes." Ally laughed as Ted shook his head, his expression inscrutable. "Does that bother you? Sounding like a normal person, a regular human being, and not some Essex-educated elite?"

Ted continued to shake his head. "No, of course not. If anything… I mean, whatever. I am a run-of-the-mill Mass-hole, right? Isn't that what you think?"

Ally laughed. "No, I think you're something special. Your very own breed of—" But at the hopeful, open look on his face, she couldn't help but take a sudden left turn, away from bitterness. "You're your own person, Ted. And not a bad one at that."

He blushed faintly, or maybe it was just his face flushing from all their talking-while-running. Even if they were currently walking. "Is that a… compliment? Coming from Allegra Bryant?"

She tore her eyes away from his, focusing instead on the path that lay before them. "Don't get used to it…" she mumbled, feeling entirely uncertain of herself and yet utterly sure of one thing—strange as it was—him. "Come on, let's pick up the pace. We've got a ways to go before we hit the pool where they sail the toy boats."

Ted acquiesced, running a hand through his increasingly damp hair. "Honestly, I have no idea where we are. Do you?"

Ally shook her head, amused despite herself. This run was turning out to be not such a terrible idea, after all… Not that she would ever admit as much to Wren. Or Ted. It was probably just endorphins, but she was beginning to not hate Ted with the fire of a thousand suns. Maybe not even one? If she wasn't careful, she might end up liking him. Or at least tolerating his presence with uncharacteristic amounts of equanimity and grace.

"Of course I know where we are. We're…" She looked around her, not recognizing any landmarks. "Well, we're certainly not lost."

Ted chuckled. "Whatever you say, partner. Do you want me to look up our location on my watch?"

Ally tossed her ponytail. "Don't be ridiculous, Harvard. Central Park is hardly the wilderness. We'll be fine."

"Oh, I know we'll be fine."

"You do?" She cast a dubious glance in his direction. How was he always so chipper? And why did she like his sunniness so much? Well, not *so* much. But… enough? Enough not to abandon him to the maze that was the footpaths toward the southern center of the park.

"Yeah, I do."

Ally stared at him, ducking to avoid a low-hanging branch. "Why? How?"

He shrugged, his eyes tracking her sudden movement with mild concern. "I just do. Maybe I trust you. I mean, everyone else does." He looked back at the path, his lips curving. "What's the harm in a little interpersonal leap of faith?"

Ally's mood darkened instantly. "You should be more careful, Ted. It's like I said before."

He glanced over at her as they rounded a corner and she wasn't sure if he'd clocked her sudden shift in mood. "Oh?"

"Never mind. Just check your watch or whatever. I'm thirsty and I didn't sign up for a marathon."

Ted shuffled into the locker room with his bag and stick ten minutes after the appointed time the next night. "Sorry, cap." He waved to Wren. "Trains were delayed."

She nodded, pulling her jersey on. "No worries, Lewis. Just find a seat and start getting ready. You can tell me all about your cardio later."

Ted looked around the locker room. It was a mess of strewn-about gear and half-dressed teammates. There were a couple open spaces, but he zeroed in on the one next to Ally. After their run, he felt closer to her. And he was pretty sure the feeling was mutual. He set down his bag and slid onto the bench beside her.

She paused in the process of fastening a shin-pad. "What are you doing?"

"Sitting next to the woman who called me her soulmate," he answered with a smile he knew was cheeky but couldn't help.

"That was a joke. Wren, is this necessary?"

Ted frowned. Something was off. Ally had seemed so... chill during their run. But maybe that had just been the exercise-induced endorphins.

Wren snapped her chin strap in place. "Absolutely, Bryant. In fact, you'd better bond on that bench because you'll be skating on the same shift."

"What?" Ted and Ally asked in unison.

Wren chuckled. "You're playing together tonight. I changed the line up."

Ally groaned and Ted wished they could go back to yesterday, when she had been more inclined to laugh—and not just *at* him. What had changed in one day? What had made Ally remember her earlier hatred for him?

"Don't even think about asking me to switch you, Bryant. You're partners, now."

"What about Madison?" She protested.

"She'll still be on your shift. And she doesn't mind Lewis' presence."

Ted shrugged. This was great, even if Ally didn't share his opinion. He'd been itching to skate alongside her ever since he'd seen her take down both Brooklyn defensemen in a breakaway.

"Oh, and Lewis?"

Ted snapped to attention. "Yes, captain?"

"Don't let Bryant hog all the glory. I expect some shots on net from you, too. Back of the net, not the goalie's glove." Wren slid her mouthguard in. "I'll be on the ice, team. Get your asses in gear. I'm looking at you, Lewis. The trains are always delayed."

"Yes, sir." Ted immediately shucked his sweats and started rummaging in his bag for his athletic socks.

Beside him, Ally sighed as she secured one of the velcro straps that held her shoulder pads together.

"What's wrong?" Ted glanced over at her, concerned and increasingly curious about this mood swing. Or maybe the run had been an exception, rather than a change of course...

"Don't look at me like that."

Ted stepped into his padded pants. "Like what? Ally, you're fully dressed."

"Not like *that*." She dragged her jersey over her head, struggling to get it around the swell of her shoulder pad. "I already told you, I don't need fixing. I'm fine."

She didn't sound fine. She sounded furious for some reason.

"Did I do something, to piss you off? I thought—"

"Your existence pisses me off. Whatever you thought, you thought wrong." She reached for her helmet. "We can talk about this after the game. Better yet, never." And just like that, she strode off in the direction of the locker room door.

Ted was genuinely mystified. He'd thought they'd gotten on well yesterday. Sure, she kept him at arm's length, but she'd laughed at his jokes and hadn't bitten his head off after he'd let them get lost. He'd gotten a glimpse of her good humor, her competitive wit. He'd enjoyed her company—and she'd enjoyed his, he was pretty sure, if only for a bit. So why was she sighing and snapping at him now?

Well, Ted was determined to find out. "Stop." He reached for her arm. "Ally. Allegra!"

She whirled around, stepping just out of reach and shouting, "*What?!*"

He couldn't help himself—he raised his voice in return. "*What* is your problem?"

She took a step back, so that she was pressed against the door to the locker room. All eyes were on them. Except Wren's, because she'd left a minute earlier. More's the pity, Ted mused; their captain was probably the only one who could diffuse the tension in the room.

After a long moment and some murmuring, Matt stood and addressed them both. He held up his hands like he was dealing with an angry stallion and not two of his teammates. "Hey, hey." His voice, too, was calculated to soothe, but it seemed to inspire further ire in Ally, who turned her glare on him. "Why don't you two—"

"Why don't you stay the fuck out of it, Matt?" Ally erupted. "Just because you're assistant captain now doesn't mean you can tell me what to do."

Matt watched her with a calm that must have been infuriating for Ally, given her emotional state. "Actually, that's exactly what it means, so long as you're a player on this team." He glanced around. "Everyone, hit the ice." Giving Ally a stern look, he said in a nevertheless slightly softer tone, "Ally, let them through."

Ally stomped away from the door and past Ted in the process, knocking her shoulder into his. She sat down by her bag in a huff. The rest of the team—some still clutching their jerseys, gloves, and helmets—exited the locker room with haste. Madison was the last to leave, giving Ally a worried once-over.

Matt turned to Ted, his expression stern. "Talk this out, you two. Don't come out until you do." He opened the door. "And Ally? Try not to kill the second-best player on this team."

Ally gave him such a look, Ted was surprised Matt didn't wither like a hothouse flower in winter. Instead, he shook his head and closed the door behind him.

Ted exhaled slowly. "Allegra…"

She looked up at him then and he was shocked to see tears welling in her hazel eyes.

"Are you alright?" He made to cross the space that separated them.

"*Don't* come any closer." Her voice was thick with an emotion that refused to reveal itself to him. It couldn't just be rage. Embarrassment? Shame?

Ted sighed. A memory flashed in his mind, something she'd said as they stretched. Something that had stuck with him, even more than the adorable way she squinted in the sunshine or the hypnotic swish of her ponytail whenever she took the lead. *Bad men aren't a fictional phenomenon, Ted.*

He lowered himself to the nearest bench, directly across the locker room from where she sat. "Please, Ally. Talk to me."

She let her head fall into her hands. They looked so small without gloves, and her wrists so thin and breakable where they extended from within her thick elbow pads.

In this moment, Ally was fragile. Ted could see that. And he had a sudden and overwhelming urge to protect her, to shield her from harm. But right now what she needed was for him to listen.

"Fine. I'll talk to you."

Ally took a deep breath, grounding herself in the stale sweat smell of her surroundings. It was now or never, she supposed. "You remind me of my ex."

"Oh." Ted bit his lip, his brow furrowing. "I see."

Ally exhaled harshly. "No, you don't see. This ex, he... hurt me. Not physically—" She held a hand up, anticipating his confusion, his heroic horror. "Emotionally. Psychologically." She huffed a humorless laugh. "And that shit leaves scars, too."

Ted watched her for a long moment. His voice was quiet when he spoke, but his eye contact was unwavering; Ally found calm and earnest concern in those twin pools of pale blue. "We don't have to talk about it, if you don't want to. I'm sorry I put you on the spot like that, making demands of you. In front of everyone, no less. I know you don't owe me your story."

"I—" Ally paused, a little disarmed by his quick retreat but appreciative of the space—the truce—he was offering her. "No. I do owe you. I mean—I don't, but you deserve answers. I treated you badly and you… You were patient with me, beyond rhyme or reason. Persistent, even. Anyone else would have just dismissed me as a jerk and moved on with their life."

Ted flashed her a small smile, a peace offering she was sure she didn't deserve. "For better or worse, I'm not anyone else. I'm me."

Ally sucked in a breath, suddenly aware of the space that separated them. It felt cavernous. And yet…

She could still hear the rhythm of his breathing, the soft sound of his gear shifting against the bench. She wished he was closer, for some strange reason; she wished he was sitting beside her, his arm around her shoulders, even. But she'd need distance if she was going to do this, and do it right.

"Right. You're… you. Which is why I actually do feel comfortable sharing this with you," she continued.

His eyes widened and he sat up a little straighter.

"But don't get cocky, Harvard. A little heart to heart in the locker room doesn't make us besties."

"Cocky? Me?" His smile was gentle and a little lopsided. "I don't even have a celly!"

Ally lifted one eyebrow. "You punch your glove in the air and hold it there for three seconds every time you score."

Ted shrugged, apparently unfazed by the fact that she'd been watching him so closely. He might be unfazed, but her tendency to focus on him was alarming to her, at the very least. Wasn't that why they were sitting here, missing out on warm ups? "It's too simple to be a true celly."

Ally couldn't help but roll her eyes. "Whatever. I refuse to argue about this with you."

His smile faded. "Then why don't you tell me what it is that I do that reminds you of him. So I can stop doing it and you can feel safer. Besides, it might make both our lives easier if I were different."

"How would assuming a false identity make your life any easier?" And would she want him to be anyone other than himself?

"Well, first of all, before we even get into prosthetic noses and accent coaching… I don't believe you hate me as much as you think you do."

"Oh? And why do you think that?"

He smiled again, that lopsided slip of a thing. "Because you still managed to have fun with me yesterday morning and I was just being myself then."

She nodded, reluctantly conceding his point. The run *had* been fun. Much more fun than she'd expected. She'd even let her guard down, and laughed at his dumb jokes. Of course, that had only made her feel worse. Like she'd betrayed herself, somehow. Which had landed them here, alone in the locker room. "And second?"

"What?"

"You said, 'First,' so I assume there's a 'Second?'"

"Right. Second of all, assuming a false identity—presumably, one that erased all history of my higher education—"

"And prep school."

"This goes back as far as high school? Christ…" He ran a hand through his dark brown hair, rumpling it further. "Well, as I was saying, assuming a false identity would make my life easier because then you wouldn't constantly be glowering at me. You might even let me sit with you at lunch."

Ally scoffed. "My glowering at you can't be that much of an inconvenience. And I'm sure you have people with whom you can sit at lunch. Senior management people."

"Au contraire. Your glare is like an eclipse of the sun. And sure, there are other people I could sit with. But that doesn't mean I wouldn't be pining after you from across the cafeteria. Très *Twilight*."

Ally couldn't help herself. She giggled. And then she clapped a hand over her mouth.

This was supposed to be a serious conversation. And besides, she wasn't supposed to be *giggling* at the prospect of Ted's pining after her! That came perilously close to flirting and flirting led to feelings and feelings, well, frankly they weren't something she could afford to have, for him. For her own sanity's sake, not to mention safety's.

Although, truth be told, she felt safe with Ted. She wouldn't be here, alone in the locker room with him, about to spill her darkest secrets to him, if she didn't feel safe. With him. But that didn't mean she was going to date him.

"Look, Ted. *Twilight* aside, I don't know you well enough to go dumping my trauma on you."

He sobered. "I understand."

"But I will do you the courtesy of revealing the resemblance. Because that's what has me so on edge. That, in your words, is 'my problem.' You remind me of him."

He frowned. "Is it something that I do? The way I look?"

"He was handsome—a bit like you, but blond. Still is, rather, although I haven't seen him in years so I can only imagine, and, as you can imagine, I don't like to imagine."

If Ted heard her confess she thought he was handsome, he kindly did not comment on it. "I can't change the way I look, other than to avoid ever bleaching my hair, which isn't exactly on my bucket list."

"It's not just looks. And you don't *really* look like him.

Sometimes, when you're being arrogant, you carry yourself the way he carried himself. But that's rare."

"Then what is it? What's the big red flag?"

Ally groaned. "Crimson, more like it..."

Something sparked in Ted's eyes. "Wait... He went to Harvard? *That's* why you're such a dick about my alma mater?"

Ally nodded, grimacing. "And he went to prep school."

"Not Essex... If he went to Essex, I might..." Ted appeared horrified. "What's his name? What year was he?"

Ally shook her head hastily. "Everett Dalton. He was a Brixley boy," she added bitterly. "But he was the year above me, so you might have crossed paths with him at Harvard."

"Or played against him, before that. Do you know what sports he played in high school?"

"Hockey, briefly. And lacrosse—he wouldn't shut up about lacrosse. I don't know the rest." Ally sighed, allowing her head to fall into her hands.

It was painful, talking about Everett. But it hurt in the way that irrigating a wound with a salt water solution hurt. She had been trying to heal her heart and mind for years, had worked hard in therapy and even talked about it, very occasionally, with friends and family. Talking to Ted was strange because she didn't really know him. But, for some reason, possibly his persistence, possibly his patience, she had started to trust him.

"He was a real asshole, Ted. But not on the surface. On the surface, at least around others, he was charm incarnate. My mother never liked him, but she has a sixth sense about these kinds of things. My friends all thought we were happy. And we were, when he wasn't putting me down or lying to my face or manipulating me into doubting my reality." That last one was a doozy. And Ally probably should have explained, but she was tired and they had to go play a game.

"The point is, I've been feeling so *guilty*, for—" She paused.

He waited until it became apparent she needed prompting. "For what?"

She dug her fingers into the scarred bench and forced herself to look Ted in the eye. "For not hating you."

He shook his head in disbelief. "But you *do* hate me, Ally."

"No, I don't. You said it yourself. I don't hate you. Not really. Not anymore."

They looked at each other for a long moment. Something passed between them, some secret truth, that went beyond truce. All Ally knew for certain was that she could spend eternity staring into his pale blue eyes, the color of the summer sky reflected in a still river. But she shouldn't. Lord knew, she shouldn't.

Finally, quietly yet with conviction, Ted spoke. "I'm not him, Ally. I never will be."

It was a promise; it was a pact.

Ally stood abruptly. Her light and breezy tone was a blatant lie and she told it regardless of the fact that the darker truth was obvious even when she asked, "Shall we?"

Confusion replaced conviction. "Shall we what?"

She rolled her eyes in an attempt at levity, or at least the resumption of a pattern. Not that things would be the same between them, ever again. "Get out there and win this game."

CHAPTER 7
SPEAKERPHONE

"Thank you for accommodating my schedule, Ally. Ally?"

Ally jerked her head up and out of the confusion that clouded her thoughts. Her therapist was watching her with a faintly amused expression. "What?"

"I was just thanking you for coming in today, instead of our usual day."

Ally shrugged. "I didn't mind the wait. It was only three days."

Linda continued to watch her, catlike in her curiosity. "Are you sure?"

"Okay, fine." Ally sighed. "I was annoyed that we couldn't meet on Monday. I needed to talk to you!"

"About what?"

Ally bit her lip. "Remember Harvard?"

"The…" Linda mentally checked her notes. "Arrogant, entitled, narcissistic boor? With two o's?"

Ally nodded, a little embarrassed by her past self's passionate prejudice.

"Ted, was it?"

Ally nodded again.

"What happened with Ted that made you need to talk to me?"

Ally closed her eyes. "I told him the truth."

When she opened her eyes again, Linda's eyebrows were raised slightly, but other than that her therapist's expression was carefully neutral.

"The truth?"

"About why I hate him. Hated him." Ally let her head fall into her hands. "Oh, I don't know, Linda. I don't know how I feel about him! I just…" She peeked at Linda through her spread fingers. "I felt so guilty."

Linda leaned forward on one elbow, her chin propped up on her closed fist, so that they were almost level. "Guilty for hating him?"

Ally sat up like a bolt. "Guilty for not hating him at all!"

Silence fell in the wake of Ally's outburst.

Linda sat up and stroked her chin thoughtfully. Then she stood, crossed the room, and collected her cup of tea. She always had a mug during sessions. She rarely drank from it, however.

Ally watched wordlessly as her therapist returned to her seat and sipped the tea slowly. When she had finished, she set the mug on the small coffee table. Steam rose from the remaining tea's surface in soothing tendrils.

Ally's gaze darted back to Linda as the older woman rested her elbows on the arms of her chair and templed her fingers in the air.

"Ally… Does Ted know that you're attracted to him?"

"What?!" Ally clapped a hand over her mouth but it was too late. She'd shrieked. "Sorry. Sorry, that was really loud."

Linda smiled gently. "It's my fault, for springing that on you. I just hope none of my neighbors was napping."

"I know you have soundproofed walls but seriously, Linda. What the fuck?"

Linda shrugged. "You still haven't answered the question, Ally."

"That's because it's a ridiculous question!"

"Oh?"

Ally narrowed her eyes. "Yes. It is *ridiculous*. So ridiculous that I don't feel the need to answer it. I mean, first off, I'm not attracted to him."

"Mmmm." That was disbelief if Ally had ever heard it.

"We've been over this! I told you last week, I would never sleep with him!"

Linda cocked her head. "That's not what I recall…"

"Fine, I said I would. And can you blame me? He's got a jaw that could cut glass and abs like moguls on a ski slope. Yes, I've been skiing, I know what a mogul is."

"And what about his personality? What is it about him that you find so… persuasive?"

Ally scrunched her eyebrows. "You are killing me here, Linda." She drew out the syllables for emphasis. "*Killing me.*"

"You were the one who brought Ted up."

"Yeah, so we could talk about the fact that I told him about Everett! Not so you could grill me on how patient he is, or how funny, or how he never gives up on me, no matter how rude I am—how he seems to believe in me, despite *barely* knowing me—"

Linda sat forward in her chair. "You told Ted about Everett?"

"Yes, Dr. Boyd. I told a guy I barely know—barely even like!—about my biggest trauma."

Linda nodded. "I see."

"What do you see?" Ally asked, somewhat sarcastically.

"You must trust him, to tell him something you keep so hidden."

Ally scoffed. "I do not *hide* my history with Everett. I just… bury it. Deep, where the sun doesn't shine."

"Because you want the worms to devour his decomposing flesh?"

"Linda!" Shocked, Ally stared at her therapist. "That was dark! I'm impressed!"

Linda gestured towards her bookshelf. "I've read my fair share of Gothic novels. At the end of the day, aren't almost all of them about abuse?" She paused. "But back to Ted. What exactly did you tell him, and why?"

Ally shrugged, intrigued by her therapist's analysis. "Not much. I felt he deserved the truth. After the way I've treated him…"

"How have you treated him?"

Ally bowed her head. "I've… been pretty rude. I wouldn't say *mean*, but like… I've not been nice. And it has nothing to do with him. Well, almost nothing. It's just that he reminds me of Everett, and that scares the shit out of me."

"Because you have feelings for him? Feelings you think you shouldn't have?"

"Whoa, there." Ally put her hands in the air. "I never said I had feelings for him."

"Alright," Linda offered. "I retract that question."

"Leading the witness, your honor…" Ally grinned, but her smile faded as she recalled her conversation with Ted. What must he think of her? Unloading and off-loading on him like that?

"Earlier, you said you felt guilty." Linda was watching her again. "Can you tell me more about that guilt?"

"What do you wanna know, doc?"

"I want to know where it comes from."

Ally frowned. "I dunno. We went for this run together and I had fun even though I didn't want to have fun and I guess… I guess I feel or, rather, *felt* guilty for not hating him—because if I didn't hate him then I liked him and if I liked him, even though he reminded me of Everett, wasn't that a betrayal of myself? After all I've been through, all I've survived? I mean, I got myself out!"

Ally's voice was steadily rising, again. She tried to keep it under control this time. "I got myself out of that relationship safely, eventually. I didn't let it escalate into physicality. Not that other people *allow*—you know what I mean. I kept myself sane and stable."

She took a deep breath. "What happens if now that this guy's come along, this guy who reminds me of Everett, a little bit—what happens if I go for it? And what happens if it ruins me? If *he* ruins me? I won't go through that again, Linda. I won't suffer any more abuse."

Linda exhaled slowly. "Two questions, Ally."

Ally took a deep breath before nodding for her therapist to continue.

"First of all, are you attracted to him *because* he reminds you of Everett, or in spite of the fact?"

Ally didn't even have to think about it. "The latter."

Linda nodded. "As for the second question... Do you believe Ted could ever hurt you? Seriously hurt you? Do you think he has the capacity to abuse you?"

No.

The answer came as quick as lightning. Ted would never do what Everett had done. She didn't know how she knew, she just knew. But was that good enough?

"Ally?"

"No. I do not believe that Ted could ever abuse me. But I trusted Everett, too!"

Linda frowned. "There is no easy answer, here, Ally. Life is full of risks—love is, too. But know this: you have me. And your friends and your family. And, most importantly, you have *you*."

Emotional abuse
  Manipulation in romantic relationships
  Gaslighting
  And, last but not least:
  Everett Dalton Harvard

❄

He'd searched the terms ten times or more, varying the vocabulary and the word order. He'd found definitions for the first three, as well as personal essays, strategies, and help hotlines. He'd found some social media profiles for the fourth. Ted was relieved to see that he and the evil ex had no mutual friends. And that the piece of shit now lived in Palm Beach. The distance must be a blessing for Ally.

It had been four days since his and Ally's conversation in the locker room. Her words had been gnawing at him. Her voice, thick with anger and hurt. Her tears, blinked back but on the brink.

He'd been worried sick about what she'd endured at the hands of her ex. Ted didn't have anyone to ask about the behaviors she'd described—no therapist, no friends who did social work, certainly not his little sister or his mother, who would both be concerned past the point of simply calling if he started asking questions about "intimate partner violence." As a result, Ted's search history was... Well, he had certainly had an education, albeit a brief one, informed solely by the internet.

Ted was working late tonight. Really late. It was nearing ten and the office was empty. He'd sent his team home two hours earlier, in an attempt to reward them for their hard work all week and to salvage something of their work-life balance. Ally had left early too, saying something to Vanessa about an appointment, a conversation he couldn't help but overhear. The office layout—rather, the lack of walls— allowed sound to travel as well as it would in a rink.

He would have gone home with the rest of his team, but he had a report to write on how GreenLight's latest partner- ship was affecting company revenue, a report that he had to present in person tomorrow afternoon at the weekly leadership meeting that was held just prior to the Keg Friday festivities.

He'd known about the report all week, but writing it required him to first pull data from across the company—product, sales, finance, etc.—which in turn required him to wrangle various employees he didn't yet know and who didn't yet know him, and in the end everyone had been exceptionally slow in getting the data to him. So slow that he'd only been able to sit down to write the damn thing as of eight o'clock tonight.

Ted sighed, taking his hand off the trackpad of his work laptop. He needed to close the tab he had open on IPV (a Planned Parenthood fact sheet) and log back into GreenType, GreenLight's secure online word processing software. But first, he needed a break.

Clicking the little 'x' on the corner of the tab, Ted pushed back from his desk. He rolled his neck once before standing to stretch properly. A yawn escaped him as he bent to touch his toes. Ted grabbed his suit jacket, because it was a little chilly in the office tonight, and shrugged into it. Then he set off for the snack bar at the far end of the floor.

As he walked, the soft padding of shoes against the carpet caught his attention. That wasn't the sound of his own steps. Ted looked around, on edge—no doubt due to his recent reading. Soon, however, he relaxed. It was only Ally, returning from the printer. She must have come back to the office after her appointment. Ted wondered what she was doing here so late.

Suddenly, their eyes met and something crackled like electricity between them.

She froze, mid-step. "Jesus, Ted!"

He put his hands up in apology.

She exhaled slowly. "What are you doing here? It's almost ten."

Was that concern he heard, or mere confusion? Ted

shrugged. "Harold wants this report by tomorrow afternoon, and I have meetings all morning."

She narrowed her eyes. "So you just left it until tonight? What happened to that Puritan work ethic of yours?"

Ted chuckled, recalling their eventful first meeting. "As I told you then, all that stuff is bullshit." She graced him with a small smile and it hit him like the morning sun, seven hours early. But then a cloud passed over the metaphorical sky, when his search history came to mind. "Listen, Ally... If you ever need to talk—"

She shook her head, cutting him off before he could begin. "Look, Ted. It's like I said in the locker room. Just because we had a little heart-to-heart doesn't mean we're lovers, much less friends."

Lovers? He hadn't been about to make a move on her, merely offer her his ear and shoulder. Maybe he'd been too forward when he'd admitted to pining, before. He hadn't been serious! Well...

"Besides, you're hardly competition for my therapist."

Ted nodded. "Got it." Her past wasn't his business. Except when it bit him in the ass. "Just... try not to trip me anymore?"

Ally rolled her eyes, sass replacing suspicion. "That's ancient history, preppy."

It had only been a few weeks!

Reading his mind, she added with a slight smile, "Get over it already." After a long second, in which neither seemed to so much as blink, Ally's smile faded. She shuffled the papers in her hand. "Now, if you'll excuse me, I have to revise this web copy before tomorrow morning or Harold will kill me."

"You revise web copy by hand?"

Ally nodded, looking pleased with herself. "Most copy-writers keep it on the screen, especially when it's for the website, but I've found it's easiest to catch typos when you mark it up the old-fashioned way." She pulled a red pen out from where it was stuck in her ponytail. "Not that I make typos often."

"No, of course not." He scuffed the carpet with his shoe. "Right, well. I'm just off to refuel."

"Cool." Before Ted could reply, no doubt awkwardly, she turned on her heel and strode in the direction of her desk. As she passed him, he caught a whiff of orange blossom. The scent was like sunshine, warm and welcome on this long October night.

Ally was wrenched from sleep by the sound of ABBA's "My Love, My Life." It was jarring to hear such a sweet song when she'd been in the middle of such a bad dream.

Everett, again. He seemed to have been resurrected by her discussion with Ted. Rolling her neck, Ally unlocked her phone.

Kaitlin Fielding's voice sounded over the static. "Ally? It's me. Kait."

That was strange. She hadn't heard Kaitlin use her nickname in years. The other woman had made a point of asking all her friends to stop calling her 'Kait' around the time they'd graduated college. Stranger still was Kaitlin's voice. It was stuffy, like she'd had allergies all day.

Kaitlin stifled a sob and suddenly Ally understood. The woman on the other end of the line didn't have allergies. She was crying.

"Kait? Are you okay?" Ally's own voice came out scratchy with sleep. She'd been napping in one of the office pods before getting back to work.

"Oh, shoot. Did I wake you?"

Ally checked her wrist watch. "It's midnight, Kait. On a Thursday."

"I'm sorry. I was working late." She sniffed. "I should let you get back to sleep…"

"No, no—I wasn't sleeping," Ally lied, hoisting herself into a sitting position lest she be lulled back into slumber. "You didn't answer my question." She stifled a yawn. "What's wrong?"

"It's Paul," Kait said after a long, sniffly pause. "Or, well, maybe it's me," she added, hopelessly.

Ally perked up. "What happened?"

She spoke on a half-sob. "We're getting a divorce."

"Oh my god." Ally swung her legs over the edge of the pod. "Are you okay, Kait? What happened? I mean, you don't have to talk about it, if you don't want to…" She trailed off, uncertain as to what she should be saying. Ally didn't know anything about marriage, much less divorce. But she knew that Paul had always been a bit of a dick. And if he wasn't treating Kait right, well, he'd have Ally to answer to.

"I want to talk about it," Kait said at last. She sniffed. "I have to talk about it or I'll go mad."

Ally put Kait on speaker then set the phone down. She stood and started to pace the little room the pod resided in. Thank god it was late and the walls were soundproofed.

"Okay. Where do you want to start?" She tried channeling her therapist, whose calm voice was always a balm.

Kait sighed and the sound was so weary, so full of sorrow and disappointment, that Ally had to put her hand on the wall to steady herself. "I don't know, Ally."

"You don't know where to start? That's okay. How about the begin—"

"No, I mean… I don't know what happened." Kait sounded so small and vulnerable, Ally wished she were in Boston so she could pour her friend a glass of pink wine and pull her into a much-needed hug. Screw software, GreenLight should be working on teleportation technology.

"Whose idea was it? The divorce, I mean." Ally tried to tread carefully.

Kait was silent a moment. "His. But…"

Ally could hear the shame and self-loathing in her friend's voice, but she couldn't understand it. "What did he say, what reason did he give?"

Kait blew her nose. "It's my fault."

"Kait, I'm sure it's not—"

"No," she insisted. "That's what he said. It's my fault. He said I was a—a frigid workaholic who didn't care about him."

Ally clapped a hand over her mouth. Fury rose in her faster than a lightning strike. "That fucker—"

Kait started to cry again. "He's right, Ally."

"No, he's not. You are a warm and loving person who cares deeply for the people—and pets—she knows. It's not your fault Paul is an insensitive asshole."

"But Ally…"

"You listen to me, Kaitlin It's-Embarrassing-That-I-Don't-Know-Your-Middle-Name Fielding."

"Elizabeth," she supplied on a sob.

Ally nodded. "Right, well. Paul's a loser, and losing him will hurt but if that's how he talks to you, if that's what he thinks of you, you'll be well shot of him in the long run."

"But I *am* a frigid workaholic," Kait protested. "I never want to have sex when Paul does, and even my boss says I work way too much."

"It's okay to not want to have sex, Kait. You're not frigid for not wanting to fuck a man who doesn't deserve you." Ally hoped she was saying helpful things. She was speaking from the heart. "And yeah, maybe you do work a little too much. But there's nothing wrong with loving what you do, and giving it your all. You're a lawyer, Kait. You help people for a living!"

Kait snorted. "I'm a paralegal, Ally. I help lawyers help people for a living."

"That's important. *You're* important. But if you need help taking a break, just come hang out with me in New York for a bit. My couch is pretty comfy. And free of cat hair," she added —and it wasn't entirely a lie. She had bought some lint rollers on Tuesday.

"Okay." Kait sounded unconvinced. Ally thought it probably had more to do with her lack of self-confidence than her awareness of Heathcliff's nonstop shedding.

"Trust me, Kaity. You're not what Paul says you are. Do you want me to come up to Boston next weekend? I have a game, but it's not a big deal. We've got a hottie from Harvard who can easily make up for my absence."

Kait laughed a little. "I thought you hated guys who went to Harvard."

"I do!"

"Then why'd you call this one a hottie?"

Ally shrugged, delighted to hear her friend emerging from her misery. "You'll just have to come and see."

"Okay." Kait exhaled slowly. "I feel a bit better. Thanks for talking to me."

"I don't have anywhere to go, you can stay on with me for a while."

"No, I should sleep. I've got a meeting at nine and if I get less than seven hours it'll be a nightmare."

Ally nodded. "Sweet dreams, Kait. Please, please take care of yourself. And let me know about this weekend. I'm happy to hop on a train."

Kait hesitated. "Don't come. Thank you, but... I don't want you and Paul to fight."

"Are you sure? I could easily teach him a lesson or two about love. With my fists."

Kait laughed again, an encouraging sound. "I'll visit you."

"Okay, sounds good. Night, Kaity. I'll text you tomorrow."

"Night, Ally."

Ally hung up, a sour taste in her mouth. She shoved her

way out of the nap room and glanced around the office. It was empty except—Ted was just standing there, not ten feet away from her, watching her every move.

"What the hell do you want?"

He looked startled and embarrassed.

Join the club, Harvard.

"I'm sorry—I couldn't help but overhear…"

She'd assumed it was soundproofed. It had always seemed soundproof. Maybe that was just the pods. Fuck. "Eavesdropping, eh? Should've guessed you'd be the type."

"No, it's just—" he blushed and Ally was drawn momentarily out of her anger by the mesmerizing sight. "Your phone must have been on speaker."

Color came to her own cheeks as she remembered the adjective she'd used to describe him. "You should have said something."

"I know, but I didn't want to interrupt. Your friend sounded like she was really going through something, and you were being so supportive, and I—"

"Didn't say anything." Ally sighed, choosing to let go of her ire. Wren would be proud. "Go home, Ted. It's late."

He nodded. "Be safe." And then he gathered up his things and headed for the stairs. Never mind that they were on the seventh floor. Ally went back to her desk to collect her own belongings, confused by Ted's persistent kindness and shaken by her friend's situation.

CHAPTER 8
PRIORITIZED

"Seriously, guys, another round and you'll be carrying me back to my apartment."

Frank, another senior manager working on a different team, laughed. "I refuse to believe that you're a lightweight, man. What are you, six two?"

"Six three, and I skipped lunch to tidy up that report so my tolerance is seriously hindered. Plus, I worked late last night. But if you think you can lift me…"

"Bro, you have no idea what I can lift."

Ted shook his head. Frank had shown himself to be a decent guy in the weeks that Ted had known him, but he was a little toxic on the masculinity front. "It's cool, dude. I've got things to do." He tossed his empty cup in the recycling and sent Frank and his friends a casual salute. "Catch you on the flip."

As Ted crossed the rooftop deck, making his way to the exit, he searched the crowd of coworkers for Ally. He spotted her just as he reached the door to the elevator. Her hair was loose about her shoulders, shining in the sun and blowing in the slight breeze. Ted watched as she pulled it up off her neck into a high ponytail, not unlike the one she'd worn on their run.

Ally turned suddenly, as if she'd had a sixth sense that someone was watching her. She caught his eye.

Ted blushed.

Ally raised an eyebrow.

He smiled and she turned away. But not before he noticed a warmth in her gaze, a heat that she usually tried to hide. A heat that belied her words of warning last night.

Just because we had a little heart-to-heart doesn't mean we're lovers, much less friends.

All the way home, Ted thought about that fleeting flicker, and the way her white teeth had grazed her plump lower lip mid-way through the word 'lovers.'

Having taken off his shoes and traded his suit for joggers and a t-shirt, Ted entered his aunt's study with apprehension. It was time to sort through her things.

Lorraine Lewis had left behind an immaculate apartment, with the exception of this one room. As Ted stood on the threshold, he teetered slightly, overwhelmed by the sudden surge of memories. All the summers he'd spent with her seemed to swell inside of him. It was like a tsunami of suppressed grief.

She'd been gone for a while now, but that didn't mean he didn't miss her.

One of the greatest things about his aunt—and there had been a lot of really great things about Aunt Lorraine, including but not limited to her pecan pie recipe, her ability to fold a fitted sheet with ease, her tendency to sing along with the radio, whatever the station, and her fondness for cats, despite her allergy—was how she always made Ted feel like he was on a path to becoming the best version of himself. She had been whatever he needed her to be: a mentor, a friend, even someone who meted out discipline—although the latter happened rarely. Ted had been a pretty good kid.

Aunt Lorraine's passing had been especially difficult for Ted because it left him feeling untethered, like the current was pushing him back, taking away his personal progress. It was also tough because she'd been one of the few people who saw his loneliness and didn't judge him for his difficulty connecting with others.

The strange thing was, with Ally—ceaselessly, he thought with a sigh, like the boat at the end of *Gatsby*, he was borne back by the current of his emotions to the subject of Ally—he didn't feel like he had any trouble with that. Even when she'd hated him, he'd always felt a kind of connection. And once she'd told him the truth about her hatred for him—and for *him*—well, that connection had grown stronger.

Honesty is like butter in that it binds us all together, his aunt had once said, during one of the many cooking lessons she'd given him as a teen. And Ted appreciated the fact that Ally was willing to be honest with him, to show him the real Allegra Bryant, behind the defensiveness. Of course, her idea of defense was a good offense. And he'd been on the receiving end of that forecheck for a few weeks now. But he understood her anger now and her hostility. He also understood that there was more to her than that. She was a fiercely loving friend, for example. He'd seen that last night. Heard it, rather.

Ted shook his head. He could sit around and think about Ally all day, but nothing would get done. He surveyed the study in all its cluttered glory and set to work picking up papers off the floor. He could sort them later. Maybe with a friend, over a cup of tea. Would Ted feel comfortable letting someone see his aunt's inner world? Was that too private to share? Maybe not with Ally. Ally, Ally Ally... But certainly with someone like Frank.

Ted wasn't so sure about Frank, the senior manager from earlier. Rather, he was starting to be sure, just not in a good way. Frank seemed a bit douchey, like the 'friends' Ted had left behind in Boston. Back when he'd been a bit of a 'bro' himself, before the milieu of casual misogyny and toxic masculinity had become too much for him, and he'd quit his social club. But there were other fish in the sea, other (real) friends to be made at GreenLight, hopefully.

His phone buzzed. Ted pulled it out of his sweatpants' pocket to check the screen. Speaking of fish—of friends, rather…

Yo, are you up on the roof deck? Jordan and I just wrapped and are heading up. We should hang.

Sam Lyons, one of the copywriters on Ted's team, seemed like a decent person. Decent enough for Ted to give him his number, when he had asked.

Ted frowned as he texted Sam back, *Sorry, I had to take care of some personal things. I'll see you guys Monday.*

Damn, okay. Sam paused, or maybe he was typing, because all Ted could see was a row of bouncing dots. *Jordan says he has a lunch meeting on Monday.* Jordan was also on Ted's team, bringing to it a vast array of sales knowledge. *Can we do Tuesday instead?*

Sure thing, Ted replied. He hated lunch meetings, which always felt like an encroachment on his personal life. He was already working 9-5, sometimes later; he had a right to spend his lunch break however he saw fit. Apparently, on Tuesday at least, that would be with Sam and Jordan. *Do you want to eat in or go out?*

Sam's reply was instant. *Out. I don't love our restaurant of the month this month. Not enough spice.* Another pause. *Jordan says he knows a place. You like tacos?*

Who didn't like tacos? Ted's aunt had used to make them for him and Belle, whenever they visited. *Of course.*

Cool, cool. Catch you on the flip.

Ted put his phone back in his pocket, breathing a sigh of relief that he wasn't the only one who still said goodbye like that. Then, he resumed his work.

He couldn't leave this monument to his aunt's messiness up forever. It was time to move forward—never forgetting her, but at the same time not allowing the past to overwhelm the present. It was only an office, after all. His aunt lived on in other rooms—rooms he'd already tidied because this apartment was no tomb—and in her recipes, many of which he knew and the rest of which he was learning. But, most of all, Lorraine Lewis lived on in Ted's memories.

He'd like to share those memories, he rather thought, with someone special. But for the time being he'd have to content himself with quietly sorting through sheets of scribblings.

Screw quietly. Ted reached for his phone.

After fiddling with his music library for a moment, he found the right album. Ella Fitzgerald and Louis Armstrong, singing away the world's sorrows. He hoped, absently, that Ally's friend—the one from the phone last night—had a similar playlist, some kind of musical talisman. He hoped, fervently, that she was okay. But then, he thought, she had Ally. And so he knew that she would be okay.

Ally grabbed Vanessa by the arm and steered her away from the conversation she'd been having.

"Hey! I was talking there!"

Ignoring her friend's complaint, she brought them to a secluded corner of the rooftop deck. "V, can you keep a secret?"

Vanessa rolled her eyes. "I write fanfiction under a pseudonym, Ally."

Ally's brows knit. "And?"

With exaggerated patience, Vanessa continued, "In the years that you've known me, you've never once figured out my OTP."

"I've never asked!"

Vanessa smiled and shrugged her slight shoulders. "That's your own fault, honey. Now, tell me the secret."

Ally bit her lip. "It's not really a secret. I mean it's not common knowledge, but…"

"What is it?" Vanessa's voice went breathless. "Oh my god! Did you and Ted… you know!"

Ally jerked back, nearly spilling her beer. "What? No!"

Vanessa sighed. "A girl can dream. Besides, you did say you both stayed late last night…"

"Right, well, nothing happened. Not between him and me."

"So, what's the secret?"

"Have I ever told you about my friend Kaitlin—Kait, from college?"

Vanessa feigned a gasp. "You have other friends besides Madison from your hockey team and me?"

Ally rolled her eyes fondly. "Yes. Although, Kait and I haven't been as close the past couple years."

Vanessa peered at her suspiciously over the flared rims of her glasses. "What happened?"

"Nothing! We just sort of got busy with our own lives. The group chat got quiet."

"No, I mean last night. What happened last night?"

Ally sighed. "She called me up around midnight. She told me," Ally lowered her voice, "she's getting a divorce."

Vanessa's expression grew pensive. "Hmmm. And are we happy about this or sad?"

Ally thought about that. Kait had been pretty torn up, but what Paul had said… It sounded like their marriage had been on the rocks for a while now. "Happy, I think?" She frowned. "I mean, Kait's inconsolable. But her husband—"

"Her soon-to-be-ex-husband," Vanessa interjected.

"Yeah, he said some pretty awful things about her, apparently. To her face."

Vanessa raised her eyebrows. "Fuck him. She's better off without him."

Ally agreed; she didn't want Kait staying with someone

who considered her—much less called her, to her face—a frigid workaholic. She'd never been Paul's biggest fan, but that comment was unforgivable. Kait deserved better.

"So, what are we doing to help her?"

Ally smiled at how thoughtful, how free with her affections, Vanessa could be. "I dunno, V. I'm going to make a point of checking in with her more often, from here on out. She lives in Boston but I invited her to come down here for a weekend, but maybe I'll extend it to a week."

"Or forever," Vanessa offered, sincerely. "Let me know if she takes you up on that. We could have a girls night out!"

"Thanks, V. It means a lot to me." Ally had really lucked out when she'd been paired with Vanessa for training when she was first hired by GreenLight.

"Sure thing. But what about you?"

Ally frowned. "What about me?"

"I mean, how are you doing with regards to your awful ex?"

Ally shrugged. "I told Ted about him. I felt I owed him the truth."

"Good girl." Vanessa smiled warmly. "Ted's not so bad, is he?"

Ally narrowed her eyes. "Don't you have a boyfriend, V?"

Vanessa laughed. "My, aren't we territorial."

"I am not—"

"I was being friendly, Ally. He's a nice guy."

Ally swallowed, feeling as though she'd accidentally shown her hand during a game of high-stakes poker. Not that she had a hand to show. "I can't go down that road, Vanessa."

Vanessa pouted. "Why not?"

"Because…"

"Because you're afraid of letting him in? Because you're worried it'll happen again?"

"Yes!" Finally, someone understood.

"Listen, Ally." Vanessa put her hand on Ally's shoulder.

"Lightning doesn't strike the same girl twice. And if you're scared of commitment, or don't want to risk it, just have sex with him. Nothing more. Get it out of your system and then you'll be over him!"

"There's nothing to get out of my system!"

Vanessa leveled Ally with a look. "Bullshit, babe. I've seen the way you watch him when you're supposed to be writing email blasts. I saw the way you looked at him today before he left."

Ally sighed. "Fine. Fine! I'm attracted to him. Okay?"

Vanessa smiled like a cat that had gotten the cream. "So, what's the plan? Another late night at the office? Ooh! What about sweaty, locker room sex?"

"Vanessa!" Ally could feel her cheeks burning. She glanced around the rooftop deck, but no one was paying any attention to them. Most people were on their third beer, and the older crowd had started to trickle out. "There is no plan. If anything happens..." She flushed a deeper hue. "Nothing is going to happen. He's probably not interested, anyway."

Ted couldn't get Ally out of his head. He'd sorted through his aunt's things all evening, but even fond memories couldn't dislodge the gnawing need he felt to sweep Ally off her feet. But she didn't want him. She'd made that clear.

Except...

Ted shook his head. She hadn't been watching him the other day. He'd imagined that. Just like he'd imagined her finding him on Flutter, imagined the little buzz as his phone notified him that he'd been prioritized by the only person he'd found remotely attractive on that app. Imagination was one hell of a drug.

Sighing, Ted pulled out his phone, unlocked it, and opened the dating app. It took him a moment to find her profile; he'd buried it in his pile of potential matches, a little worried he'd take to checking it, obsessively, for changes. For evidence that she was active or, worse, that she had suddenly taken her profile down—which could only mean one thing. Ted knew exactly why that possibility had the power to sting.

Fortunately, he soon found her. She hadn't changed her profile at all.

Ally Bryant. 28. Interested in men. Ted was a man, wasn't he? With a sigh, he continued to read. Almost immediately, as he arrived at the little snippet of astrology, he ceased to frown. Ted had asked his little sister to ask a friend what "scorpio with a fire moon" meant and the eventual answer hadn't surprised him. According to Belle's friend, and confirmed by Ted's own account, Ally had a "hot temper" and could be "extra-emotive." You could say that again.

Personally, Ted liked Ally's passionate nature. She was so... alive. So vibrant, so intense. He wanted to be close to her, to bask in her smile's sunlight—even if that meant he risked getting burned by her anger sometimes. Besides, she'd stopped subjecting him to her scorching stares, ever since he'd confronted her in the locker room.

Briefly, Ted wondered what would have happened if he hadn't worn that Harvard jersey that first day. How she would have treated him if he had attended a different college, altogether. What their relationship would be like if he didn't remind her of the man who had abused her. Ted knew that the similarities weren't his fault and that they were superficial —the buck stopped there.

So he wished, instead, that she had never gone through what she went through, never suffered, never endured. But, as his aunt had always said, wishing was for wells. And he couldn't travel back in time, not with a mere MBA to guide him. Ted would just have to support Ally, in whatever ways she would accept, while showing her with his actions, not just his words, that simply put he wasn't her ex.

A little ping alerted him to the fact that someone, apparently, had prioritized him. For a moment, Ted allowed himself to imagine it was Ally. For that brief moment, he couldn't breathe. Then, another ping. Someone—presumably the same person who had prioritized his profile—wanted to message him. Ted sighed. He opened his eyes.

Sarah wants to flirt with you! read a little banner across the top of his screen. With great reluctance, and about a gallon of guilt, Ted opened his Flutter inbox and prepared to apologize.

The woman's message was short and sweet. *Hey! You're cute.*

Ted accepted the message and typed out a response. *Thanks, so are you.* And she was, he supposed. *But I'm just looking to make friends.*

Sarah sent a confused emoji, followed by a shrug. *Wrong app, bud.*

Ted began to spell out "I'm sorry" but before he could, Sarah withdrew her message, meaning Ted couldn't talk to her anymore. It was his turn to shrug.

Ted tossed his phone across the couch. It landed facedown. He looked around, studying the over-stuffed bookshelves, the possibly priceless paintings. His uncle had had an eye for art, whereas his aunt had been the book-lover. Ted knew he didn't need another half to make himself whole, but he longed for companionship, the kind his aunt and uncle had shared, in his very soul.

Another ping. Ted frowned and reached for his phone. Maybe he should deactivate his Flutter account. It wasn't fair to anyone for him to advertise as though his heart were open, when it was closed to all but one. Christ, he couldn't believe he'd allowed himself to fall for someone who could never, would never want him.

Because he had, hadn't he? He'd fallen for Ally.

He liked her humor, liked the sound of her laughter. He liked that tote bag she carried around, the one with the cover of *Wuthering Heights* painted on it. He liked how carefree she was with Vanessa, how competitive she was with Madison. He was endlessly amused by her faux arguments with Wren. He liked the face she made when she wound up for a slap-shot, which was rare, and the fact that she preferred to make a last-minute pass, to assist her teammate even when she could just as easily have put the puck in. He liked that her sense of injustice was so strong that she sometimes started a fight on the ice. He liked her sharp edges, even when they scratched him. And he liked the soft side she'd scarcely let him see, except in unexpected flashes, like the glimpses he had upon waking of his dreams.

But he wouldn't go there, with her. Not unless she went there first.

Ted picked up his phone to check the notification. It wasn't actually a Flutter match or message. It was a text. From the devil herself. Ted smiled. He hadn't even spoken of her—aloud.

Allegra Bryant: *Hey, just thinking—maybe we should go for another run tomorrow?*

Ted's smile widened with delight and surprise. *Absolutely. Shall we run by your place, this time?* He really wanted to enter her world, if only for an hour's exercise.

Let's stick to Central Park. The Met, this time. Meet you on the steps?

Ted didn't even bother to wait the customary two minutes to text her back—lest he seem over eager. *10am, Met steps. Maybe we can get a coffee, after?*

Her reply was short and not so sweet. *In your dreams, Harvard.*

CHAPTER 9
KINGS

ALLY CUT up the ice coming to a sudden stop. She pulled the puck back, lifting her stick. Then she came down on it hard. Instead of hurtling toward the net like a low-flying UFO, the puck did a little flip and skittered off out of reach. Ally lunged for it, then pulled back when she felt her shoulder go.

"Shit!" Ally bit back a string of worse profanities—the ref had already chastised her once for her language tonight. Something was wrong with her shoulder. Beckoning to Madison to cover for her, she made a dash toward the bench.

"What's wrong?" Nikki stood to open the door for her so she wouldn't have to climb over the boards. Ally shot her a grateful look.

"My shoulder—I seriously screwed up that slapshot."

Ever present, ever helpful, Ted had a suggestion. "Do you want me to take a look? I've seen a lot of shoulder injuries in my time."

Ally rolled her eyes as she settled in beside him. "At Harvard, yeah, we know."

"Not just at Harvard." Beneath the stench of sweat, he smelled like cloves and cinnamon, like mulled wine on a winter night.

Ally shook herself, regretting the movement almost immediately as pain radiated around her shoulder. "I'm fine," she bit out, a blatant lie.

"Come on, I can treat a wound."

Ally sniffed, suspicious. "Where did you learn to, if not at Harvard? Wait. Were you a Boy Scout?!"

"No," he answered, averting his eyes.

Ally laughed, even as she winced. Bullshit. "How far up the patchwork ladder did you get?"

He mumbled something unintelligible.

"What was that?"

He cleared his throat. "Eagle Scout."

Ally stared at him. "You are a walking parody of yourself."

Ted looked defensive. "Look, it's good training for—"

"Getting your hot teammate to take off her shirt?" Ally wasn't quite sure why she'd gone so far with her taunt, but Ted blushed furiously in response, which made her forget about her pain. For about five seconds.

Wincing, Ally announced, "I think I'll let Madison's boyfriend do the honors. He's, ya know, a doctor. With a real license, not just an embroidered patch." Ally raised her good hand and waved it in the direction of the stands. Sure enough, a man wearing a bright red puffer jacket jumped to his feet and headed for the stairs.

Technically, Hardit was a doctor for baby humans, but he'd done his residency like the rest. Besides, the team depended on him so much that he'd started reading up on sports medicine in his free time. He hurried round the long end of the rink and approached the bench.

"Ally! You okay? That last shot didn't sound right." Hardit had watched enough of Madison's games to know what a slapshot should sound like.

Ally shrugged, then immediately hissed. "I think I done messed up my shoulder, doc."

Ted jumped to his feet. "I've gotta run," he announced. "Well, skate." It was his turn to take the ice.

Ally looked up and caught a glimmer of concern in his round eyes.

He smiled down at her. "I'll be back in a minute. Scout's honor. Try to let the good doctor do his job."

Hardit nodded at Ted, who was in the process of hoisting himself over the boards and onto the ice. Ally marveled at the way he made everything, from stick-handling to board-jumping, look effortless and smooth. Probably all that muscle, she mused, watching him skate toward center ice, and those long limbs.

"Does it hurt when I do this?" Ally's attention was dragged back to the present by a shooting pain as Hardit gently lifted her arm and rotated it.

"Like a bitch."

Ignoring her crass language, Hardit continued his examination. "What about when I do this?" He reached underneath her pads and gently probed the skin around her shoulder.

"A bit."

Hardit frowned. "It's swollen. I think you might have strained your shoulder."

"That's not too bad," Ally reflected. Surely she'd done it before. "Can I play third period?"

"Absolutely not," Hardit answered, adopting a stern expression. "Have a PT take a look at this and in the meantime stay off the ice."

Ally rolled her eyes. "Hardit, I'm fine—"

"You won't be, if you play on that. And you won't be able to play on it well. Don't make things worse for yourself and your teammates, Ally. We need a win and we need you in peak condition."

She sighed. "Fine. But you get to tell Wren."

"Tell me what?" Wren vaulted over the boards and slid

onto the bench beside Ally. "How's Bryant's shoulder look-ing, doc?"

"Not good," Hardit said. "She needs to rest it, ice it, and possibly wear a sling."

Wren nodded. "I've got one of those in my bag. We'll strap her in between periods."

"Good."

"Thanks, Hardit." Ally forced a smile, even though she felt like throwing something. Not that she'd be able to lift much, at the moment.

"Anytime, Ally." Hardit smiled fondly at her, blew Madison—who was just returning from her shift—a kiss, and went back the way he came.

Once again, they won.

Once again, it was thanks to Ted Lewis.

Ally tried not to think about how much it galled her to be bested by a man who had barely been on the line up for Harvard's men's team. But if she didn't think about how badly she wanted to beat him on the ice, she was forced to think about how much she wanted to sleep with him off of it.

Yup.

She had it bad for Mr. Ivy League. Especially now that he was singing a song straight off her favorite Maroon 5 album, conjuring a scene of post-coital serenity and trust in a rela-tionship that was familiar from her fantasies yet which she had found elusive in reality.

Ally found in Ted's rendition an earnestness that made a plea of the song's smooth, sensual promise of stolen covers and shared skin. His interpretation was sweet, seductive, and yet soul-baring and vulnerable. There was a timeless truth to his singing, an honesty to his stripped down rendition; he seemed to lack some of Adam Levine's pop-star confidence, and instead allowed the lyrics' aching loneliness to come alive, to linger in the low-lit room.

As Ally listened, she became aware of a strange sensation, like a bruise beneath her breast. Ted's version of the hit that had defined her school days was soulful, sorrowful. But there was determination, too, a hope that he didn't hide. Ally found herself hoping for him, for her, for them—except, Ted wasn't serenading her. He hadn't even chosen the song.

After the game, Wren had taken them all out for a night of team bonding and celebration in the form of karaoke. She had bought the first round and sang the first song: Queen's iconic "We Are The Champions" (naturally). Having brought the house down, Wren had wandered off stage and in the direction of the booths, where a pair of attractive young women were watching her, a little more than admiration in their eyes.

Ally had had to laugh. Wren could pull like no one else. And she was still, somehow, a decent person. One of the most decent people Ally knew. It had been fifteen minutes, however, and she still hadn't emerged from the booth. Ally was about to go and subtly investigate with a walk-by when Madison appeared with three beers.

"You drinking all those yourself?" Ally asked, a little in awe of her usually sensible friend.

Madison laughed. "No, two of these are for you and your new running partner."

Ally couldn't even bring herself to grimace; instead, her friend's words inspired a certain giddiness. "Thanks, Mads." She carefully lifted two of the beers out of her teammate's cold hands. "Where's Hardit?"

"He had to perform a house call."

Ally frowned. "Hope everything's alright..."

Shrugging, Madison sipped her beer. "I'm sure it's just new parents overreacting. Oh, Ted's just finishing up," she said, redirecting Ally's attention to the stage. Like Ally hadn't had one ear trained. Madison gave her a gentle shove. "Go on, go give the man his reward. He deserves it, after his performance on the ice tonight—not to mention, on the stage."

Ted deserved more than a lukewarm beer, Ally thought to herself. She turned and caught his eye—his stare was particularly smoldering tonight. Ally smiled, a tad mischievously. Maybe it was just the fact that she was tipsy, but if he kept looking at her like that, she might just have to bring him to her bedroom, where Teddy-bears belonged.

Giggling slightly at perhaps the worst pun she'd ever mentally made, Ally strode over to Ted's side. "You looked thirsty," she said, willing the innuendo into the words. What could she say? His performance had inspired her, as had the two previous beers.

Massaging his throat with one hand, Ted accepted her offering with the other. "Thank you." His voice was husky, probably just from his performance, and his pupils were dilated due to the low light, darkening his eyes. Or, perhaps, there was desire there in that slight rasp, in those oceanic depths… "Although, it's a little late for liquid courage."

Ally swayed slightly, caught up in the idea of his desiring her. "Hmmm?"

"I just finished my song," he explained, raising one hand to her shoulder, steadying her.

She leant into his lingering touch. "I know, I was listening."

Ted smiled, his cheeks tinging pink. "Were you?"

"It was hard not to hear, what with the microphone and all." *Smooth, Ally. Real smooth.* But was she trying to seduce? As Ted let his hand fall from her good shoulder, Ally thought back to her conversation with Vanessa. It couldn't hurt, if they did it just once. And then, like Vanessa said, they could move on with their lives.

"Earth to Ally," Ted murmured, looking amused. "Are you still with me?"

"Oh, I'm with you. Partner." Ally smiled and tried to look sexy as she took a swig from the bottle in her hand, her lips lingering on the rim.

Ted's eyes tracked the movement and swallowed hard, his Adam's apple bobbing. "Do you want to play a game, Allegra?"

Ally shivered at the sound of her full name, coming out of his no doubt capable mouth. He said it the way a lover might, at the beginning of what he knew would be a long and luxurious night. "What kind of game, *Theodore?*"

Ted smiled enigmatically.

Ally raised an eyebrow in reply.

Preempting any percussive action, however, Matt called out from the corner of the bar. "Oy! Who wants to play Kings?"

They both glanced over Ted's shoulder to see Matt wave a pack of cards in the air.

Ally watched Ted, who seemed to have suddenly lost some of his suavity. "Well, Ted?"

Looking back at her, he shrugged. "Kings it is." He offered her his arm.

After a moment's hesitation, Ally slid her hand into the crook of his elbow. He flexed slightly, definitely for her benefit, but perhaps for his, too, as the gesture pulled them closer together.

For once, Ally allowed herself to think about Ted's towering height, and the post-game scent of him—sweat tinged with spice.

"Shall we?" He sounded like an actual prince.

"We shall," Ally announced, a scullery maid playing at princess.

Together, they approached the table where Matt was now sitting, flanked by Madison and Wren, who had emerged from the dark booth with a smudge of lipstick on her jaw. All three were watching Ally and Ted with evident amusement.

"Come to join us in our little game?" Wren asked, her grin giddy and knowing.

Ally cleared her throat. "In the name of bonding."

"Is that what we're doing?" Ted whispered, his lips brushing the shell of her ear so that Ally had to suppress a shiver. Then, at a normal volume, "If you'll have us, we'd love to play."

The way he said 'us' and 'we' did something to Ally. How had she managed to tamp down her attraction to him all this time? And how would she keep it in her pants long enough for them to leave without causing a scene?

"Sit," Matt commanded, gesturing to the two remaining chairs. They were side by side.

Reluctantly, Ally relinquished Ted's arm and slid into the seat he had already pulled back from the table for her. Then Ted folded his long limbs to settle into his own chair.

Matt smiled, shaking his head at Ted's gallantry. "You know the rules?"

Ted inclined his head, setting his beer on a stained paper coaster.

"Would you care to elaborate for the benefit of anyone who may have forgotten?"

Ted nodded again, glancing around the table. His eyes lingered briefly on Ally's. "It's a drinking game. Whether, and how much, you have to drink depends upon the card you pull." He gestured toward the deck next to the can of light beer at the table's center, rattling off the individual cards' meanings from memory. "And when you pull a card, after you've drunk accordingly, you slide it under the tab of the beer beside the stack to discard. If, in the process, you pop the tab open, you have to drink the beer."

Matt nodded approvingly. "With us, you have to chug it."

"Fair enough."

Wren tapped her own drink twice on the table. "Let's get started. Ally, you're up."

Ally jerked her eyes away from Ted's princely profile. "What?"

"You're starting. And your 'mate' is Ted, because we're playing with our cardio partners."

Trying not to think about all the different things that 'cardio' and 'partner' could mean, Ally pulled a three. "Ugh," she slumped in her seat. "Me."

Laughing, Matt went next. At the sight of the seven of spades, everyone's hands shot into the air—except for Ted's, because his eyes were on Ally instead of the deck.

Ally's gaze met his, and her every nerve seemed to switch *on*; the tension between them was like an electric current that connected them and coiled low in her belly. Sparks seemed to light up the space. When Ted, flushing, finally glanced around, he groaned and took a swig from his sweating bottle.

Ally couldn't help but stare as he swallowed, then licked a stray drop from his lips.

They went round and round. Wren was the first to pull a face card. Jack of Diamonds. Grinning, she glanced at Ally, who immediately tore her eyes away from Ted's long fingers, curled loosely around his drink.

"Drink or Dare," Matt observed, smiling. "Who's the lucky victim, Wren?"

Wren pretended to think about it, but it was obvious whom she had in mind. Ally shrank into her seat. Except, apparently, she had no need to hide.

"Lewis," Wren announced, with a wicked gleam in her eye.

"Yessir," he answered, automatically straightening in his seat.

Wren leaned over the table. "You remember how this one goes, don't you? I come up with a suitable dare, and if you're too much of a coward to do it, you have to drink. It may seem minor, but rest assured we'll all think less of you if you don't follow through."

His eyes flicked to Ally and back. "Yeah, I remember. And I don't doubt it. What's the dare?"

Wren grinned and any relief Ally had felt at not being chosen dissipated like the morning dew. "I dare you to tell us who you were singing about."

"I wasn't." Ted's answer came too quickly. So he had been singing about someone, after all...

And here Ally had thought he was single, available—that he had been singing about a fantasy that they both shared, not a reality that was his and some other person's alone. She deflated a little, tabling her planned seduction. And then she shook herself. What business of hers was it? She had no claim on him. If anything, she'd probably scared him off with all her Harvard talk. Not to mention, the whole Everett thing. He'd been handling her with kid gloves ever since she'd told him about her ex.

"You sure you didn't leave anyone behind in Boston?"

"No one." Ted shook his head, looking down at the scarred wooden table, sticky with god knew what. "And there hasn't been anyone, not in a long time."

A wave of relief crashed over Ally, with more force than she'd been expecting.

"Lewis, are you lying to your captain?" Wren's tone was sly. "You sounded awfully convincing, up there on that stage..."

"Leave him alone, Wren." Ally surprised everyone, even herself, with her quick defense of Ted.

"But lying is against the rules, Bryant." Wren was as stubborn as a dog with a bone.

Well, Ally didn't want to know the truth. She didn't want to hear that Ted was still in love with someone else, especially not when he'd been looking at her, well, the way he'd been looking at her. It would hurt. And it would make him the kind of guy who could sing about one person and make eyes at another, all in the same night. She hadn't thought he was that kind of guy.

Sure, she had hated him at first—and been irritated by him later. But... she'd finally gotten to the point where she could admit to herself that he might just be what he seemed— a thoroughly decent man, with a jawline that could cut a diamond.

"Lewis..."

"No one!" Ted stood suddenly, looming over the table. "There's no one. And I—I need some air. Excuse me." He sounded frustrated, and confused.

Ally tore her eyes off his retreating figure to glare at Wren. "Nice going."

Wren affected innocence. "Well, aren't you going to go chasing after him?"

Fuming at Wren, at the situation, at her own predictability, Ally shoved back from the table. Narrowing her eyes, she searched the dimly-lit room for Ted and finally caught him slipping out the side door. She hesitated. Should she go after him? What would she even say? 'I'm sorry Wren decided it was okay to treat you this way?'

It was better than nothing, she supposed. He was her teammate and she was supposed to be there for him. However awkward or painful the increasingly impossible-to-ignore truth of her feelings for him might be.

"Ted! Wait!" She hurried after him, catching the door before it closed. She ran out onto the sidewalk. "Ted —please."

He stopped suddenly and she crashed into him. Turning, he caught her in his arms before she could stumble backward. "Ally—" He held her for a long moment, taking care not to jostle her shoulder, and for once she allowed herself to be held.

"Ted, I'm sorry. It's just a game and Wren took it too far. I don't know why, but—"

"You don't know why?" He released her to rake a hand through his dark hair. "I'll tell you why, Ally. Because it's obvious!"

Her brows knit and the knot in her stomach tightened. "What is?"

"This... *thing* I have for you! Everyone knows about it, except, apparently, you! Even though I as good as told you once before—not to mention, tonight's performance..."

Ally's jaw actually dropped. Suddenly, a snippet of their conversation in the locker room surfaced. When he'd joked about pining after her. "You... *like* me?"

His eyes were wide with desperation. "Ally, this isn't high school. I don't just like you. I *want* you. And Wren knows —*everyone knows*—and that's why she was needling me. But no matter how much anyone else wants us to—to happen, no one can make you want me. And I don't want you if you don't want me." He started to turn away.

"Wait!" Ally's hand, seemingly of its own accord, shot out to snag his sleeve. "Wait, Ted."

"Ally, I'm not in the mood for—"

"Shut up, Harvard."

She wasn't in love with him. This wasn't some movie. It was lust, plain and simple. But she'd be damned if she didn't do something to satisfy the aching in her belly, ignoring the aching in her heart. Besides, one time and it would be out of both their systems.

She took a deep breath, then reached for his cheek. "You know you're smart, but you're not that smart."

Confusion wrinkled his brow. "What—"

"I want you, too." Then she pushed up onto her toes and pressed a kiss to his stupidly perfect lips.

CHAPTER 10
SATURDAY NIGHT

ALLY FUMBLED WITH HER KEYS. "*Fuck*—No, hang on, I've got it."

She could practically hear Mr. Responsible frowning behind her. "Are you sure you're sober enough for this?"

Successfully opening the door to her apartment, Ally nodded emphatically. "Are you?"

Ted grinned, closed the door behind him, and caught her up against his chest. The air left Ally's lungs in great, giddy gasp. "Sober as a priest."

"Now there's a fantasy I don't have the costumes for…"

They laughed and some of the tension between them eased. The attraction, however, blazed on.

Ted angled his head, leaning in to capture her willing lips in another wondrous kiss. Each had been better than the last, ever since the first.

Ally put her hand on his chest, a staying motion. "There's something I need to tell you, Ted."

He stopped immediately. "Yeah?"

She tried to focus on her words, and not on the press of her palm against his sternum, or the heartbeat she could feel beneath the bone. "I can't, um, come," she confessed, a little embarrassed—not to mention, unpracticed. This wasn't a conversation she usually had with one night stands.

When he cocked his head in confusion, she let her hand fall to her side.

"Okay. I mean, as long as that's okay with you—I—that's okay."

To her surprise, he seemed to mean it. Still... What if he was one of those guys who tried to prove that he was the exception to the rule?

"Sex doesn't have to be about orgasms," he continued, surprising Ally further by speaking with the calm confidence of someone who'd read several books, or perhaps taught a class, on the subject.

"I know, I know. And I, mean, I *can* come." She forced a smile. "It just takes a *while*. Or a battery," Ally added wryly.

"Oh."

Oh. Was he one of *those* guys? The ones who were intimidated by toys? Christ...

"Thanks for telling me."

She grimaced, feeling a sudden urge to explain herself, to salvage some of her dissipating dignity. "I just, my ex. He used to get... impatient with me? I don't want you to feel like I'm not enjoying myself. Or whatever." If they even got to the sex part, which, after this conversation, was uncertain.

"No, I understand." Ted frowned. "Do you want to talk about it?"

"No." She laughed, the sound slightly forced, even to her ears. "He was an asshole. Let's get this show on the road."

"Okay. But I just want you to know... I don't consider sex a contest or a competition. If you can't... If you want to take it slow, or incorporate toys, or... Listen, however you want to do this, that's alright with me. So long as we're communicating."

Ally let out a breath she'd been all too aware of holding. "Right. Communication. Our strong suit!"

He laughed a little at her joke, and she relaxed back into his embrace.

This was okay. This was more than okay.

She smiled shyly up at him.

He grinned eagerly down at her.

Unable to take their stillness any longer, Ally wrapped one hand around the back of his neck and brought him down to her level. Ted went willingly, his eyes fluttering closed even as Ally felt the puff of his breath against her lips. He smelled like cinnamon. Would he taste as sweet? Forgetting the fact that they'd spent the past twenty minutes making out, Ally wondered whether that scent of his, that signature spice, was deodorant or cologne or gum or what. Then, she stopped thinking altogether as their lips met.

Once, twice, she brushed her lips against his in the tender precursor to a kiss.

Licking his lips, Ted angled his head to better capture her mouth with his. Gently, with a touch so light it was a tease, he licked the seam of her lips. Ally inhaled sharply, opening for him. Letting him in. The two of them began to explore each other's mouths with eager curiosity, kindling their mutual desire.

He didn't taste like cinnamon, but Ally found—remembered—she wasn't disappointed; he was still as sweet. Her breathing was heavier now, to mirror his. She tugged his lower lip between her teeth, biting down with enough force to draw a slight gasp from him.

"Shit, sorry. Was that too hard?" She pulled back, cradling his face in her palms.

Ted shook his head, grinning again. "Are you by any chance a vampire?"

"Oh, shut up," she said with affection instead of ire, drawing him into her arms once more. She kissed him hard, holding him close like she might never let go. For a moment, she imagined it—never letting go.

But this was casual. This was one and done.

Ted slid his hands down her back to cradle and knead her ass. In one swift movement, he pulled her flush against him, letting her feel his arousal for herself. Ally's mouth fell open in a gasp of delight and Ted seized the opportunity to sate his evident hunger, supping from her like a man starved.

Having pushed Ted's shirt up until he got the hint to take it off himself, Ally set to work on the button at the front of Ted's trousers. When that popped free, she rushed to unzip him. Trapped beneath taut fabric, his dick was hard and looked heavy with need.

Her fingers flexed, eager to feel its weight. She skimmed the surface of his boxers, eliciting a groan from him, then hooked two of her fingers into the elastic waistband and tugged it loose.

"What do we have here?" Her tone was coy and it sounded strange to her. Strange, but not wrong. She just wasn't accustomed to talking to Ted like this. But she could get used to it...

"Oh my..." She looked down, licking her lips.

"Do you like what you see?" Ted murmured, his voice a roll of latent thunder.

Ally grinned, glancing up at him. Then she started to kneel.

Ted put his hand on her good shoulder, slowing her. "You don't have to—"

"I *want* to." And she did. She sank down to her knees, pulling his down his trousers, his boxers, too. His hard cock twitched to attention, flushed and swollen with arousal. Ally licked her lips again. "I want to taste you."

"Christ," Ted muttered, as she took him in her hand.

He was hot, and smooth like velvet. Slowly, leisurely, she caressed his length. Her other hand gently cupped his balls, reveling in the way they spilled to fill her palm. "Can I kiss you?" She asked, all innocence.

"You just did," he replied, a beat belatedly.

Ally just smiled. Ted was no longer following the plot. "Not there," she murmured, before pressing a chaste kiss to his leaking tip: "*Here*," she hummed happily.

Ted hissed his pleasure.

"Salty, slightly tangy," she announced, as though this were a Zagat review. Her lips curved. "And all for me." Then she flattened her tongue and licked him from base to tip, catching more of the pearly white precum between her lips.

"*Fuck*," he muttered, watching her from above. The way he swore, the way he shivered—she felt sexier than any porn star. "I can't do this."

Ally pulled back. "Can't do what?"

"I need more. I need *you*." Ted helped a suddenly grinning Ally to her feet, and gave her a sound kiss. Then he set to work on the fastenings of her jeans.

Ally laughed, and pulled her shirt over her head. Pain bloomed like a carnivorous plant. "Shit shit *shit*."

Immediately, Ted stilled. "What's wrong?"

Wincing, Ally answered, "My shoulder." She probed the swollen joint.

"Should we stop?"

Such a Boy Scout... "Are you kidding?" Ally leaned forward, nipping at his neck. "You'll just have to take this off for me, Harvard."

Shit, that endearment sounded sweet on her lips. Ted grinned. "Whatever you say, Lestat."

Ally's mouth dropped open, and she swatted him with her good arm. "Do *not* compare me to—"

Ted cut her off with a zealous kiss, unzipping her jeans in the process. He paused to take a look at her panties, peeking through the splayed opening. They were pink, with little rainbows and unicorns dotted all over them. "Cute underwear," he said with a smirk.

"It is, isn't it?" Smiling, she shimmied out of her skinny jeans.

"It'd be cuter in the laundry hamper," he murmured, clearly trying to be smooth.

Ally snorted. "That's definitely not the line."

But Ted didn't answer, nor did he appear to give a damn. Taking care not to touch her injured shoulder, he swept Ally off her feet and into his arms, carrying her to the bed. Not that he had to walk far—if her apartment was small, her bedroom was tiny.

Ally took a deep breath. "I want you to fuck me, Ted."

The confession caught him off-guard. They were well on their way to having sex. According to some definitions, they already were in the process. It was just the bluntness of her confession, edging into the territory of command. He'd been hoping for some slow and sweet love-making. Ally clearly had other ideas.

They tumbled onto the bed and she drew him on top of her, reaching for a bottle of lube on her bedside table and a condom from a drawer. She handed him both.

Obediently, Ted rolled the condom down his hard cock, hissing at its tight caress. Then he took the lube and slid down the length of her body, taking her rainbow panties off as he went. Before applying any of the cool liquid, he spread her legs and inhaled the rich scent of her. Then he dove in, licking her labia in long, lapping strokes and sucking on her clit gently.

Ally whimpered, and Ted was consumed with a desire to get to know her and her body, to hear all her sounds and feel all her textures. To taste all her flavors.

"Hurry up," she moaned, impatient in her pleasure,

having none of his thorough exploration. Another time then, he thought, refusing to be disappointed.

Ted warmed the lube between his palms, then spread it along his stiff length and inside her velvet walls. She gasped, pulling him up so that his mouth met hers, and their bodies were aligned.

"Fuck me," she begged.

Ted eased himself into her, wincing with pleasure at the vice-like clutch of her glorious cunt.

"Faster," she demanded, again an empress. "*Harder.*"

Less gently, Ted started to thrust.

In tacit approval, Ally bit down on his shoulder.

He tangled his fingers in hers and stretched her good arm above her head. He sucked on the sensitive skin between her uninjured shoulder and her neck. Pumping his hips with increasing abandon, he moved to make her moan. And she did. Beautifully. The sound was even sweeter than her celebratory shout whenever she scored.

"Oh, god."

Ted thrust harder and faster—as previously requested. Ally slipped her wrist free of his grasp to scrape her nails gently down his back. One of her legs folded and her heel dug into his ass, offering encouragement.

"Are you close?" He asked, feeling the tide of an orgasm build within him.

Ally laughed, but it morphed into a gasp as he drilled into her with new intensity, giving her all that he had in him. "No, but I'm not going to be. Just fuck me, don't worry about me."

"Whatever you say," he murmured reluctantly, sweat beading at his temples. He was tired and sore, but he'd be damned if he didn't give her his everything.

"You're so fucking hot," she muttered, almost to herself. "I just want you deeper, deeper, *deep*—" She cut herself off, crying out as he adjusted his angle to better penetrate her.

He wanted to reach that spot, that secret spot, the one that would give her the most pleasure.

"Come for me," she whispered, nipping at his earlobe. "Ted, please!"

Never one to disappoint, Ted gasped her name—her full name, not her nickname—and allowed the pleasure to surge within him, erupting in hot spurts within her.

"Oh, god." She groaned, as he slowed, holding himself over her so as not to crush her. "That was good. That was really good."

"But you didn't—"

She smiled dreamily up at him. "Like you said, orgasms aren't everything."

Ted rolled off of her, taking care not to land on her injured shoulder. Stripping off the condom, he tied it tightly, then tossed it in the nearby bin. Once more, he made to hold her, to gather her up in his arms and nuzzle her neck where he'd sucked hard on it earlier, but she squirmed away.

He pulled back. "What's wrong?"

"Nothing!" Her tone was bright, too bright.

Ted settled himself on the bed, thinking hard. Had he done something to make Ally uncomfortable?

"I'm going to go to the bathroom and clean myself up," she said, standing. "There's glasses in the kitchen cabinet and water in the tap, just don't look at all the dishes in the sink. Ice in the freezer, too," she offered, like the cubes were a truce.

Had they fought, though? Ted frowned as Ally slipped out of the bedroom. He needed to clean himself up, too, but he supposed he'd better wait. Ally seemed to have withdrawn and he didn't want to overstep a boundary—although, he worried, it might be too late? Maybe she wasn't ready for a relationship, or even a one night stand, after what had happened with her ex.

The faucet was running when Ted knocked on the bathroom door. "Ally?"

"Out in a minute!"

He nodded and, after throwing on his wrinkled clothes, made for the kitchen, where he splashed some water on his face and ignored the dirty dishes. The only reason his own sink was currently empty was because his aunt had taught him—over the course of his teenage years, when he used to spend a month each summer with her in New York, being her sous chef and going to museums and exploring the city—to clean as he cooked.

"Oh." Ally sounded disappointed, but also—a bit relieved? "You got dressed."

Ted lowered the washcloth with which he'd been drying his face and turned. "Yeah. I, uh, think maybe I should head home."

She crossed her arms over her bare breasts. "Are you sure?"

Ted suppressed a sigh. Yes, he was sure. Not because it was what he wanted but because it seemed like, for whatever reason, it was what she wanted. "Sure thing."

"Okay!" Ally nodded. "I'll just—Feel free to use the bathroom before you go."

"Thanks." Tonight had not gone as planned. "I'll be out of your hair in a minute." And then, later, as he left her apartment for what he hoped would not be the last time, "Don't forget to ice."

CHAPTER 11
THE RIGHT CALL

ALLY WATCHED Ted go with mixed feelings. She didn't acknowledge the mix, however, choosing to focus only on the relief, which was temporary and soon replaced by horror.

What had she done?

She'd slept with the enemy!

Okay, she'd stopped hating him at least a week ago, and one might argue that she had never *really* hated him, but still.

The actual problem was, having sex with him hadn't cured her of the desire to do it again. She'd been counting on a one and done. She hadn't been counting on continued, confusing cravings…

Oh god. Oh god. Oh, *god.*

Her mind thus occupied, she went back into the bathroom, brushed her teeth, and settled in for some scraps of sleep.

She didn't truly freak out until the next morning, when her mother called.

"Mom! Hi."

"Hi sweetie, how was the scrimmage?"

"Game, and we won." No thanks to her. Entirely thanks to him. Oh god. He'd seen her bedroom. He'd seen the dishes in the sink. He'd seen *her*—naked!

"Fantastic! How was Harvard?" Ally had told her mother a little bit about Ted and her mother had picked up Ally's nickname for him.

How *was* Harvard? On the ice? Smart, quick, ruthless, calculating, a star as well as true team-player. In bed? Amazing, considerate, attentive, strong, eager to please, well-endowed, sexy as all hell.

Shit.

She was so screwed.

"Sweetie?"

Ally hadn't answered her mother's question. "Oh, um, he's great!" Ally winced. That sounded fake.

"Hmmm." Her mother had heard it, too. "What aren't you telling me?" And then, with the prophetic wisdom that, combined with an invasive curiosity, was the hallmark of her mothering, "Did you sleep with him?"

"Ma!" Ally was outraged. But she was also… relieved? Maybe her mother could talk her out of doing something crazy, like calling Ted up and asking him out on a date.

"Well, Ally?" Her mother's tone was gentle, yet stern. This would quickly turn into an interrogation if Ally didn't cooperate.

"Yes, Mom." Ally dragged her feet across her bedroom floor, gathering worn and unworn clothing on her toes. Christ, she couldn't believe she'd let Ted see her like this. A mess. What would he think? He wore a suit to work—in this day and age! And how could she forget the pocket square? They worked at a tech company, for god's sake! Ally wore leggings most days! At least she had, before he'd shown up that fateful Monday.

"How was it?"

"Mom!"

Her mother laughed. "I'm not asking for details, sweetie. In fact, I'd really rather know nothing about your sex life." Just hearing her mother say the word sex made Ally cringe.

"But you seem pretty worked up about it. Did he hurt you?" This last question she asked with gentle gravity and tact.

"No, no." Ally went into the kitchen, where Heathcliff was waiting expectantly by his bowl. He'd been surprisingly unobtrusive last night. Did that mean he approved? Or did cats just suddenly develop tact when they sensed someone was having sex? Or, maybe, Heathcliff was disappointed in her. Maybe he was traumatized by the sight of Ted's sizable—

"Then what's wrong, sweetie? It sounds like you like him, at least more than you used to; does he not like you?"

Ally frowned. She was pretty sure the feelings were mutual. And not the mixed ones, either. "I think he likes me… I mean, this isn't high school. But, like…"

"Do you no longer like him? Sometimes, when you add sex into the mix, this can happen…"

"Ma, *please*. Lay off the sex stuff."

She could hear her mother smother laughter on the other end of the line. "You millennials, you're so sensitive. Talk to me about your feelings, sweetie. Or else I'll be forced to tell you about your father's antics at the Cortelluccis' dinner party last night. Honestly, why I married him…" She spoke with a combination of frustration and fondness.

"If you and Dad are fighting, I don't wanna hear about it." Ally opened a can of cat food for Heathcliff, who jumped up onto the counter. "Down, Heathcliff. Off the counter!"

"That cat of yours… He lives up to his namesake, that's for sure. Absolutely no manners."

"Mom, I think you missed the point of *Wuthering Heights*."

"Well, whatever. You were the English major, not me. So, tell me. When are you seeing him again?"

"Monday."

"I meant outside of the office, sweetie. Although maybe you'd better talk to HR. Is it that serious?"

Ally shook her head, and then remembered that her

mother couldn't see her. "No, Ma. It's not that serious." And it wasn't. Was it?

"Still, I think you should go out on a date with him. A real date. An outing without your teammates or coworkers. It's complicated enough without office *and* hockey politics. Just go out on the town! Have some fun. And be *safe*!"

"Mom, New York is not what it used to be." Ally rolled her eyes.

"I meant sexually."

Ally gasped. "Ma! That's it, this conversation is over."

"Okay, okay. Embarrassing Mother Alert. Love you, hun."

"Love you, Mom."

She hung up, feeling slightly queasy. Not about the sex stuff—her mother had given her the talk in first grade; she could handle whatever Bianca Bryant threw at her—but about the idea of asking Ted out on a date.

Should she do it?

Could it make things worse?

Could it make them better?

Ally shook herself.

Heathcliff meowed, having finished his breakfast.

"I don't know, Heathie. It could be dangerous."

Heathcliff tilted his head skeptically.

"What if I fall in love?"

Laughing at the absurdity of her little joke, Ally opened the fridge and foraged for breakfast.

Ted's first alarm went off at an unholy hour. Well, it was early, Ted confirmed as he glanced at his smart watch, but not really —not for him. Ted sat up in bed, rubbing the sleep from his eyes.

He was up, now. Might as well make a smoothie.

In the kitchen, Ted turned off all of his alarms. And then

he pulled the blueberries—frozen fresh from his last road trip through Maine—out of the freezer. The bananas, too. And, on second thought, the strawberries. He wanted something sweet after last night's sour.

Not that it had been all that sour. Just that he was a bit sad, disappointed by the distance that still separated Ally from him. Still, he shouldn't complain. He'd had great sex with a great girl—woman, that was.

Smiling to himself, he replayed their first and second meetings in his head as he prepared the smoothie. Ted tossed the fruit, some yogurt, a dash of honey, and a handful of chia seeds into the blender. Then he pressed the smoothie button. Fruit, and globs of honeyed yogurt dotted with black seeds, flew everywhere.

Fuck.

An hour later, he had cleaned the kitchen, eaten an emergency bowl of sugary cereal, and watched some cartoons as a kind of consolation. But the television couldn't hold him for long. Ted had all this nervous energy he needed to express and walking seemed the best way to get it out.

Ted checked the weather app on his wrist. He'd need a fleece.

He took the stairs down, two at a time, and exited onto Park Avenue. From there, it was a couple of blocks to Central Park, which was relatively empty, with the exception of joggers and dog walkers, given the hour. The leaves were still on the trees for the most part—it had been a warm autumn thus far. Yellows and oranges and only the occasional crimson met his eye when Ted raised his head.

In his fleece pocket, his phone started to vibrate. Fishing it out, he picked up on the third ring.

"Teddy!" Belle sounded altogether too alert.

"Belle…"

His sister laughed. "Did I wake you?"

"No, I'm on a walk."

"Getting those steps in? You know, I'm not so sure a random tech company needs to know your daily routine."

"Belle, it is entirely too early to get political."

"I'm just saying. Besides, I heard that ten thousand is an arbitrary number."

"Belle!"

She went silent.

"I'm not in the mood."

"Are you okay?" Belle asked, after a beat.

Ted frowned "Yes, I'm fine."

"How'd the game go?"

"We won."

"Are you sure? You don't sound too happy."

Ted sighed. "My teammate got injured."

"Oh dear…" Ted could hear his sister's concern. "Are they okay? Did they see a doctor?"

Ted huffed. "I was with her the whole night, Belle; she's fine. She just needs some ice, and some time." Her injury wasn't half as bad as it could have been.

"The whole night?" Belle parroted, and Ted realized his mistake. "Is *that* why you didn't pick up when I called you last night?"

"We went to the bar, I texted you!"

"No, after. I called and it rang through to voicemail."

"Belle, please drop it."

"Oh my God, you're *blushing!*"

"How the hell do you know? You're in a different state."

"I have a sixth sense about this stuff." She sniffed. "It's a younger sibling thing. Anyway, what happened? Did you make a move? Did she *reject* you?" Belle's tone turned pitying.

"She did not reject me, thank you very much." Well, not at first. But after… Ted couldn't be sure.

Belle went suspiciously silent, and Ted fervently wished

he'd kept his mouth shut. "Then why are you on the phone with me, and not whispering sweet nothings in her ear?"

Ted checked his watch. "Don't you have class?"

"It's a Sunday, Teddy."

"They had weekend classes in my day..." He muttered, uncertain as to whether or not that was the truth.

Belle laughed. "Bullshit. If they did, you didn't go to them. Besides, you are not getting out of it this that easy." Her voice entered a wicked pitch. "You like her."

It wasn't a question, so Ted didn't have to answer.

"Oh my god, you like her. Teddy!" Belle squealed with glee, and the sound was so loud it startled a nearby squirrel on Ted's end, which scampered up a sycamore tree. "You haven't had a girlfriend in *ages*. At least not one you've told me about."

"Maybe I don't tell you about my girlfriends because this is how you react. Like a mad hatter." Or, maybe, he didn't tell her about his girlfriends because he never had any. Maybe Ted struggled to make connections, to form deep and lasting bonds. Maybe dating was hard as an adult. Maybe he tried but his heart was never in it. Maybe Ally was the exception.

Christ, what if she was the exception, and he'd somehow screwed it up? I mean, why else would she freeze up after what they'd shared? Not that the sex had been profound, mind you. Ted was convinced Ally was holding out on him. But that was okay. Not everyone was as open, as willing to share, as he was. He could work with walls, if she threw them up. He could also back off, if she wanted him to give up.

His phone beeped. Another call on the line.

"LOL! What if it's her?" Belle teased.

Ted pulled the phone from his ear. "What if it's *she*."

He blinked down at the screen.

Holy shit.

Allegra.

Ted picked up on the fourth ring, just before Ally decided to abandon everything and go live in a cave by the sea. There was silence on the line for a second, and then a muffled, "Jesus."

"...hello?"

"Hey! Ally." His voice was dark and deep, and she wanted to be enveloped in its rich timbre. "Sorry about that, my sister..." He trailed off. "She's nosy."

Ally laughed nervously. "Like all good little sisters should be. Listen, I can call you back later, if you're busy—"

"No, no, not at all. I was just on a walk and my sister called. But she had to go, so."

"Oh, where are you walking to?" Ally's voice sounded artificially bright to her own ears and she winced.

Ted paused. "Nowhere in particular. Rambling around The Ramble, I guess."

"Ah, Central Park." She recollected teasing him about living uptown, but it must be nice to be so near a sizable park. Not that Tompkins Square Park was anything less than perfect. "Um, listen."

"Yeah?" He sounded nervous, beneath his tone's clearly calculated levity.

"About last night..."

"Oh." Ted's pitch plummeted and Ally almost freaked out again. What if he didn't want to go on a date with her? What if he regretted what they'd done?

"What about last night?" He asked, patiently. There was no hint of accusation, no dusting of disgust. Just, calm. And a slightly gentle touch. Not like last night, when he'd been deliciously rough...

Ally cleared her throat. "I just wanted to ask... Do you maybe wanna go on a, I don't know, a date with me?" Oh god. She could die right now. Right here on this sidewalk in front of the basement tarot card reader. She should never have asked, she should never have called, she should never have—

Ted cleared his throat, and his voice shook slightly when he spoke. "I'd love to."

"What?"

He laughed on the other end of the line, a warm and welcome sound. "I said, I'd love to. What did you have in mind?"

"Um, nothing yet," she confessed. "I actually didn't expect you to... you know."

"Ally," he said, and then corrected himself. "Allegra."

She wanted to melt at the sound of her name on his lips. Ally squirmed, wishing she were at home with her vibrator. She didn't know why, or how he knew, but *damn* the way he said her name did it for her.

"You may not realize this, but I'm crazy about you."

Ally's mouth opened and closed like a feeding fish. What was she supposed to say to *that*? Perhaps he realized he was being unfair, because he took pity on her.

"Why don't we talk tomorrow, once we've both had time to come up with some ideas?"

Tomorrow. Monday. Right. "Okay!"

"Until tomorrow, then." His voice was warm, like mulled wine.

"See you," she veritably squeaked. And then the line went dead.

Ally, too, felt liked she'd died. And, uncharacteristically, gone to heaven.

CHAPTER 12
PESTO ON PARK

"You slept with him."

Ted was walking past the open kitchen when he heard Vanessa's accusation. He slowed, hiding behind the refrigerator for a moment. Vanessa didn't sound angry, however, or judgmental, to his surprise. Instead, Ted heard in her tone amusement, excitement, and not a small amount of pride. From Ally, he heard nothing. Nevertheless, Vanessa responded as if her friend had spoken in confirmation of her accusation.

"I knew it! Why didn't you text me? Were you incapacitated by your fifteen orgasms?"

Ally sighed. "I didn't have fifteen orgasms," she said flatly. "That's physically impossible. Well, difficult. Anyway." She pitched her voice a little louder, "Ted, you can come out from behind the fridge."

Ted did as he was told, a little embarrassed to have been discovered. "How did you know I was—"

Ally smiled, a triumphant gleam in her eyes. Ted felt his heart flutter. "I saw you walk over."

"I was just—"

"Eavesdropping? Again?" Ally put her hands on her hips. "We'll have to work on that."

Vanessa's eyes widened. "You say that like there's a future for you two! So it wasn't just one and done?"

Ted grinned. "In fact, she asked me—"

"Zip it, preppy." Ally sent him a threatening, yet fond, look. She turned back to Vanessa. "I asked him on a date, alright? It's just a date, not a marriage proposal."

"It's not just a date," Ted interjected, feeling a little wounded by her choice of words.

Ally wheeled around, her eyebrows high on her forehead. "Oh? What is it, then?"

Ted fumbled for the right words. Technically, it was just a date. But... but it might be so much more! Still, he didn't want to scare Ally off by moving too fast. "It's a dinner date," he said, at last.

Vanessa cocked her head. "How is that different from a date?"

Ally's eyebrows stayed raised. "Yes, Theodore. Do tell."

"It's different because..." Shit, he really hadn't thought this through. "Well, because it's not just overpriced drinks. And because..." He glanced around at the glorified snack bar. Inspiration struck. "Because I'll be the one cooking for you!"

Vanessa's mouth opened, a perfect 'o.' "That is so thoughtful—"

"Do you even know how to cook?" Ally sounded skeptical.

Ted smiled smugly. "I think you'll find I'm quite proficient in the kitchen."

Vanessa's eyes lit up. "As proficient as you are in the bedroom?"

Ally flushed, as did Ted. He probably didn't look nearly as pretty as she did when embarrassed. Ted wondered, briefly, as he watched her, if this was the color she turned when she came. He prayed he'd one day have a chance to find out. To earn the sight of her, lost to pleasure.

"V!" Ally screeched belatedly, drawing the attention of more than one passerby.

Ted nudged her and, noticing their new audience, she flushed a deeper hue.

More quietly, she continued, "This is why I didn't immediately tell you!"

"I would have found out eventually, Ally."

"Maybe, but—but do you have to be so, so... *you*?"

Vanessa flicked a lock of her long black hair over her shoulder. "Yes, I do."

Ted couldn't help himself; he started to chuckle. It was just so nice, friendship. He wished he had more of it.

Both women rounded on him. "What are you laughing at, Harvard?"

"Yeah, what's so funny?"

Ted shrugged. "Nothing, I just think it's great that you have each other. I'm jealous, honestly."

"Of our fighting?" Ally demanded.

"Of your friendship," Ted answered. He turned to Vanessa. "Vanessa, would you give us a minute? And then I'll disappear, I swear." He checked his smart watch; the screen was bright with a calendar notification. "I have a meeting in five."

"I'll leave you two lovebirds be," Vanessa replied in a tone that was sugary sweet.

Ally rolled her eyes. "I'll see you in a sec, V." She addressed Ted, as soon as Vanessa left in the direction of their desks, "You wanted to speak to me? Alone?"

Ted laughed. "Alone as can be, given that we're standing in the center of the office, in the middle of the workday."

"Sound doesn't travel as well over here," Ally said, the bright light of conspiracy in her eye. "Vanessa and I have performed tests."

"Tests?"

"We have lots of secrets we're interesting in keeping secrets."

"While still gossiping about them in public?"

Ally shrugged. "A girl's got needs. Anyway, that's why we were over here. It's the best place to talk on this floor."

Ted frowned. "What about the nap rooms, aren't those soundproofed?"

"As you and I learned the other night, that soundproofing is limited to the pods themselves."

"Right." Ted was still slightly embarrassed at having overheard such a personal conversation, when Ally clearly hadn't thought anyone was listening. "Sorry about that, by the way. I—"

"Don't worry about it, Ted. Who would you even tell?"

She'd meant it as a jest, a jovial insult, but it struck home. Ted had started to make friends. Matt, Wren, and some of the guys from GreenLight. But the only person he'd really clicked with was Ally.

Ally, Ally, Ally…

"So." She was looking up at him, expectantly. "After work, Friday?"

Ted was lost, for a moment, in her eyes' warmth. Like embers, they lit a fire in him he'd long thought banked. Shaking himself, he considered her question. She was obviously asking about their date.

Their date!

Trying to sound cool, calm, and collected, Ted teased her. "And miss out on the keg?"

Ally arched her brows. "I'd rather you cook for me than spend my Friday evening drinking mediocre beer. Besides, we can show face for a few minutes, if it means that much to you."

"Nah," Ted said, brushing her suggestion aside. He stepped closer and, after checking that the coast was clear, tucked a loose lock of her hair behind her ear. It curled around the pink curve of her lobe. "You mean more."

Her answering smile was uncharacteristically shy. She ducked her head. "Don't you have a meeting to attend?"

Ted groaned. "Yes. I'll see you Friday."

Ally laughed. The sound was as sweet as water after a long shift. "We work together. You'll see me before then."

"True," he ceded, "but all I'll be thinking about until then is, well, then."

Ally pouted. "You won't be thinking about me?"

Ted threw caution to the wind and, hooking an arm around her waist, pulled her in for a brief but beautiful kiss. He didn't let his lips linger, however. He let her go—quickly, lest anybody see them, but reluctantly.

Her eyes were wide with wonder and surprise.

"You're all I ever think about, Allegra Bryant." Then he turned on his heel and made his way toward the meeting room, his mind on the velvety softness of her lips.

"You have a doorman," Ally observed, half in awe, half in judgment.

"Albert," Ted offered, waving at the man.

"Albert," she echoed. Then, finding her stride again, "How do you have a doorman but holes in your socks?"

Ted laughed. "So you noticed. I didn't realize you had such a thing for feet," he teased.

Ally flushed, protesting, "I do not! It's just hard not to notice when your big toe is poking out like a pig in a blanket! Must be why your skates smell..."

It was his turn to protest. "My skates do not smell."

"Like a teenager's laundry hamper."

"Bold of you to assume any teenager puts their laundry in their hamper."

She grinned. "Point taken."

They stepped into the elevator. Ted inserted a key and pressed a button. The doors closed. Suddenly, they were alone.

They hadn't been alone together since that smoldering kiss, on Monday, and then they hadn't really been alone then because they had been in the office. Technically they had been alone together on the street earlier, as they walked here from the subway, but that was out in the open. They had been alone in her apartment, almost a week ago now, but that was under the influence of sex and alcohol. And that was before she had asked him out. That was before she'd put her cards on the table.

Now, they were sober and alone together in an elevator with the knowledge that each was interested in the other.

Ally tore her eyes away from Ted and inspected the small control panel. The elevator was fairly small and decidedly old fashioned.

"Are you sure this thing is up to code?" Ally asked, allowing her anxiety to break the tension at last.

Ted smiled reassuringly. "Check the date on the maintenance sheet." It was set in a frame below the columns of buttons. Last inspection: August of that year.

"Oh."

The elevator dinged and its doors opened. Into a foyer, not a hallway. She'd been expecting a hallway. What *was* this place?

Ted gestured for her to exit and she did. He followed, close on her heels. Close enough for her to catch a whiff of the spiced cologne he wore. Or maybe it was a deodorant. Ally focused on her surroundings.

"Is this... yours?"

Ted nodded.

"All of this?"

He nodded again.

"What about the other tenants?"

"Owners," he corrected. "It's a co-op. And each of us has our own floor. Or two, if you're the Hoffmans."

"But that's..." Ally wheeled around, feeling suddenly accusatory. "You must be some kind of millionaire! But why would a millionaire dress like *that*?" She added, under her breath.

"Excuse me, but I happen to like the way I dress."

"Mark Zuckerberg does too, and you don't see him on the catwalk." Her jaw dropped. "Wait. You're not a *billionaire*, are you?"

He laughed. "Christ, no."

"Good, because I couldn't associate with you anymore if you were."

"Oh, is that what we're doing?" He said, smirking. "Associating?"

Ally sniffed. "It's as good a word for it as any."

"What ever happened to 'dating?'"

"Whoa, cowboy." She put her hands up. "This is our first date, if you must call it that, and I'm only here because you promised me fresh pesto." That, and the fact that this had been her idea. Ted was kind enough not to point that out, though.

Ted shook his head. "Come on, Bryant. Let me show you around."

To Ally's surprise, he took her hand. His grip was firm, yet gentle. His fingers were long and felt strong as they enveloped hers. She tried to ignore the butterflies that had started flipping cartwheels in her stomach.

"So, how do you afford the mortgage on this place? Do they really pay senior managers that much more?" Ally asked, noticing a small chandelier hanging from the foyer's ceiling. It looked an awful lot like the one she'd seen at the opera, the one time she'd gotten tickets, but smaller. It had been a modern production, experimental, and she'd hated it.

The chandelier, though, that she had loved. It, like the one above her, resembled a star shattering into light. Or at least, that's what she thought an exploding star would look like; Ally was no astrophysicist.

"My aunt died," he said, simply, recapturing her errant attention.

Ally nodded. He'd mentioned it once before. "I'm so sorry…"

"It's alright. It's been three years, so I've mostly stopped sobbing in the middle of the night."

Ally didn't know whether or not to laugh at his dark humor. Instead, she plunged ahead. "So, what? She left you a small fortune?"

"Not exactly. She left me this apartment."

"You mean, this entire floor of an apartment building."

Ted ceded her point with a slight incline of his handsome head. How humble.

"Honestly, you might as well be a millionaire!" Ally wasn't going to ask him about the taxes on a place like this, but she was mighty curious.

"So you've said. Twice now. I wonder, would it make you more or less attracted to me?" He pulled her closer, coming to a halt in front of an open doorway. Their bodies were inches apart.

Trying not to inhale any more of his intoxicating scent, she resorted to immaturity. "Shut up," she said, pushing at him playfully. Ted let her go, and she regretted the loss of his body's heat.

"What was she like?" Ally asked, her curiosity getting the better of her. It was smarter, too, to keep things in the realm of questions. It might save her from having to offer him any answers.

He smiled fondly, gazing off into the distance. "A little bit crazy. A lot quirky. At times, strikingly serious; at times, utterly silly. She was a very private person, but she wasn't afraid to be affectionate. Or to let me in on her secrets." He met her gaze, and held it.

Ally struggled to remember how to breathe. "What did she do, to afford all this?"

"She wrote cookbooks."

Her brows knit. "You'd have to be an heiress to survive on selling cookbooks. Or be famous."

Ted smiled abashedly, and looked down at his clasped hands. "My aunt was Lorraine Lewis. Maybe you've heard of—"

"*The* Lorraine Lewis?" Ally gasped. "I have a copy of her *Country Vegetables for City Girls* in my kitchen! Well, if you can call it a kitchen… But you've seen it. You've washed up in it." She quirked an eyebrow at him. "Not all of us are living in the lap of luxury."

"I know," Ted responded, earnestly. "And believe me, I know I'm lucky. More than lucky."

Ally nodded. "As long as you're aware. So, did she teach you any tricks?"

His smile returned, slow and sultry.

Ally inhaled deeply and caught another whiff of his warm, spicy scent.

"Who do you think taught me how to make pesto?"

"Google?" She suggested, shrugging.

They laughed together, reveling in the sound of their shared pleasure, and then he took her by the hand again and continued the tour.

Ted unplugged the food processor before lifting its plastic lid.

Ally inhaled deeply, enjoying the fresh fragrance of finely chopped basil and extra virgin olive oil. She opened her eyes again to admire the pesto's vivid greenery. "Yum."

"Yeah, I think we did a pretty good job." Ted reached for a silicone spatula.

Ally raised her chin. "I think we nailed it."

Ted laughed and gave her a gentle hip-check. "You haven't even tasted it, yet, hotshot."

"No, but I'm rarely wrong about pesto."

"I don't doubt it." Ted started to scrape the sauce into a glass container. "If you get a fork out of that drawer—"

"In a minute," she said, making for the kitchen's door. "Where's your bathroom again?"

He answered without ceasing to scrape. "Down the hall, take two lefts."

On her way back from the sparkling guest bathroom that was papered with a Morris print, Ally spied a swathe of bright pink in the crack of an open door. She wasn't normally one to snoop, but... Ally pushed the door open a little wider and found herself standing at the edge of what she could only assume was Ted's bedroom. Ally bit her lip. She really shouldn't be in here, but curiosity had already gotten the better of her—she stepped over the threshold and onto the soft carpet, taking a good look around.

The pink, it turned out, was a dress shirt that had fallen off its hanger, out of the tall cherrywood wardrobe, and onto the floor. Ally felt compelled to rescue it, so out of place amidst the room's general neatness. Nothing like her own bedroom. Ally picked up the shirt, shook it out, and opened the wardrobe a bit more in order to replace the garment on its hanger. Her eyes widened, however, at the impressive sight of Ted's clothing collection. Then again, she'd known the man was interested in fashion. She'd seen the evidence every day of the work week.

"You sure do own a lot of shirts, old sport." And yet, owning them wasn't the point for Ted. Clothing was a form of creative expression for the man, not a means of impressing his socioeconomic status on strangers.

Ted's voice was muffled by the several walls that separated them, but nevertheless it shocked Ally out of her sartorial musings. "What?"

"Nothing! Be right there." She admired Ted's shirt collection a moment more before hanging the shirt back up and gently shutting the twin doors of the wardrobe, which appeared to be an antique, and making her way back to the kitchen.

Ted was still scraping pesto from the processor's blades. He glanced at her over his shoulder. "Did you say something about shirts?"

"Keep your eye on the prize, Harvard. Wouldn't want to have to take you to the hospital. They'd assume I had something to do with it!"

He huffed a laugh but returned his gaze to the twin curved blades. "And they'd be right. You're very beautiful."

She shifted nervously before reluctantly allowing herself to accept the compliment. "Thanks."

"Anytime. So, why were you in my bedroom?" His voice was absent both accusation and innuendo. Ted wasn't upset about her snooping, and he was clearly being very careful not to spook her, sexually speaking.

Ally shrugged. "Got lost on the way back from the bathroom. Which one of these is your silverware drawer?"

"Second one to my right. And I don't believe you."

She dipped a fork into the pesto, its tines disappearing into the sea of green. "It *is* a big apartment."

Ted nodded, placing the blade extension gently in the sink. "I know. The taxes are a lot," he added sheepishly. "But I've been thinking of getting a cat."

Ally snorted. "To help with the taxes? You do realize that cats don't come with their own income."

Ted rolled his eyes but suppressed a grin. "Most animals, no. But not my dream cat. He'd quickly become a celebrated stunt actor."

Ally couldn't help but laugh outright at that. "And who would train this stunt actor cat of yours? You?"

Ted seemed to think about this, standing tall and handsome in his apron—never mind the several errant bits of basil that were stuck to his broad chest. "I suppose I could quit my job and start an agency. Do you think Heathcliff would be interested in signing with me?"

Scoffing, Ally quickly shook her head. "The only thing he's interested in is treats. And sleeping. And shedding little black hairs all over my clean laundry."

Ted smothered a smile, his eyes traveling up and down her figure. "In fact, I think I've found one..." He stepped closer to her, close enough for her to feel the warmth of his body, to smell the faint hint of his cologne beneath the scent of pine nuts and parmesan.

Ally's breathing hitched and her heart beat faster.

Ted raised his hand to pluck something from her shoulder. "There," he murmured.

Their eyes met and locked. Ally found herself forgetting her fork altogether, abandoning it and the container of pesto in favor cupping the back of Ted's neck and bringing him closer to her. Close enough for her lips to meet his in a gentle yet generous kiss.

His hands snaked around her waist, pulling her to him. Ally's mouth opened on a languid moan. His tongue slipped between her parted lips to stroke hers. Ally pressed up against Ted until she could feel him harden against her hip.

Suddenly, her stomach let out an enormous rumble.

Ted broke the kiss, laughing against her lips. "Come on, Ally. Let's eat."

Ally sighed, cursing her hunger for getting in the way of the satiation of another, rather less literal form of starvation. "Oh, alright. The pasta's at least al dente by now, anyhow."

CHAPTER 13
SKITTISH

"That was delicious, Ted."

He inclined his head, not bothering to hide his smile. "My pleasure. Besides, you did half the work. I should be thanking you." Ted liked to cook for and with the people he cared about. And Ally was rapidly becoming one of those people. Or, rather, she had been for a while…

"So, what other *Hidden Treasures* do you have hiding here?" Ally nodded at the Amy Winehouse CD Ted had left on the kitchen counter that morning.

He laughed. "None, honestly. Unless you want to see my uncle's matchbook collection."

"I think I'll pass," Ally said, in a high-pitch that Ted suspected was her attempt at being polite. "But I don't believe you. I mean, look at this place. It's certainly unexpected."

"I can't tell if that's a compliment or an insult," he said, frowning. "But really, there's nothing more to know about me."

Ally smiled mischievously. "We'll see."

She wandered away from him, in the direction of the living room, but extended her hand for him to take. Ted caught her wriggling fingers between his, a spark of static electricity passing between them. Was that all that was? Ally stopped on the threshold and turned back to face him. "What shall we do now?"

Ted wasn't sure if she was toying with him, because all he wanted to do was to pull her into his arms and kiss her. "What would you like to do?"

Ally's answer was little more than a whisper as her eyes met his. "You…" Ted started to tug her closer, but as soon as she was pressed against his chest, she continued quickly, "… have a really big TV."

Huh. He rather felt that last part had been an improvisation, but he wouldn't protest. If Ally wasn't ready to begin where they'd left off on Monday, he was more than happy to help her warm up. "Your profile says you like Katharine Hepburn movies…"

She stepped back, into the soft light of the living room. "My profile?"

"On Flutter." Ted shifted, feeling slightly self-conscious. "We have a lot of things in common. That's why I wanted to prioritize you."

"You found me on Flutter? You clicked-and-held on me?"

Ted chuckled, his revelation rewarded by the excitement in her eyes. "Ally, I said I *wanted* to."

"What stopped you?" She was quiet in her confusion.

"I would never have presumed…"

"So you were just waiting for me to make the first move?"

Ted shrugged. "I wasn't sure how you would have received the information, honestly."

Ally grimaced, looking away. "Fair enough." She took a breath and raised her eyes to meet his gaze. "I'm sorry about how I've treated you, Ted."

"You were trying to protect yourself. That, I can understand." Well, mostly. He still had a few questions—but all in good time, he supposed, not wanting to let a good thing go.

"Even though I was an absolute asshole to you in the process?"

Ted smiled cheekily and stepped forward, his toes touching the threshold. "No one's perfect."

She pushed playfully at his shoulder. "Yeah, okay, Mr. Always Scores The Winning Goal…"

Ted's eyebrows shot up at this apparent admission. "Oh? So you think I'm perfect?"

Seeming to realize her mistake, Ally backtracked into sarcasm. "Oh, yeah. I mean, you went to Harvard, didn't you?"

Ted laughed outright, overjoyed that what had once been an obstacle between them was now their private joke. "How the tables turn… So, what Hepburn movie are we watching tonight?" He ushered Ally into the living room, letting his hand linger on her waist.

She smiled up at him. "What about *Bringing Up Baby*? I've always liked the bit where she steals his clothes and he has to wear her sheer feathered robe to answer the door."

"'Because I just went *gay* all of a sudden!' Eh?"

Ally laughed. "An iconic delivery! Cary Grant was a comedic genius."

"I'm just impressed that line made it past the Studio Relations Committee, or whomever was in charge back then. Its ambiguity probably helped." Ted bit his lip. "Unfortunately, however, I just watched *Bringing Up Baby*… Literally, I caught the tail end of it last night. I mean, if you really want to watch it, I'm happy to—"

"Ted." She put a hand on his shoulder and his skin tingled under her touch. "I'm not a tyrant. What about *The Philadelphia Story*?"

Another Hepburn-Grant masterpiece. "Perfect. I have it on DVD." Ted plucked a plastic case from a nearby shelf.

She laughed, fondly. "You and your antiquated technology…"

"You and your antiquated taste in movies!"

Ally sniffed. "My parents raised me to appreciate a classic. And a class act."

"No wonder you like me," he teased.

She narrowed her eyes at him as he drew her deeper into the living room. "You are a bit, well, old school. Or maybe you're just old."

Ted's jaw dropped in an outrage that was only half-mock. But before he could splutter a protest about their relative proximity, in terms of age and experience, she had abandoned him in favor of inspecting his sizable DVD collection.

An hour later, they were settled cozily on the couch, watching Katharine Hepburn perform a fit of practiced pique.

"You remind me of her," Ted said with a smile, snaking his arm more securely around Ally's shoulder, which had—she had assured him—fully healed. "And I'm not just talking about your temper…"

Ally sighed tragically. "Ah, but I'm not a style icon."

Ted shrugged. He didn't know as much about women's fashion as he did men's, but he liked the way Ally dressed. She wore her clothes with a slightly unkempt confidence— and her strong sense of self was one of his favorite things about her. "You also don't have a costume designer person- ally dressing you."

"Touché." She snuggled closer into the crook of his arm. A few minutes later, she whispered, "Ted?"

He did his best Cary Grant impression. "Yes, dear?"

For a split second she grinned, but then her expression grew shy again. "When are you going to kiss me?"

Surprise lifted his brows. And something far sweeter flut- tered in his stomach. "Whenever you want me to, Ally."

She reached up to cradle his cheek, the silvery figures on the screen forgotten. "Now, please."

Ted bent his head, and pressed a chaste kiss upon Ally's lips. It was a prelude, unpracticed and understated. But before he could pull away, and better angle himself to resume, she bucked up in his arms, her mouth crashing into his.

It was clumsy, this second kiss, full of need and necessity. Ted felt the tension that had been coiling between and within them for the past few hours—the past few weeks, even—felt it break free and burst over them like a shower of sparkling gold. That was how good a kisser Ally was—he saw stars explode against his closed lids.

Ted moaned, his mouth opening as their kiss deepened— as Ally's fingers fumbled around the first button on his shirt.

"May I?" She whispered against his lips.

He nodded eagerly. "But it might be faster if I—"

"Shush. I want to undress you myself this time."

Ted cocked his head as best as their half-continued kiss would allow. "It's not like you weren't a participant last time."

"I know, I just..." Suddenly, she pulled away from him. Sitting back on the couch, she bit her lip.

Ted hauled himself up, shifting on the cushions to give her plenty of space. He watched her worry her lip beside him in devastating silence and, after a reluctant minute, he made a decision. "Hey."

Her eyes darted to meet his. Ted didn't think she was even aware that her fingers were fidgeting, furling and unfurling like a woodland fern played back at a high speed. "Hey."

"Maybe... Tonight's not the night."

Her eyes widened, but he thought he caught a flash of something like relief, behind the confusion and clear, albeit sexual, frustration. "Why?"

Ted shrugged, but he knew why. "Because we still haven't really talked about what happened last time. And I don't want to make any mistakes with you." When had anything good ever come of rushing into sex?

Hurt colored her cheeks as well as her tone. "What do you mean? You left, last time. *After* we had sex. Are you saying that sleeping with me again would be a mistake? Do you consider last time a mistake?" Her voice hitched up half an octave as she spoke.

Ted reached for Ally's hand and, to his surprise and relief, she let him take it in his. Intertwining his fingers with hers, he met her eyes and prayed that the words he chose would be the right ones. "No. I don't think that sleeping with you a second time would be a mistake. I don't think that the first time was a mistake, either!" He took a breath but held her gaze. "Allegra, I like you. I really do. And I have since I first met you, even though you were, well, mean to me and more than a little rude."

"I—"

"Just let me say this, okay? And then it's your turn."

She nodded, not breaking their fixed gaze. "Okay."

"I know you like me more than you used to, or at least more than you used to let on. And I know that I want to have sex with you again. Believe me. But... I also know that I won't feel comfortable doing that if I think you're not comfortable, too. And last time…"

God, he really hoped she was hearing him because her expression was frozen, her lips parted and her eyes wide with emotion.

Clearing his throat, he continued. "I left because I was pretty sure that you didn't want me to stay. I left because I saw this look in your eyes, like maybe *you* thought sleeping with me had been a mistake. I left because you seemed uncomfortable, suddenly, like you regretted having sex with me. Like you regretted ever meeting me. And I—don't want tonight to end the same way."

Ally twisted her lips and said nothing. Which, Ted supposed, was better than an empty protest.

"Well?" He squeezed her hand. "Come on, Ally. It's your turn. I'll take anything. And I won't judge you and I won't get mad at you for having had cold feet—or whatever your feelings were that night. I just need you to tell me what's going on in your head tonight. Before we go any further." Sexually, but also romantically.

After a long moment, Ally nodded. "Right. Okay. My turn." She withdrew her hand from his to brush back a curling lock of her hair, dark in the low light of the living room. "I—I didn't regret having sex with you that night, although the next morning I did feel a bit... freaked out?"

Ted steeled himself against the crushing feeling in his chest.

"Because you were the enemy," she rushed on, "and I wasn't supposed to have sex with you. I wasn't even supposed to like you! But we've already had this discussion, in the locker room, the other week. Before that game."

"I know," Ted murmured, glad they were using their words but still not reassured. "I remember. But if it had been resolved after that, why was having sex with me an issue?"

"Because it wasn't resolved!" Her outburst caught both of them off-guard. Ally ran a hand through her hair, her frustration evident. "Just because we talked about it once doesn't undo years of abuse, or make it any easier for me to look at you and not see him."

Her words were like an icicle plunged into Ted's heart. "You—you still see him when you look at me?" He pushed to his feet, shoving the couch back an inch in the process. Ted turned to look down at Ally, who had startled slightly. "Why are you here? This must be torture—I thought—I don't want to hurt you, Allegra!"

She quickly rose to her feet and reached for his hands before he could cross his arms. "And you aren't going to! You haven't, and I know you won't." Her fingers hesitated, then wove between his. "I mean, I don't *know*, but I trust you. And, no. I don't still see him when I look at you. I shouldn't have said that. When I look at you, all I see is you. When I close my eyes at night to go to sleep, it's you. Not his shadow, not his creeping specter."

She shook her head, the ghost of a smile curving her lips. "I see your smile, and the way your eyes crinkle when you laugh. And that makes me want to make you laugh. And make you smile. And," she made a flippant gesture, "fuck it, make you come! I *want* to have sex with you. I *want* to spend time with you."

Ally took a deep breath and grimaced. "But I'm—I'm skittish, okay?"

Ted nodded, not trusting himself to speak amidst all the emotions he was trying and failing to keep contained, in their proper place.

She ran her palm up and down his forearm, and he rather thought the motion soothed her as much as it was intended to soothe him. "It's been bad before, real bad, and I'm scared it'll be bad again—*Not* because I don't trust you, though. Just… because." She shrugged, almost helplessly. "Half of it's PTSD, probably. *None* of it is a reflection of you. And none of it factors into what I'm beginning to feel for you."

Ted nodded and nodded and continued to nod. Then, wordlessly, he pulled Ally into a close hug. She tensed momentarily before relaxing into his embrace. "Thank you," he murmured into the soft, loose strands of her hair. "I needed that."

Her words were muffled as she spoke into his shoulder. "Needed what?"

He sighed. "I don't know. Communication, maybe. Clarity."

She huffed a laugh. "That was clear?"

He couldn't help a smile. "Well… It was clearer than nothing." Ted gently released Ally and stepped back. "I still think we should take it slow…"

Ally nodded, if a bit reluctantly.

"I'd like to call you a cab. On me."

Ally snorted a little. "God, you're gallant. But how are you going to pay for my cab?"

Ted cocked his head, confused by her apparent ignorance. "They have an app, you know."

"The ride share platforms, yeah. But not the taxis. Not the yellow cabs."

He shook his head. "It's funny how you've lived here all your life, and yet somehow I know more about yellow cabs than you."

Ally bristled playfully. "Nonsense. It's like with the movies—I'm just old-fashioned. And I thought you were, too."

Ted led her into the foyer. "Only cinematically. And maybe a bit musically."

She paused, one shoe on. "Do you want me to stay and help with the dishes, at least?"

He smiled and gestured for her to resume. "Maybe I am old-fashioned because I refuse to ask a guest to do the dishes."

Ally grinned. "Fair enough. It's not like I'm dying to do them myself. Just be careful with that food processor blade."

Ted called the elevator. "Of course. It's sweet that you're concerned for my safety."

Ally scoffed, but Ted got the sense that she was playing up her protest. "Am not. I'm just... I just want to make sure the Manhattan Monsters don't suffer any more injuries."

"Yeah, okay." Ted stepped into the elevator after Ally, feeling light as air. "The cab's here. I'll take you down and make sure you're set before I do anything irresponsible with a sharp object."

Ally raised her eyebrows before darting in to press a quick kiss to Ted's cheek. He caught her and held her to him, peppering her with kisses until the elevator doors opened. Then, with a show of reluctance that was entirely real, he let her go—lest Albert be shocked by their shameless display of affection.

Ted closed the car door behind Ally gently but firmly. She waved through the window before greeting the driver, who already had her address in his system (per Ted's app). As they pulled away from the curb and down Park Avenue, Ally settled back into her seat with a smile and a sigh. Oh, what a night.

Suddenly, her phone buzzed. She checked the screen and saw several missed texts from Kait, who was now calling. Ally picked up immediately; they talked a lot more now that Kait was getting that divorce. "Hey, Kait!" She cringed at the sunshine in her own voice. But how could she help what she felt?

"You sound quite... I don't know, chipper? Having a good night?"

"I, uh, just, um... went on a date?" Ally wasn't sure if she should be bringing it up, what with Kait's situation. Her friend *was* still in the middle of filing for divorce.

Kait laughed, although the sound was a little watery. "You don't have to keep stuff like that from me. I want to know what's going on with you! After all, you know plenty about what's going on with me."

Ally twisted her lips. "Yeah, I guess I just didn't want to..."

"Rub it in?" Kait supplied, her tone amused and absent any bitterness. "Please, Ally. I'm not so self-centered as to think I'm the only one in the world whose problems are real. Not that you have any problems. At least, it doesn't *sound* like you do."

Ally laughed a little. "Not with this one." Was that the truth? Ally thought it might just be.

"Are you being safe?"

"We're not—I went home tonight, instead of, you know."

Kait was silent for a second on the line. "I see. I meant generally, but... Is that a good thing? Bad thing? You sounded really happy when you picked up. I assumed—"

"No, no—it's good. It's all good. We talked about it and he wants to take things slow. Which is definitely the right thing to do. Even if it is, well, frustrating. Sexually, I mean. I'm not frustrated with him!"

"Mmmhmm. Ally, I think he might be right, whoever he is. Taking things slow might be a good idea, especially, well, considering."

"Everett?"

"Wow! I wasn't even going to go there, much less say his stupid name, but... Yeah. You haven't—to my knowledge, which admittedly might be limited, because we hadn't really talked until recently, and that's all my fault, I know, but—"

"Hey. Kait. Not your fault. You've been through the wringer lately and I've been a bad friend."

She could hear Kait's outrage. "You have not!"

"Have too."

"Have *not*. I stopped reaching out. That's on me."

Ally wanted to put up a protest, but Kait kept on talking, showing Ally that she would brook none.

"Anyway, the point is, you haven't really been in a real relationship since Everett. And that was years ago. And he was an abusive *fuck*. I still can't believe I ever let you move in with him."

Ally's eyebrows went up, but her heart warmed at Kait's strong display of anger. Then again, Kait had always had Ally's back, especially when it came to her abusive ex. "No one could have talked me out of that, Kait. I was stubborn and scared of losing him. And once I was in, I couldn't get out. He held that shared apartment over me like a guillotine."

Ally swallowed. She didn't usually talk so freely about things she desperately wanted to forget.

"And if I hadn't been too much of a coward to put my foot—"

"Kait, come on. We're not re-litigating this. Although I am curious… Were you about to say 'down' or 'up his ass?'"

Kait thought about this. "I really don't know… Sorry, I'm quick to anger these days. It's tough, suppressing all my feelings at the office, even though I can still hear the whispers, and then coming home to *him*."

"Do you want to talk about it?"

Kait's answer was immediate. "No! I told you, I want to hear about you. Where were we, before I started fantasizing about kicking Everett's ass?"

Ally laughed, surprised that she could given the subject of their conversation. "I was going to say that you're right. It's been a bit of a dry spell. Well, I mean. I've had one night stands. But yeah, I've never taken them back to my place."

"Wait." Confusion clouded Kait's usually crisp tone. "I thought you were just leaving his place. And I thought you *hadn't* slept together."

"Uh, not exactly." Ally grimaced. "It's kind of a long story."

"And apparently one you've felt the need to keep from me the last few times we've spoken," Kait scolded.

Ally grimaced. "Sorry…"

"Well, you can tell me about it now," Kait announced. "I needed a break from looking at documents—I'm doing discovery for a case in order to distract myself from my ice cream cravings, which are a self-pity spiral waiting to happen."

"Kait, you're allowed to eat ice cream." Ally felt strongly about this.

"No, I know. I get that it sounds like some draconian diet but the fact of the matter is, if I go into the kitchen, I'm going to bump into Paul. He's always in there, since I've taken over the office we used to share. That's why I called. Not because I'm in crisis, again. Although I probably am, if the cravings are any evidence. Whatever. I just wanted to hear your voice."

"Aw, Kaity. I miss you, too. And fine, I'll tell you the whole story if it'll cheer you up. Well, maybe not the whole story? I'm in a cab and I don't want to scandalize the driver." She waved to the man in the front seat; his eyes didn't meet hers when he waved back however, as he was intent on the road. Conscious of her doubled audience, Ally launched into a PG-13 account of the past few weeks.

Kait was an excellent listener, as always. And telling her about Ted, and about her own actions and choices... it boosted Ally's confidence a bit. Ally was embarrassed by her early-on hostility—although it amused Kait endlessly—but proud of the way she had told Ted about Everett in the locker room. And she was proud of the way she had handled herself this evening, when Ted had wanted to talk instead of, well, fuck.

Kait asked questions occasionally, and offered some input, but mostly she just let Ally talk—and in doing so, figure some things out. Like the fact that she was capable of using her words to communicate, instead of spiraling into embarrassment, (passive) aggression, or silent shame. Or the fact that she felt comfortable around Ted—comfortable enough to tell him the truth about herself and her history with Everett. To be fair, she'd already known she felt safe with Ted, already told him as much, but talking it through with Kait confirmed it for Ally beyond any doubt, reasonable or otherwise.

"I think—I don't know. I think I might be ready for this," Ally concluded, at last.

There was a smile in Kait's voice when she replied, "Honestly? I agree. It sounds like you're in a good place and Ted's a good guy. I'm—I'm really happy for you, Ally. And I'd love to meet him, sometime."

The cab turned onto Ally's block.

"I'd love that! And thank you, Kaity." She paused to direct the driver to her apartment building. "I appreciate the assurance, because, I'll be honest, I still get nervous."

"Of course you do, Ally." Kait sighed. "Everett did a number on you. But you are not the sum of your trauma. You are a person, a real and wonderful person who deserves good things."

Ally sniffed as she slid out of the car. "So are you, Kait. Now, enough about me. I'm about to be home and I want to hear all about you—the good, the bad, and the Paul."

Kait giggled. "Did you just substitute my soon-to-be-ex-husband's name for 'ugly?'"

Ally shrugged, unlocking the front door of her apartment building. "Sorry, babe, but if the shoe fits…"

CHAPTER 14
TAKE OUT

"You had sex with him," Wren observed placidly as Ally came to a sudden stop beside her.

Panting, Ally planted her palms on her bent knees and looked up at her captain. "What?"

"I said, you had sex with Ted." Wren's lips curved into an amused half-crescent.

"Friday? No, he made me dinner and then I went home. It was very chaste! Well, somewhat."

"I meant last week, after karaoke." Wren raised her eyebrows. "Wait. Lewis cooked you dinner? You went on a date with him? Damn."

Ally realized her mistake. "Fuck. I, uh, I forgot I hadn't told you…"

"I'd be insulted, but it's so obvious you've got feelings for each other—"

Ally held up a gloved hand. "No comment."

Wren leaned against the boards in sardonic disbelief. "Sure. The fact remains, however, that you slept together. And then he cooked you dinner. And you didn't bother to tell me."

Ally straightened, glancing around. The rest of the team

was doing stick-handling drills between the blue lines. "Uh, sorry. But how *did* you know? About the sex, that is. You weren't exactly in the locker room to observe…"

Wren's eyes widened. "You did it in the locker room?"

"No!" Ally gulped the icy air. "No, I just meant, it's not like you were around us earlier, when we were getting dressed, to detect a difference."

Wren's half-smile grew into a full grin. "Ah, but that's where my experience as a coach and captain comes in handy. It's in the way you play."

"What do you mean?"

Wren shrugged, her shoulder pad shifting beneath her practice jersey. "You've started passing to him, even when the drill doesn't demand it. You're willing to work with him, in the end zones and when you're racing up the middle. You've started to rely on him, to trust him to have your back. In fact, I wonder if it's more than that."

Ally looked Wren in the eye warily. "More than what, cap?"

"More than sex and a single dinner. You're starting to play like partners, on the ice. I wonder if that seismic shift in dynamic extends to off the ice, as well…"

"He's not my boyfriend," Ally blurted out. And it was the truth! For all her revelations the other night, regardless of the conversations she'd had with Ted and later Kait, one date did not a boyfriend make.

Wren watched her for a moment, then turned her eyes to Ted, who was picking up cones in the distance.

Ally couldn't help but remember the body beneath the bulky gear. His bare skin like silk beneath hers… She shook herself.

"Does he know that?"

"Listen, Wren. It's not that serious." Even if their conversation the other night had been. "We slept together, once.

We've been on one date since then. One. *You* made us do cardio together. The sex thing? It's just not that serious! He knows it and I know it. We're just… blowing off steam! Having some fun. Nothing to tell HR about."

"Ah, that's right. You're coworkers, too."

Ally scoffed, ready to retreat into her spiky shell. "I wouldn't exactly call it co-working. He's leading a sales team, which puts him in a different department *and* a more senior position."

Wren tried to stroke her chin, realized her cage was in the way, and settled for a contemplative frown. "I bet you two still *interact* at the office."

"No!" Ally flushed, remembering the time Ted had kissed her in the middle of the floor. The way his strong arms had stolen around her. For one brief moment, she'd forgotten time itself, lost in the luxury of his lips…

They were so lucky no one had seen them. Still, there was a thrill in things forbidden.

"Well, a little. It's hard to focus sometimes, when he walks by."

Wren smirked. "I can't imagine what it must be like in the locker room for you. For him, for that matter. How *hard* it must be for him, to strap his shin pads on straight when you're sitting there, shirtless, directly across from him."

Ally didn't miss the double entendre. Still, she scoffed. "He's not a creep, Wren. And I'm not some mythical siren."

Wren barked a laugh. "No, that's true. No feathers on you. And you certainly can't sing. But don't underestimate your sex appeal. Especially not to someone as smitten as him." She gestured at Ted, who had finished cleaning up the cones and was now waving in their direction. He had a goofy smile on his face, which on any other man would have been irritating but on Ted…

Well, everything he did was endearing.

Ally rolled her eyes reflexively. "He's not smitten. And I'm not that sexy!"

Wren rolled her eyes in return. "This false modesty doesn't do you any favors, but otherwise... If we weren't friends..."

Ally swatted at Wren. "We both know I'm not your type."

"I don't have a type."

"Fine, but you've never been into me."

Wren shook her head. "No, and you've never been interested in me, so I'd say we're even. Now, go help loverboy with those cones."

"How do you want them set up this time?"

"I don't. The two of you can put them away. We'll be practicing penalty kills next."

"Sounds like a plan." With something strangely akin to butterflies fluttering in her stomach, Ally skated off in the direction of Ted, who looked like he was struggling to balance his bounty of orange cones. "Hey, Harvard!"

He whipped his head around, nearly dropping a cone in the process. "Allegra," he said, his smiling growing, changing. From goofy to smoldering, in a second and a half.

Ally blushed. She wouldn't ever tell him, but she loved it when he used her full name. It made her feel special, made her feel seen. It also reminded her of the time they'd spent together in the privacy of her bedroom.

She was still a bit torn between regret and relief that they hadn't slept together after their dinner date. Ted was something different, and he was right; they shouldn't take things too fast. But her attraction to him was undeniable... "Cap told me to help you put away the cones. We're switching to penalty kill drills."

She waited for him to tease her, for him to remind her that she was the reason they so often skated a man down, but mercifully all he said was, "You don't think I'm strong enough to carry a couple of cones?"

"We both know they're heavier than they look."

He shrugged, again nearly losing his grip on the stack. "Come and get 'em." And then he pushed off backwards, away from Ally, his skates carving crescents into the ice.

Shaking her head at his antics, but unable to hide her amused smile, Ally gave chase.

"So… Where do you wanna go?" Ted popped up behind Ally as she was entering the empty GreenLight elevator. Its doors closed on the two of them before she turned to face him.

"I said, wait five minutes and then come find me! We don't want the whole office to know."

Ted grinned, and took a step forward, closing Ally into the corner. "Know what? That you're my girlfriend?"

She scoffed, as expected. "You should be so lucky. We're just dating!"

"Whatever you say…"

Silence fell for a second as she suddenly seemed to realize how close he was standing. Ally took a step back only to find herself pressed against the stainless steel wall. Rather than panic, however, her eyes were bright with excitement.

"What are you doing?" She asked, a bit breathlessly.

"I don't know," Ted said, honestly. Then he watched as her tongue darted out to wet her lips. "What do you want me to be doing?"

She inhaled sharply, her nostrils flaring. "Ted…"

"Ally…"

Her eyes flicked up to the numbers above the closed doors. His followed. They were getting closer and closer to the ground floor. "Kiss me. Quickly."

She didn't have to tell him twice. Ted stepped closer, closing the gap between them entirely. He put his hand against the wall next to her head, his other hand snaking around her waist, pulling her flush against his body. Ally gasped and Ted seized the opportunity, closing her open mouth with his.

Moaning, Ally threaded her arms around his neck, standing on the tips of her toes so as to better access his lips. Ted felt himself harden, felt the pulse of his own erection. Ally must have noticed it too, because she slipped one hand down his chest, stroking his tie, sliding her palm along his length. She groaned, swirling her tongue around his, withdrawing and biting at his lower lip. Ted's hands found the hem of her dress and started to climb...

The elevator dinged and both of them jumped. Ted stepped back hastily as Ally tugged on her dress to straighten it, her other hand wiping at her swollen lips.

Ally cleared her throat and gestured to the open doors. "After you, Mr. Lewis."

Ted pulled on his loosened tie. "I insist, Ms. Bryant." He held out a hand to stop the doors from closing, letting her exit. As she stepped out of the elevator and started across the atrium, he admired the swish of her dress, the authority of her stride.

In an attempt to respect her rather frustrating wish that they not be seen leaving together—for his part, Ted was ready to burst into song about their budding relationship— he waited until she had exited the building to catch up. The sun was just starting to set, casting a burnt orange glow about the Chelsea streets that was reflected and refracted by the wall of windows that marked GreenLight's NYC location.

The light caught Ally's loose curls, which she'd worn in a low braid today, styled as though she were ready to play, and illuminated the gold and auburn highlights in her otherwise dark waves.

"Permission to speak freely, sir?" He teased as he caught up with her.

She stuck her nose a little higher in the air, which only made him smile wider. "Granted."

"Good. It's exhausting, having to act like I'm not wildly attracted to you, when all I really want to do is catch you up in my arms in the middle of the office—again—and kiss you."

She bit her lip, clearly suppressing a smile. "Mmhmm?"

"Mm*hmm*. Have you decided where we're going for our next date? I only ask because it's supposed to be tonight— right now, in case you'd forgotten—and you still haven't clued me in. I'm starting to worry you'll cancel."

"Relax, Harvard. I haven't forgotten and I'm not going to cancel."

He relaxed. "Good. Because I've been looking forward to tonight all week."

"It's been like five days since our first date, and you've seen me four out of the five of those days."

Ted smiled breezily. "Mmm, the perks of dating a coworker who also happens to be your teammate."

Ally came to a slow stop. "What if... What if my idea of a date is different from yours? What if it's not as... fancy?"

Ted slowed too, but not out of any concern. "That's fine by me. I just want to spend some more time with you. Off the ice, away from the office, alone—together." He turned to face her. "What's your idea of a date?"

She bit her lip again and Ted envied her teeth their unfettered access to her sweet skin. "My idea of a date is take out from the Ukrainian restaurant across the street and a six pack from the bodega downstairs." She shifted slightly, her eyes on her feet. "It's really good Ukrainian."

Ted tipped up her chin, stepped closer, and pressed a chaste kiss upon her worried lips.

She jerked her head up but didn't step out of his embrace. "Ted!"

He stroked her chin, lost to the softness of her skin. "What?"

She swatted at his hand half-heartedly. "Someone might see!"

He shook his head. "Ally, it's your turn to relax. We're several blocks from the office. And the sidewalks are busy." Extending his fingers to graze the line of her jaw, he ran his thumb along her cheekbone in a delicate caress. "Now, about your date idea." He shrugged. "It sounds nice."

She looked up at him, her eyes round. "Really? Because I know you're fancy and good at cooking whereas I mostly just cook because daily take out doesn't fit into my budget, and—"

Ted couldn't contain his chuckle. "Allegra."

Her eyes widened with something else, something far more encouraging than anxiety. Desire.

"If you keep looking at me like that, I'm going to make love to you in the middle of the sidewalk."

She blinked, surprise flashing across her features. "You want me that badly?"

Ted groaned. "Wasn't it obvious in the elevator?"

Smirking a little, Ally said, "Maybe we should skip dinner and head straight back to my apartment."

Despite his desperate desire to take her up on her offer, Ted shook his head. "I want to court you properly, Ally."

"*Court* me? What is this, a Regency romance novel?"

He smiled, shaking his head. "We're American, Ally. They don't write Regency romances about Americans. Maybe something set in the Gilded Age, but..."

"Point taken. Still, what's with the antiquated vocabulary? I don't exactly have a dance card for you to fill."

"I just..." He frowned. "I want to earn the right to call you my girlfriend." He held up a hand. "I know, I know you aren't ready for that yet. And that's fine. I would never want to rush you. But, someday... in the not too-distant future, I hope... I'd like to be able to call you mine. And be yours, in return. Exclusively, all strings attached. So, in a way, I consider this—our dating—a courtship. A prelude, if I'm very lucky and I don't utterly mess this up with my antiquated terminology and preference for contemporary romantic fiction." He held his breath.

To Ted's infinite relief, Ally rolled her eyes. "You're so dramatic, Harvard. Come on," she offered him her hand and he took it gladly. "Let's go get some Ukrainian food."

"This smells amazing." Ted had stopped in the middle of the sidewalk to stick his nose in the opening of the brown paper bag.

Ally grinned, stepping aside to let a woman with a toddler in a stroller pass. "It's delicious, especially the veal goulash. I can't believe in all those summers you spent in New York, your aunt never took you to Kotliarevsky's Kitchen." The historic restaurant was named for the so-called founder of modern Ukrainian literature—apparently its owners were big into books, as well as food.

Ted shrugged, picking up his pace again. "I don't know. I mean, maybe she did and I just don't remember?"

"Huh. Well, if that's the case, you'll know as soon as you bite into your first pierogi. They are heaven—and unlike any I've ever had elsewhere." Ally turned down onto her street, gesturing for Ted to follow her. "Come on, my apartment's over here."

"Yeah, I thought this corner looked familiar…"

As soon as she'd turned her key in the front lock, Ally rushed up the stairs; Ted followed her, taking the steps two at a time. Her own stomach was growling and she could've sworn she'd heard his, too. Ally jiggled the stuck key until it slid into the lock more easily, at last opening the door. "It's a bit messy, but—"

Ted interrupted her with a chuckle. "Allegra, relax. I've been here before, remember?"

She stepped inside, shut the door, and started shucking her shoes. Ted followed suit, albeit in a more orderly fashion. "Yes, well... We were drunk. I wasn't sure how much of it you remembered."

Ted bent to scratch an inquisitive Heathcliff behind the ears and under the chin. "It's not like we were blackout, Ally. And I hardly would have blocked that night from my memory."

Ally felt her cheeks heat. "Right." God, he looked good in this light—the sun was in its final stage of setting, basking Ted in muted rays of red and gold and ochre. His eyes were especially brilliant, sparkling in the low light. Ally wanted kiss him again, to take him inside of her—right there, on the kitchen counter—but she was really hungry.

Ted looked like he was hungry, too. And not just for the food. "Come here, you," he murmured.

Ally slid a little, her socked feet slick against the wood floor.

Ted caught her easily, one arm wrapping around her waist, the other brushing a stray lock behind her ear. "I'm glad I'm here," he whispered as she clasped her hands behind his neck. "In your apartment," he continued, "and in your arms."

Ally pushed up onto her toes, extending herself until her lips were level with his. "I'm glad you're here, too." She brushed her lips against his—once, twice. "In my apartment, yes. But especially in my arms." And then she kissed him with all the sweetness she could summon, with all the tenderness that she felt towards him. The enormity of her emotions scared her a little, but she knew that she was safe in Ted's embrace.

Suddenly, his stomach rumbled like a roll of thunder. Ted broke their kiss, laughing. "Not again..."

Ally couldn't help but grin. "I want it on record that this time it was you and not me."

He let go of her, raising his arms in a gesture of resignation and surrender. "Alright, alright. But you're hungry, too!"

Her stomach growled cooperatively.

"See?"

Ally narrowed her eyes at her belly. "Et tu?"

Ted laughed. "Come on, Caesar. Let's dig in."

She let go of the joke and banked her arousal—for the time being—stepping into the tiny, open-plan kitchen. "I'll get plates and utensils if you pull everything out and put it on the coffee table." She grimaced. "Sorry there isn't like an actual table we can use. I don't—I don't normally have dinner guests."

Behind her, a rustle of paper told Ally that Ted was doing just what she'd asked him to do. "No need to apologize, Ally. A coffee table counts." And then she could hear his sly smile, warming his low voice. "You don't often have dinner guests, huh? So you're saying I'm… special?"

Blushing, Ally shut the cabinet with an accidental bang. She took a deep breath. "I suppose you could say that…" She turned and offered him the plates, which he placed on the low table. "But I wouldn't want to inflate your ego any further. It's already dangerously large."

Ted grinned wickedly and, taking her hand, drew her down onto the couch. "You know what else is dangerously large?"

Ally rolled her eyes, but her lips twitched. "The portions at Kotliarevsky's Kitchen?"

He huffed a laugh. "That, maybe. But I was referring to something else."

Ally raised her eyebrows innocently. "Oh? Something else I can put in my mouth?"

Ted gave her a doleful look as his stomach growled again. "Let's revisit this conversation, shall we?"

She smirked. "Absolutely." And then they both began to pry the tops off their dishes—they'd ordered too much, but who would say no to leftover Ukrainian food? A little kielbasa with some fried eggs sounded like the perfect breakfast.

Ted picked up a pierogi, examined it carefully, then popped it in his mouth.

"Unlocking any memories?" Ally inquired, ladling herself some pork stew with a side of sauerkraut.

He shook his head. "Nothing, alas. But dear *god*, that's good."

Ally smiled, then took a bite of the stew and moaned.

Ted eyed Ally appraisingly. "I'll have what you're having."

Ally chewed, swallowed, then laughed. "So you're not culturally illiterate. Good."

"Obviously I have seen *When Harry Met Sally*. I can't believe you'd imagine otherwise! That's slanderous, quite frankly."

"Culturally literate, but doesn't know what constitutes slander."

Ted's eyes widened, and not just because he'd just bitten into the veal goulash. "It's not like I accused you of *libel!*" He huffed. "Back to your first insult—why did you think I might not have seen Meg Ryan's best picture?"

She shrugged. "I don't know. I didn't think you *hadn't* seen it, but… You like a lot of old things, Ted."

"So do you."

"Fair. I just didn't want to assume."

Ted shook his head, swallowing another heaping bite of the goulash. "Ally, sweetheart… I *know* about rom-coms. And not just the ones from the early aughts."

Ally nibbled on a pierogi of her own. "Oh yeah?"

"*Yeah.*"

"Well, maybe we should watch one tonight." She

shrugged, getting up to grab a couple of beers from the fridge. "It's a good sign for a couple, right? Shared interests?"

Ted grinned, accepting a bottle from her as well as the opener. He popped off the metal top. "What decade are we thinking?"

CHAPTER 15
FRIDAY NIGHT

AN HOUR into *The Cutting Edge*, Ted couldn't stop laughing. He had his left arm around Ally, who was snuggled up on the couch beside him, Heathcliff sitting on her feet, and in his right hand he held his second, half-empty bottle of beer. It had grown warm and flat because Ted kept forgetting to drink it, he was having so much fun.

"Toepick!" Ally shouted as Doug Dorsey went down for the umpteenth time. Startled, Heathcliff shot off the couch and into the bedroom.

Ted, meanwhile, winced at the hockey player's fall—but the movie was too funny for him to actually fear for any of its characters. "This was a good choice," he announced, taking a swig of his lukewarm beer.

Ally sat up to set her empty bottle down on the coffee table, which they had cleared of plates and take out boxes. "Yeah, well. That's what happens when you let me choose."

Ted raised his eyebrows. "I seem to recall having been the one to suggest it."

Ally shook her head primly. "No, in fact, you merely offered it up as one of many suggestions. I actually selected it. You would have been happy with *10 Things I Hate About You!*"

"So would you!"

Ally lifted her chin like a Byzantine empress. "That's beside the point."

On screen, Kate and Doug shared an intense glare—or was it a passionate stare? Ted couldn't tell, hardly noticed the movie, because he was too lost in the elegant line of Ally's neck, the sharp curve of her jaw, the subtle purse of her supple lips. "And what, exactly," he murmured, the words starting to lose their meaning, "is the point?"

Ally looked down at him—no longer a cold goddess, no more a marvelous, distant empress, but hot-blooded and hungry, a human being.

And it was Ally's humanity that he adored. Her humanity that he—not worshipped from a distance, but *wanted*, up close and personal. He wanted her. For the imperfect person she was, for now, for—forever, Ted realized. Forever…

"The point?" Ally's brows knit, adorably. "The point. The point is… Oh, kiss me already, Ted. Just—just kiss me."

Ted was all too happy to stop thinking and do as he'd been told. Setting down his own beer, he raised his right hand to caress Ally's soft, pink cheek. His left arm he lifted from where it lay on the back of the sofa to stroke up and down her spine, whose slight ridges he could feel beneath his fingers like the keys of a piano or polished, precious stones. Ted's right hand curled along the back of Ally's neck, coaxing her down, until their lips finally met.

He drank from her with unquenchable thirst. And she returned his kisses with a ferocity that spoke of an arousing insatiability, a hunger that had him hot, heavy, hardening.

Ally moaned, her mouth opening to let him in. Ted treaded lightly at first, tracing the inner curve of her lips with the tip of his tongue as though this territory weren't familiar at all. Because it wasn't, not really. Every time they kissed, it felt like the first time.

She took his lower lip between her teeth and bit and Ted groaned, crushing her to him. Ally's hand slipped down the side of him, setting him alight, until she found his erection. She gasped into their kiss when she felt his rigidity—when her fingers gripped his cock, trapped beneath layers of clothing.

Ally pulled back, breathless, and whispered, "Can I?"

To which Ted nodded and allowed his head to fall back, gulping down the cool air like it was water. He was burning up; she had set him ablaze.

And now she was unbuttoning his trousers. And now, unzipping his fly. Now, she was tugging at the placket of his boxers. Now, her fingers found him. Took him in hand, stroked and caressed him. She freed him from his clothing only to trap him in her cage of pleasure, her fingers like bars against which he strained, whose torturous restraint he craved.

There was only one thing he wanted more than her hand on his cock, and it was his cock in her mouth. Christ, but the stroke of her tongue, the suction of her lips, the rhythm of her throat, constricting around his straining length…

"Ally…"

"Yeah, baby?" The endearment was rare, precious, breathless.

"Will you—" He groaned as she wrapped her fingers around him and squeezed. "Will you—" He moaned as she repositioned herself, his cock grazing her hard nipple through the fabric of her dress. "Will you—" He whimpered as suddenly he felt the teasing tip of her tongue trace the throbbing vein that ran along on the underside of his aching dick.

"Will I suck you off?" She finished his question for him, reading his goddamn mind.

Although, Ted mused through the thick haze of his thoughts, it had probably been fairly obvious. Everything about his need for her was obvious. Blatant. Bared. Exposed. She held him in her hand—no, her mouth, now closing around his tip, all hot and wet and soft and— "*Fuck,*" Ted hissed.

Ally moaned, her mouth widening to accommodate his swollen head, sinking down his shaft. He could feel her lips, supple and smooth as silk. He could feel her tongue, questing and inquisitive, swirling along his length. He could feel—he could feel the back of her throat, tight and soft and hot as her cunt—her cunt!

Christ, he wanted to be inside of her. Even deeper than he was now. And before that, he had another idea. It pierced through the pleasure that had flooded his brain, filling him with a new and aching need.

He'd been wrong, before, when he'd thought that there was only one thing he'd wanted more than her touch. He'd loved every second of it, to be sure, when she took him into her mouth, when she let her tongue and lips do the work of her fingers, when she'd worked her throat and caressed his cock with every swallow. But now, he knew what he really wanted. What he wanted more than anything she could do to him. He wanted to taste her again.

"Allegra!"

She immediately pulled back, letting his cock fall from her dripping lips into her warm hand. "Ted? You okay?"

He nodded, struggling to find words past the pleasure, to make sense, to speak. "That was—amazing. I just…"

"Do you need a second?" She smoothed her hair and adjusted her dress, the neckline of which had slipped so low as to nearly reveal the straining bud of her left nipple.

Ted shook his slowly clearing head. "I need *you.*"

Ally cocked her head, a half-smile curving her lovely lips. "What do you mean, Ted? You have me."

He clarified, "I need to taste you."

She went pink. "Oh."

"Is that—Can I?" He repeated her earlier request.

Ally nodded. "Of course. I—I'd love that." She bit her lip

and Ted cursed himself for having interrupted their rhythm. Never mind—they'd find it again. They could always find it again, he was starting to believe, so long as they both gave this—them—a chance.

"Do you want me to—" She gestured to her dress, as if to remove it.

Ted shook his head, smiling. "Let me."

She nodded and settled back into the couch.

He placed his hand upon her knee and began to move it up her leg, smoothing her soft skin beneath his fingers, letting his palm skim the curve of her muscular thigh. When he came upon the hem of her dress, he pushed it up with both hands —always keeping contact with her skin—gathering the fabric up and over the line of her panties, bunching it along either side of her ribs, dragging his pinkies over the curving wire of her bra, before lifting the garment up off her body and over her ducked head.

Ted gently draped the dress over the side of the couch before turning back to face Ally, nearly naked in her mauve bra and patterned underwear.

She twisted her lips.

"Are you nervous?" Ted frowned, raising one arm to caress her bare shoulder.

Ally shook her head, huffing slightly. "No. I just... It feels new. I know that we've done this before, that this isn't the first time you've—but... It all feels new, you know?"

Ted nodded. Everything about this encounter felt different from their first—except the raw lust, of course, but even his desire had deepened, grown more complex. "If I do anything you don't like, tell me and I'll stop, alright?"

She inclined her head. "Of course. I trust you, Ted."

❄

Ally lay back against the soft cushion of the couch, her legs splayed as Ted—simply put—devoured her. "*God*, that feels good."

He smothered a self-satisfied laugh—or rather, he buried his face in her cunt and she felt the vibrations of his good humor travel through her. Speaking of vibrations…

"But you know what would make this even better?"

He pulled his tongue from where he'd slipped it inside of her, pressing a kiss to her left labia before lifting his head. His eyes met hers, dancing with delight and desire. "Tell me, Allegra," he whispered, his breath warm on her wet folds.

Ally shivered and she momentarily lost her words.

"What would make this," he murmured, gently pushing back the hood of her clitoris with his thumb, "*better?*"

Ally swallowed a moan and searched for coherence. She was hard pressed to find it, with his tongue tracing her swollen curves. "If we—if we added a—*oh!*—toy. Into the mix."

There. She had said it. And strangely, it hadn't required much bravery. Because she did trust Ted. She trusted him with the puck on the ice and her pleasure in her bed—on her couch, rather. She trusted him not to judge her for needing a little mechanical assistance; she trusted him to try, with her, to achieve what she had never shared with anyone before.

Orgasms had always been hers alone. And maybe that was a bit of a defense mechanism. But tonight… As he'd held her in his arms, as he'd laid kisses along her limbs, she'd warmed up to the idea of letting Ted in on her private pleasure. Of letting him into her heart—or at least, between her legs.

"What do you think, Harvard?" She glanced down at him, a sudden spike of anxiety piercing her pleasure.

He gazed up at her, apparently mesmerized. "Yes. *Fuck*, yes. I want to watch you come."

His words loosened her limbs, dispelling all anxiety

therein. She reached for him and and he rose to meet her, his lips meeting hers in a crushing kiss. "There's a box," she told him breathlessly. "In my closet, next to the sweaters."

Ted was gone in an instant. After a moment's rustling in the bedroom, he returned, his expression triumphant as he brandished the shoebox that held her sex toy collection.

Ally smirked at his proud smile. "Good. Now, open it."

Obediently, he lifted the lid and discarded it on the coffee table. His eyes went wide with awed appreciation as he surveyed the box's jumbled contents. "Which—" He cleared his throat. "Which of these should I…"

Ally bit back a grin. Was he overwhelmed by her collection? Good. She had worked hard on it. "The purple one," she instructed him after a moment's drawn out deliberation. Not a bullet but a standard vibrator: more rumbly than buzzy; good for both clitoral stimulation and vaginal penetration— because Ally's desire for Ted was far from superficial.

Ted gingerly removed the vibrator in question from the box, setting said box down next to its top without once looking away from the toy in his hand. After studying it for a long moment, turning it over and running his fingers along its smooth surface, he looked up at Ally, his eyes alight, and grinned. "It's beautiful," he announced.

Ally laughed, pleased by his appreciation for her old friend. "And functional, too. Go on, press that top button."

Ted raised his eyebrows before glancing back down at the toy. His thumb found the button in question and held down. The vibrator sprang into action, increasing in speed and intensity until it hit its maximum. Ted's eyebrows shot up even higher and he looked to Ally for advice.

She shook her head, smiling. "I said press, not hold. If you hold it, it'll just keep going. And I think we should start with the lowest setting."

He managed to turn it off again. "Is that what you'd do if you were alone?"

Ally chuckled. "No, but I'm not alone. And besides, I don't want this to be a quickie." She bit her lip. "Come here, Ted."

He stepped between her half-closed legs and, vibrator in hand, sank to his knees. Then he presented her with the toy, like she was his queen and it was an offering of his fealty.

Ally leaned forward to kiss him, taking the toy only when their lips had parted again. "You're perfect," she whispered indulgently, earning herself a blush from him. Before he could speak, presumably to return the compliment with his trademark sweetness and sincerity, she continued, "And you're going to be good at this. Have you ever used a vibrator before?"

He shook his head, his eyes trained on her lips.

Smirking, Ally scolded him. "Use your words, Harvard. And look me in the eye when I'm talking to you. Have you ever used a vibrator before?"

Catching onto her imperial mode, he looked her directly in the eye and answered with the utmost humility, "No, but I want to learn." His eyes were wide with desperation. "Will you teach me, Allegra?"

Her lips curved and she felt like the cat that had got the cream. "Of course, Theodore. Now, go back to fucking me with your mouth. I want to feel your tongue inside of me." She lay back and let him gently spread her legs.

Ted buried himself in her cunt, licking her like she was a jar of honey, or the bowl in which he'd just recently whipped together powdered sugar and cream. He lapped up her luxurious moisture, sucked on her swollen lips. He fingered her with all the passion and the skill of a virtuoso. And when Ally felt that pull, that clench, that tug of bliss, she handed Ted the vibrator.

"Turn it on, Ted."

He did as he was told, his lips and chin wetter than if he'd just eaten an overripe peach.

"Stroke me with its tip," she continued and, anticipating his question, added, "lightly—along the lines of my labia."

Ted gazed at her glistening cunt for a half-second before using the vibrator as she'd instructed, dragging its cool tip along her curving folds.

Ally let out a low and lingering moan. "Yes, like that." She opened her eyes and leaned forward to watch him play with her toy—with her. "Now circle my clit—yes, yes, *god*, like that."

Ted found the bundle of nerves in an instant, tracing her anatomy with the vibrator, allowing its rumbles to penetrate her core, to spread deep along her nerves, to possess her in the most intimate of ways. "Do you like that?"

Ally nodded, whimpering but determined to watch him, to watch her, to watch *them*—because together they could do something, build something, create something—new and unknown and utterly limitless. She felt herself tremble, felt the slippage between her corporeal and ethereal selves.

"Use your words, Allegra," he murmured, the command an echo of hers. "And look me in the eye when I'm fucking you."

Ally tore her eyes from her cunt, from the toy, from the back of his hand, and looked up at his face, into his eyes like the deepest of lakes. "I am," she gasped, as he slid first one finger, then another, into her dripping cunt.

And then he pressed the button and the vibrator jerked against her clitoris and it was all too much—but not enough! —and Ally found herself falling, falling, *drowning* in his eyes' azure depths. Drowning in the pleasure he had brought her, the ecstasy that together they had earned.

Ally clenched around his fingers and raised her hand to clutch at his muscular shoulder as she came hard and fast and with the startling certainty that this was right and good, that he was right and good, that together *they* were right and good.

The intensity of it all would have scared her but she was too lost to pleasure to care.

But later, when she had caught her breath and he had washed the toy and put it back and they had tumbled onto her bed, she remembered the intensity of her feelings, physical and emotional, and felt a frisson of fear—and guilt, because no matter how transcendently good he made her feel, she still wasn't ready to call herself his girlfriend.

CHAPTER 16
FRIDAY NEXT

"You want a beer?" Ted offered, a smile in his eyes. "I can go grab us a couple."

Another week at GreenLight gone, another Keg Friday come.

Ally glanced around nervously. "Sure. Just don't be too obvious about, you know, us."

Ted laughed, although her stipulation stung. "In the two seconds it'll take me to tap that keg? Relax, Ally. We're in this together."

"Yeah, but we're not *together*. We're just dating, okay? No labels."

Ted nodded, trying not to think about how they had started to work together on the ice or what they had shared the other night. "Yep. So… is that Long Island IPA okay?"

Ally shrugged. "I don't think there's another option this week."

"Still, I bet it's delicious. You're from Long Island and you're—"

She shot him a look. "Ted, do *not* finish that sentence. We're in public!"

He sighed. "Okay. I'll tone it down. I'm just excited to be hanging out with you, you know?"

She cocked her head at him. "You had me over for dinner on Tuesday."

When he hadn't been able to recreate the ecstasy of the previous Friday. Still, the sex had been better and more open since she'd introduced him to her vibrator, even absent said toy. "I meant, in public. With other people."

She nodded, biting her lip. "Me too. I just—You're sure no one has noticed the two of us?"

Ted jerked his head in the direction of the rooftop's seating area. "Other than Vanessa?"

Ally waved a hand. "Oh, I tell her most things."

"No, I mean, she's looking for you."

"Where?" Ally scanned the crowd of GreenLight employees. "Oh!" She waved at her friend. "I'm going to go grab us a couple of seats by V. You'll get the beer?"

Ted nodded, smiling at Ally's sudden grin. "Sure thing."

"Get three, actually. V's glass looks empty." Briefly—surreptitiously—she squeezed Ted's hand before darting off to the seating area.

Ted watched her go, his smile fading a little. Dating Ally Bryant in semi-secret was a bit like walking a tightrope. Ecstasy, agony, the whole nine yards. Suddenly, a hand clapped his shoulder.

"Ted, my man!"

He spun around to face the copywriter on his team. "Hey, Sam! Did you have a chance to take a look at that—"

Sam leveled Ted with a look. "No more work. It's a Friday afternoon and we are *free*." He took a sip of his beer. "So, you and Ally?"

Ted bit his lip. Sam was a good guy, and if Ally had told Vanessa, then it was only fair that Ted could tell one of his new work friends. "Can you keep a secret?"

"I'm not a total idiot. So, are you two, you know, *together?*"

Ted nodded before he remembered what Ally had said. *No labels.*

Sam started to congratulate him but Ted must have been wearing his feelings on his face because he faltered. Sam narrowed his eyes slightly. "You sure about that?"

Ted scratched the back of his neck. "No. I mean, yes, I'm sure. We're not *together*."

"No?" Sam cocked his head before a look of understanding dawned. "Ohhh… So it's just sex. I mean, I saw her holding your hand, so I assumed—"

"What?" Ted's voice briefly visited an octave he hadn't known he could hit outside of the shower's private confines. How had Sam known about—whatever. It didn't matter. Ally wouldn't like it, but… Whatever. It was always going to come out, and Sam could be trusted. "No. It's not just sex."

Sam frowned. "So, it is sex. It's more than sex. But you're not together?"

Ted shifted uncomfortable and glanced across the rooftop at Ally, who was now seated and laughing at something Vanessa had just said. She looked so carefree, so happy. And she had been both of those things the other night, at his place. And last Friday, when they'd gotten Ukrainian take out and afterward she'd let him eat her out and experiment with one of her vibrators. When she'd looked like she'd seen stars and when she'd let him hold her afterwards.

She could be carefree and happy around him—*because* of him. But not *with* him, not when they were in the company of their peers at GreenLight or their Monsters teammates. Not when they were around anyone either of them knew.

Ted cleared his throat, realizing he'd been silent for a little longer than was appropriate. "We've been dating," he told Sam, who was watching him with some confusion and not a small amount of amusement. "But it's not—she's not—I'm not officially her *boyfriend* or anything."

Sam nodded and tactfully changed the subject to the IPA

on tap, but all Ted could think about was how badly he wanted to be Allegra Bryant's boyfriend, how much that label would mean to him. But only if she was ready for it.

"Ted?"

"Yeah?"

"You still with me?"

Ted nodded, running a hand through his hair.

Sam studied him carefully. "Do you want to talk about it?"

"No. What I really want is to get some beers." He started toward the keg.

Sam followed. "Drowning your sorrows?"

Ted laughed, but without humor. "Nah, it's just that Ally asked me to get her and Vanessa some of that Long Island stuff, too."

Sam smiled knowingly. "Not her boyfriend, though."

Ted shook his head. "Nope."

When he had acquired three very full glasses, none of which Sam offered to carry ("You'll look all the more heroic, like real boyfriend material, if you present Ally with all three!"), Ted made a beeline for the table where Vanessa was holding court. "Got a seat for me?"

"And me?" Sam poked his head out from behind Ted.

Vanessa and Ally exchanged glances, as though weighing pros and cons. Then they both broke into laughter. Ally gestured toward two vacant chairs. "Assuming one of those beers is for V and one is for me…"

Ted gently placed the glasses on the table, managing not to spill any of the beer in Ally's lap. "Naturally," he said, giving her his most gallant smile.

Ally grinned and took a glass, immediately raising it to her lips. Her lips, which she then licked…

But Ted's fantasies would have to wait, as Vanessa held up a hand. "Wait!"

Ted and Sam froze, half-settled into their seats.

"No, not you two."

Ted sat down, relieved, and reached for his beer.

Vanessa continued, "Ally, wait."

Ally lowered her glass. "What? Why can't I drink in peace?"

"You can, *after* we all raise our glasses in a toast—to GreenLight's newest, and best looking, Senior Product Partnerships Manager."

Ted caught Ally narrowing her eyes at Vanessa midway through that toast and had to hide his grin at her show of jealousy, however petty and unnecessary. In fact, he had liked it especially because it had been petty and unnecessary. Ted, like Ally, was only human.

"Cheers!" Sam raised his own, half-empty glass. "Ted, you're a real team player. I mean, the way you handled Harold today—"

"Hey! No work talk! It's a *Friday*," Vanessa protested. "The only reason the toast has anything to do with work is because I'm sapped and couldn't think of anything besides his title to call him."

What about... Ally's boyfriend? Ted smothered a sigh. No use getting ahead of himself.

Meanwhile, Ally nodded in enthusiastic agreement. "Yeah, no one wants to think about Harold over the weekend. And it is, as of ten minutes ago, the weekend."

"Sorry, sorry," Sam raised his free hand in surrender. "I know the rule. I practically invented it. I was just trying to let you all know what a great guy Ted is!"

Ally laughed. "Oh, we know."

Vanessa smirked, her dark eyes bright as her gaze fell on Ally. "Yeah, some of us more than others."

Ally blanched.

Ted twisted his lips.

Vanessa rolled her eyes. "Relax, you two. You're among friends. And nobody can hear over Dave's terrible attempt at

DJ-ing." The music wasn't *bad*, but it was clear Dave from Legal had only recently tried his hand.

Ally glanced warily at Sam, who offered her his friendliest smile.

"Besides, I already know, Ally. Ted told me."

Her eyes narrowed. "Told you what?"

"That you're in *love* with him—"

Ted interjected, "Just that we're dating! No more, no less."

Ally thought about this. "Well, that's true. It's nobody's business," she added, a bit defensively, "but we've been seeing each other for a little while now. *No* labels—it's all still very new to me!"

And Ted could appreciate that, however hard the tightrope of their semi-secrecy was for him to walk.

Vanessa snorted into her beer. "You've been doing a bit more than *seeing* one another, I do believe…"

Ally cast a withering glance in her friend's direction. "Very funny, V. Now that the proverbial cat's out of the bag, can we talk about something else?"

"I'm fairly certain Kelly in Accounting is getting married," Sam offered.

Vanessa groaned. "I had better not be invited—I've got like fifty weddings on my calendar already next year!"

Ally shook her head as her friend began to rattle off names, none of them familiar to Ted. She took a long draught of her beer before setting the glass down on the table and catching Ted's eye.

He raised one eyebrow, silently inquiring as to how she felt about being put in the hot seat because of their relationship. She answered with a shrug, but her grimace quickly turned into a grin when Ted initiated a game of footsie.

"Oh my god." Vanessa stopped listing couples to complain, "Footsie? Really? Could you two be any more high school?"

Flushing, Ally nevertheless refused to duck her head. "I think it's cute."

Ted grinned. "I think you're cute."

Ally blushed like the setting sun—but even more beautiful, thought Ted, was her shy smile.

Sam glanced at Vanessa. "And they seriously thought they could fool anyone?"

"Stop!" Laughter spilled from Ally's lips. "I can't run if I'm laughing! I'll get a stitch!"

Ted ceased his SNL-worthy impression of their boss and slowed to a walk. "Well, we wouldn't want that." He held out his hand for her to take. Brushing aside her automatic hesitancy, she slid her fingers in between his with practiced ease.

After three weeks of so-called courtship, and countless dates, Ally had grown comfortable with Ted's preference for PDA. At least, she was comfortable with it when no one she knew was around... *Whatever*. She refused to self-flagellate because she wasn't as "fast" as maybe others were.

"Hey," Ted said, softly, using his free hand to tilt her chin up so she was looking at him, face to face. "Why the frown?"

"Nothing!" Ally flashed him a forced smile. "It's nothing, really." Desperate to change the subject, she surveyed their surroundings. Almost all the leaves had changed, from glossy greens to a rich array of reds, oranges, and yellows, like a child's palette for a sunset. Summer was well and truly gone and winter was on its way. "Are you going home for Thanksgiving?"

Ted shook his head. If he was surprised by the change of subject, he didn't show it. That was Ted, willing to go with whatever the flow was. "We don't get enough time off for me to go back to Sherborn. I mean, I could do it, but I'd only have a day or two with my family, and it's a four hour trip. What about you? Are you headed back to… don't tell me… Syosset for the holiday?"

Ally shook her head, impressed but not surprised that he'd remembered the name of her hometown. "Nah, not this year."

"Why not? Long Island's not so far away as Massachusetts."

"No, but my friend's coming to town and I don't want her to have to endure my parents' pugilism. She's in a shaky enough spot as it is." Ally shook her head. "Her name's Kaitlin. Kait, rather. Do you remember her, from the—"

"From the phone call I overheard?" Ted nodded. "I'm so sorry about that, I really didn't mean to listen in."

Ally squeezed his hand. "I know. It's okay. Anyway, the point is, she's really going through it right now, and she needs to get away."

"Where does she live again?"

"Boston! South End. In a lovely apartment with her decidedly less lovely, soon to be *ex*-husband."

"Nice neighborhood." Ted frowned. "Why is she still with that jerk?"

Shrugging, Ally supposed, "She might not be able to afford to move out yet. I mean, I know they pay paralegals a decent amount, but Boston is an expensive city."

"You're telling me." Ted shook his head, smiling.

Ally rolled her eyes affectionately. "Ted, you grew up in the suburbs. A very affluent area. Don't pretend."

He laughed, rubbing the back of his neck with his free hand. "It's a good thing I have you to remind me of its existence, or I might choke on my silver spoon."

Ally raised her eyebrows and opened her mouth, preparing to roast him to a crisp.

Ted held up his hand. "No, no, please. Spare me."

She pursed her lips. "Fine. But only because you look so sexy in those tiny little shorts."

Ted's expression grew hungry. "Oh? You like these, do you?" He drew her closer.

Ally danced out of reach. "Ted! There are *children* present." She gestured to a nearby grassy knoll, where kindergarteners were taking turns jumping in a leaf pile.

He rolled his eyes "Fine." Then he ran a hand over his face, visibly changing tack. "So. What's the plan with Kait?"

"She's coming down for a couple of days—her firm gives her Wednesday off, too. She'll be crashing on my couch."

Ted looked alarmed. "Are you sure she wouldn't rather stay in my second guest bedroom?"

"Don't insult my futon, Harvard. It's survived this long. Besides, Kait will probably just sleep with me. My bed can comfortably fit two."

Ted smiled, a shy yet knowing little thing. "Don't I know it."

"Mind out of the gutter!" Ally heaved a mock-outraged sigh. "The point is, I want to make her feel better. So I'm hosting a sort of 'Friendsgiving' in her honor." Ally bit her lip. "I mean, it's just the two of us, so I'm not exactly *hosting* anything. And I doubt we'll cook much. But still. It'll be something."

Ted's fingers curled more tightly around hers. "That it will." He glanced around. "Well, I'll probably cook way too much and then I'll be eating leftovers for weeks."

"Leftovers are the best part," Ally protested.

"True. In fact, mine are so good that Belle might just steal them all, along with my favorite set of Pyrex."

Ally looked up at him curiously. "Why isn't your sister going home to your parents? Surely Sherborn is closer to wherever she goes to college than New York City." Ally knew Belle went to a New England school, she just couldn't remember which one.

"Northeastern, so yes. You're right. But she and my parents are in a bit of a fight."

Ally frowned. "What about? If you don't mind my asking, that is."

"I'd tell you anything, Allegra," Ted confessed wistfully, and then immediately looked as though he'd like to melt into a nearby grate. "Uh, yeah, so, the thing is, my sister's a bit of a radical. Well, not really. But she makes our parents look conservative—which they aren't."

Right. Belle was the firecracker of the family. "What are they fighting about this time?" Because there was no way this was a one-time occurrence. Ally knew a thing or two about getting into polarizing political debates with family members.

"This time, she's decided she's done with Thanksgiving. She says it's a celebration of genocide and, honestly, she's right."

Ally's mouth fell open. That was the first time she'd heard Ted express a controversial opinion. Well, an opinion that would be controversial to the general public. To her, most of his opinions were controversial. Like the hot pink, liberty print pocket square on the first day of work. It was pretty, but it made him look like a peacock. Which he was not. "So then why is she celebrating it with you?"

"She's not. She says she's coming to visit because she's 'in desperate need of some home-cooked food.' But no turkey. And I have to volunteer with her at a soup kitchen the day of, or else she won't come."

Ally laughed. "She's got you wrapped around her finger."

"Not as tightly as you do," Ted teased, giving her hand a squeeze. Suddenly, his eyes lit up with what she could only assume was inspiration. "Hey, why don't we combine forces?"

Ally blinked, busy trying to shove down the butterflies that were fluttering around her belly. "What do you mean?"

"Come over to my place for Friendsgiving. You and Kait won't have to cook. I'll get to meet Kait. I can finally introduce you to Belle." He shrugged. "It might be nice... And," he added, no doubt catching her sudden caution, "it can be casual. A casual, no-strings attached *Friends*giving."

"But they'll think we're dating."

"Ally, we *are* dating."

"Yes, but they'll think you're my *boyfriend*. That I'm you're girlfriend. We agreed I wasn't ready for labels like that, Ted!"

He let go of her hand, instead turning to her and placing his palms gently on her shoulders. "Ally, listen to me. They will believe whatever we tell them to believe. Kait's your best friend. Belle's family. It'll just be us, my aunt's magical cranberry sauce recipe, and a movie or something. No PDA, no presumptions on my part, I promise."

His tone soothed Ally. She put her hands on his wrists, like this was an exercise in trust. Which, well, it was. "Alright. Okay. But make it crystal clear to your sister that we are *just* dating. No labels, no strings."

Ted nodded, something sad like resignation flickering in his eyes. Nevertheless, he gave her a cocky little grin. "Yes, ma'am." Then he stole a quick kiss, leaving her breathless, and started running again before she could half-heartedly swat at him.

CHAPTER 17
FRIENDSGIVING

TED WAS PLUMPING pillows in the best guest bedroom when his sister walked into the foyer. Her footsteps echoed and he knew it was her even though his doorman hadn't called up to tell him she was in the elevator—precisely *because* his doorman hadn't called up to tell him she was in the elevator.

Albert had known Belle all her life, since Belle and Ted had visited their aunt and uncle frequently when they were kids. Rather, when Ted was a kid and Belle was an angelic baby. And later, when Ted was a teenager and Belle had turned into a terror. She still was one, although she had reduced her temper tantrum quota in favor of unprovoked and polarizing political debates.

Ted smiled as he smoothed the top sheet. He was glad she was here. Their parents would be fine without them, this year. Tweaking the corner of the pillow he'd just set down on the bed, Ted called out, "Is that you, Bluebell?"

"I was expecting a red carpet," she returned and he heard the sound of suitcase wheels dragging along the hardwood floor of the hall. "Or, at the very least, an ovation."

Ted strode out of the guest bedroom and found his sister waiting for him with her hand on her hip. "This isn't the Oscars, Belle."

"Well." Belle huffed. And then she sidestepped the suitcase and threw herself into his arms for a hug. "I've missed you, Teddy."

Ted smiled into his sister's hair. "Missed you, too." Then he released her and reached for her bag.

"I can carry it myself," Belle protested, but her tone told Ted she was quite content to let him do the work.

"Yeah, and drag dirt across the whole apartment." Ted lifted the light suitcase with one hand and led Belle to her room. "Do you have any idea the kind of stuff that covers New York City sidewalks?"

"Urine, mostly, I imagine."

"Yeah, well, our aunt's apartment is not a bathroom." Ted set the bag down on an old fashioned luggage-rack at the foot of the queen-sized bed.

"It's not hers anymore," Belle said quietly. "It's yours."

Ted sighed. "Yeah, I know. I just… I miss her, and if I call it hers, it feels like she might come back and claim it one day." But he didn't need to explain this, or his profound loneliness, to his sister. She understood. She hadn't been as close with Aunt Lorraine as he had, but he knew she understood.

Belle patted him on his shoulder. And then she broke their moment's silence by asking, "Do you have any of that fancy French ice cream in the freezer?"

Ted turned to face her. "Yes, but it's for tomorrow."

Belle knit her brows. "Tomorrow? Ted, the whole point of my coming down to visit you was to avoid Thanksgiving—"

"And we will! Avoid it, that is." He smiled, feeling triumphant. "We're going to be celebrating *Friendsgiving*, instead."

Belle's hands found their way to her hips again. "Ted, you don't have any friends."

"Ouch." He shot her a look. "First of all, not true. Second of all…" He struggled to come up with another point. "Second of all, that's mean!"

She shrugged. "I only speak the truth." Then, possibly because he pouted, she relented. "Alright, fine. But we can't celebrate *Friends*giving with just the two of us. We're not friends, we're siblings."

Ted happened to think that they were, in fact, friends, as well as siblings, but when he pointed this out, his sister shook her head.

"It's not enough. We might as well just call it *Siblings*giving, in which case it really is just *Thanks*giving. And I'm not about to celebrate colonialism."

"Well, what if I told you that it wouldn't just be us?"

She perked up. "Go on."

"I've invited a friend and she's invited *her* friend, who actually happens to be from Boston, so maybe we know her from somewhere? Anyway—"

"Wait." Belle's eyes were wide. "When you say 'friend' is that really just code for 'secret girlfriend?'" She spun away from him and out of the room.

Ted followed her, shaking his head frantically. Christ, Ally would kill him if he let his little sister think that she was his girlfriend. "No, we're just... I mean, yes, we've been dating. Going on dates, I mean. But it's not… She doesn't want—"

Now in the hallway, not so subtly making a beeline for the freezer, Belle wheeled around. "She doesn't want to be your girlfriend?"

"No! Maybe. I don't know. She says she isn't ready for labels, which is very fair considering the timeline, and I really want to respect that." He looked down at his sister with pleading eyes. "Can you respect that, for me?"

Belle crossed her arms. "Hmmm. She better not be leading you on."

"She isn't!" Ted willed his sister to appreciate Ally for the wonder that she was. "She's great, Belle. Trust me, you'll love her."

Belle's eyebrows shot up. "*Love* her?"

Ted felt himself flush. "Just, try to be open-minded. For me. And do not interrogate her at the dinner table, or anywhere else, for that matter." He slipped into a sterner tone. "Are we clear?"

Belle let her arms fall to her sides. She nodded. Then she turned and made her way to the kitchen, leaving him standing alone in the hallway. Calling back to him, over her shoulder, she said, "This is the woman you hung up on me for, right?"

Ted rolled his eyes, relieved to hear that the suspicion in Belle's voice had been replaced by her usual teasing. "I didn't hang up on you, I simply didn't stand on ceremony."

Belle had disappeared into the kitchen, but he could hear her, nonetheless. "You didn't even say goodbye! That's the definition of hanging up on someone."

Ted followed the sound of his sister's voice. "No, it's not. They never say goodbye in the movies," he offered, smiling somewhat. He'd missed arguing with his sister, face to face. Well, face to wall. "The phone call just ends, but the characters don't think it's rude."

She poked her head out from the kitchen, and spoke around a spoon that had already made its way into her mouth. "That's because they're characters. They're not like you and me. They don't exist." She removed the spoon. "By the way, I broke into the ice cream you were saving for your girlfriend. Is she a centrist? A conservative?!"

Ted heaved a sigh. "No. No! Not in the slightest. And— just don't call her that to her face. Please?"

"What, a conservative? I know, it is basically an insult at this point."

Ted's head fell into his hands. "No, Belle, not a—" He sighed again as she smirked at him over the spoon. "You know what I mean."

❄

Kait wasn't nearly as taken aback by Ted's doorman as Ally had been at first. She was used to the finer things. Well, materially speaking. Somehow, Ally doubted that divorce counted among the 'finer things' in life. But Kait was doing just fine, so far. There was a fragility about her, but she seemed determined not to break down.

"Hello, Albert!" Ally put on her sunniest smile, having read once that smiling sent happy chemicals to the brain, or something equally inane. She needed all the happy chemicals she could get—not because she was unhappy, but because she was *anxious*.

"Hello, Ally." Albert held open the door for them both. "And who is this?"

"This is my friend, Kait. Ted—"

"Is expecting you both," Albert finished her sentence smoothly. "Please, step into the elevator. I'll take you up." He inserted a key below the elevator's controls and pressed the appropriate button. The elevator started to move and Ally's stomach dropped. Had this been a bad idea? Were she and Ted moving too fast? What would his sister think of her? Oh god. What if his sister hated her?

Kait's fingers wove inbetween hers. "Hey," she whispered, "it'll be okay."

Ally nodded, swallowing the urge to be sick.

The doors opened into Ted's sparkling foyer and the two of them stepped out, waving Albert farewell.

"Oh, wow." Kait surveyed the room slowly, taking in the marble and the crystal chandelier. "This is beautiful."

"I'm glad you think so." Ted stepped out of the hall and into the foyer. "I can't take credit for the decor, however; that was all my late aunt."

"She had beautiful taste," Kait replied graciously, while Ally just stood there like a loon. "I'm Kait."

Ted smiled and Ally wanted to curl up like a lizard and

bask in his smile's warmth, even though it wasn't directed at her. "I figured. I've heard a lot about you."

Kait laughed. Ally tried not to be jealous. But Ted hadn't so much as looked at her, and here he was, making her best friend laugh! "All good things, I hope."

"Naturally. Ally?" Ted turned his full attention on her, and suddenly Ally couldn't breathe. His eyes were like pools of light, pale but deep and bright. His smile grew, and in her heart Ally knew—it was for her, and her alone.

"Ted." Ally winced at her breathlessness. Out of the corner of her eye, she thought she caught Kait's knowing smirk. But then there was a whirlwind of movement as a spry young woman appeared at Ted's side. She had the same pale blue eyes, but her hair was a lighter brown.

"Aren't you going to introduce me?" She looked up at Ted expectantly.

Ted beamed. "Ally, this is my kid sister. Belle, this is my—"

"Friend!" Ally blurted out.

Kait shot Ally a skeptical look.

Belle's eyes sparkled with barely suppressed mirth. "Mmm, his friend." She shook Ally's automatically extended hand. "Delighted, I'm sure."

Ally exhaled slowly, and refused to look at Ted, who no doubt was wearing a wounded expression. But he had no right to be hurt. They'd talked about this. She wasn't ready for labels. "The pleasure's all mine," she replied, a blatant lie.

Fortunately, Belle didn't call her out on it. "And you must be Kait. Or is it Kaitlin?"

Kait extended her manicured hand. "Kait's fine, thanks."

"Nice to meet you." Belle turned to Ted, who was shaking his head as if to clear it. "What's cooking?"

"What?"

"What's on the menu, big bro?" Belle glanced behind her, in the direction of the kitchen. "Smells like... Smells like Aunt

Lorraine's been in the kitchen." She smiled, but it was bittersweet.

Ted's smile, when Ally allowed herself to glance up at him, was similarly marred by the memory of their loved one's loss. "Yeah, I'm using a few of her old recipes. And a few of my own," he added, his lips quirking playfully. "You'll all have to do a taste test and tell me if I'm up to snuff." Ted gestured to the hallway. "C'mon, let me show you two the living room."

"Show them the dining room, too, Ted," Belle suggested. "It's not fair to make me set the table all by myself."

"Many hands make light work," Kait murmured, earning her Belle's bright and conspiratorial smile, and Ally started to think that maybe, just maybe, this would work.

Sitting around the mahogany table two hours later, placemats askew and wine glasses empty, the sound of her own laughter at one of Ted's terrible jokes echoing throughout the room, Ally knew for certain—it had worked.

Ted whistled while he washed dishes, a floral dishtowel flung casually over his right shoulder. His back was to her and he must not have heard her come in because he didn't turn or say anything.

Ally leaned in the doorway a moment, admiring Ted's ass. A professional hockey player would have been envious of the taut muscle, the tight but luxurious curve. The way his cheeks clenched against the heels of her feet, when he thrust into her, again and again and again...

She could bounce a quarter off that ass—in fact, she would, if she had any change on her. Except, the way he moved in her, she should be showering him with bills, not coins—proper Benjamins.

"Are you going to stand there and stare at my ass or are

you going to come here and help me clean?" The tenor of Ted's voice, like he was smiling as he spoke, startled Ally out of her posterior-induced stupor.

"What? I wasn't—"

Ted shut off the tap, a gesture which pretty much shut her up. Then he turned, his forearms covered in pink rubber gloves and suds, and leveled her with a knowing look.

"Oh, alright." Ally threw her arms up and stepped into the low-lit kitchen. "But you have to admit, it's quite the sight."

"What? Me, in my domesticity?" Ted grinned and turned back to the sink. "Come here, I could use the extra hands." He rinsed off a pan and set it to rest in an overflowing drying rack.

Ally made to pluck the dishtowel off his shoulder.

"No, don't use that one. There's clean rags in the drawer." Ted pointed her to the correct drawer, dripping soap all over the floor. "Oh, crap. Would you mind…"

Ally was already on it, ripping a piece of paper towel off the roll and kneeling to soak up the suds lest someone— likely, she—slip. The last thing anyone needed was to visit the ER on Thanksgiving. The line would be out the door.

Ally balled up the wet paper towel, glancing up at Ted, who was watching her with a dark, devilish hunger. Watching her cleavage, rather. She smirked. "See something you like?"

Ted nodded, his eyes flicking to hers as he licked his lips.

Ally came to her feet slowly. She tossed the wad of paper towel on the counter and forgot about it immediately. She couldn't think, she could scarcely breathe, with Ted eyeing her like he was a man dying of hunger and she was an eight-course meal. Ally bit her lip.

"I've been craving you all day," Ted confessed, in the silence of the still kitchen. "The taste of you…" His words fell away as his hand, gloved and gripping the front of her dress like he didn't give a damn if it got wet, drew her in.

Ally gazed up at him, feeling something new, something old, something strange, something familiar—just feeling *something* for him. Her arms wound around his neck, and she inhaled the sweet scent of cinnamon, beneath the soap.

A dish clattered as it fell, forgotten, into the sink.

Ted bent his head and began to make love to her lips. He sucked and bit and licked in the name of sating himself, although as the minutes stretched on it seemed he would never be satisfied. Ally gave as good as she got, nipping and swirling and exploring him like she'd never kissed him before, like she'd never get a chance to kiss him again.

Ted's arms encircled Ally, and she thought—the only thought she was capable of half-forming—that she'd quite like it if he never let her go. She slid one of her own hands south, caressing his chest, curling around his waist to grasp that spectacular—

Someone snorted behind her. "Just friends, eh?"

Dazed, Ally broke away from Ted to see his little sister leaning in the doorway. Her arms were crossed and her eyebrows were sky high.

"I, uh," Ally was embarrassed to hear herself panting slightly, "I was just helping your brother clean up."

Ted, who looked like he'd been hit by an amorous freight train, sighed deeply. "Go back to the living room, Belle."

She raised her hands, all innocence. "Sorry, sorry. Can't help being a beacon of honesty... Unlike your girlfriend, here..." Belle grinned, and Ally felt her cheeks flame.

She rapidly stepped out of Ted's embrace.

"I found another dish for you to wash, Cinderella." Belle handed the plate to Ted, who accepted it with pursed lips, then she turned to Ally. "You know he can sing as well as clean, right? That's why I call him Cindy."

Ally nodded, still not certain this wasn't a weird dream.

"Yeah, I heard him at karaoke. I mean, I didn't know about the nickname—"

Belle's eyes went wide and she interrupted Ally. "But Ted never sings in public!"

Ally shrugged.

"Wow, he must have been either drunk or desperate to get your attention. My money's on desperate, given what I just witnessed…"

His expression stern, and undoubtedly embarrassed, Ted placed his hands on his sister's shoulders and spun her around so that she faced the doorway. "Living room. Now."

Belle smirked and saluted the empty space ahead of her. "Yessir."

Together, Ted and Ally watched Belle march rigidly into the other room. After a tense moment, in which Ally made an important decision, Ted turned to her. "I'm so sorry, Ally. I know you wanted to keep things…" He started to wave his gloved hands in the air in a hopeless gesture, but she caught them. He shivered as the heat of her seeped through the thin rubber barrier.

"Hey, it's okay." She smiled up at him, her embarrassment fading. "It's not like you haven't told her about me. I can see how close you two are."

Ted froze. "I *never* told her you were my girlfriend. I swear." He hung his head. "I was… I was waiting for you to say it."

"Say what?" Ally's smile grew mischievous, and humor tugged at her heart. "Girlfriend? There, I said it."

He raised his head, cocking it in confusion. "You mean…"

"I mean I'm ready. To… take the next step, or whatever. So long as it's not a leap! I'm ready." Ally swallowed—those damn butterflies… No, this was bigger than butterflies.

"Ready to call this a relationship? Ready to call me your… boyfriend?" Ted asked, with about the amount of caution that would be appropriate if he were approaching a wild bobcat with its fangs bared.

Ally watched him for a long moment, realizing, as she scanned the sharp curve of his jaw, and searched the twin ponds of his eyes for even a trace of grey or green, that she wasn't scared. She was safe. With him, with Ted, with her *boyfriend*—she was safe. Ally put her hand on Ted's shoulder, pulling him down and closer. She nodded. His forehead relaxed and his lips quirked, as if he couldn't quite believe her. "Now, can I kiss my boyfriend?"

He drew her flush against his chest. "God, I—" He caught himself, and before Ally could dwell on what his words would have been, he swept her into a kiss so sweet, so tender, she nearly forgot her own name.

CHAPTER 18
HEATHCLIFF

"I CAN'T BELIEVE you didn't want to come home and spend Thanksgiving with your parents. We're not *that* bad!" Ally's father held open his arms for her and Ally hurried down the steps at Syosset Station to throw herself into them.

"I know, Dad, but it was really nice to hang out with my friends. Besides, Kait needed a break from Boston."

Her father released her and they started walking toward the car. "And you couldn't bring Kaity with you? Your mother and I would have loved to see her, especially given what she's going through. Poor kid."

Ally shrugged. "I wanted her to meet my friends. Don't tell her I told you this, but I think she might consider moving down to New York, once the divorce is finalized. And if she does, she's gonna need a good support network."

Her father unlocked the car and they slid into their seats. As Ally clicked into her seatbelt, her father watched her with a suspicious smile on his face. "I think you just wanted her to meet your new boyfriend."

"Dad!" Ally whipped her head around to stare at him. "How did you know about that? And he's not my boyfriend. We're just dating."

"Are you sure?" They pulled out of the parking lot and turned onto the main road. "Your mother says—"

"Mom should be keeping my secrets, not selling them to the highest bidder!"

Her father laughed. "A boyfriend isn't a secret that should be kept. Besides, you know what she's like with a little rosé in her system."

Ally sighed. She did indeed know what her mother was like. Still! It felt like a betrayal. Although, honestly, she'd have told her father sooner or later. She and Ted weren't getting *serious* serious, but he was technically her boyfriend. After all, they'd had that conversation in the kitchen. Maybe it was time for Ally to stop hiding and start... feeling.

"Okay, fine. He's my boyfriend." It felt liberating to admit. "But we're not, like, living together! It's casual. He likes me, I like him..." The sex was amazing—and Ted was a quick study with her favorite vibrator... But her father didn't need to know that. "The point is, we're whatever." If 'whatever' was a feeling that fluttered in her belly, that made her heart beat at twice its average speed every time Ted so much as entered the room. "I'm sorry I didn't tell you sooner, Dad. I just... I want to take this slow. And, if we're being honest, it's a bit scary."

They slowed to a halt in front of a stop sign. As her father eased off the brake, he asked in a quiet voice, "Why's it scary, kid?"

She frowned. "I dunno, Dad." She looked out the window at the trees that were starting to move past them again. "I guess... I'm afraid of making the same mistakes."

Her father's brow knit. "Is he a good guy?"

"Yes!" Nothing like *him*.

"Good. I trust your judgment on this, kid. But have you told your therapist?"

Ally rolled her eyes. "Yes, Dad. I talk to her almost every week. Linda knows about Ted. Likes the sound of him, too."

"As do I, if what your mother's told me is true."

They pulled into the driveway of Ally's childhood home. Suddenly, her mind was crowded with memories. Playing hopscotch on the sidewalk. Putting dents in the garage door as she practiced her slapshot. Tea parties with stuffed animals in the grass. She had a strange and sudden need to share these memories, these snippets of her history, with Ted—to tell him all about her childhood, and to listen to stories of his, in turn.

Swallowing, Ally hastily unbuckled her seatbelt and hopped out. "Is Mom home?"

"She had to run to the grocery store, but she'll be back any minute." Her father locked the car and started in the direction of the front door. "Come on in, I want to show you the puzzle I finished last night. Took me a week, but I bested it in the end."

Ally grinned. Her father loved a good jigsaw. He saw puzzles as opponents, to be both respected and thoroughly beaten. "Sure thing, Dad."

Ten minutes later, Ally heard the front door open and close. "Honeys, I'm ho-ome!"

Ally darted out of the den, where she'd been helping her father figure out how to log into various streaming services, again, and stepped into the kitchen, where her mother was unloading several overstuffed bags of groceries.

"Ma!"

"Sweetie!" Ally's mother pulled her into a warm hug. "Now, help me with the food."

Fishing a jug of milk out of the cooler bag, Ally asked, "Why'd you get so much? I'm only here for the night."

Her mother set several boxes of pasta on the counter. "Leftovers, sweetie. You don't get enough protein, you never have, so I'm sending you back to the city with a big dish of lasagna."

"Mom, I get plenty of protein. And while I appreciate the

sentiment, I don't want to be stuck eating lasagna every night for a week!"

Her mother shrugged. "Then I'll cut it into pieces and you can freeze half of them. Now, tell me about Ted. How was Thanksgiving?"

"*Friends*giving." She shook her head. "And it was… great, honestly. I met his sister, and he met Kait, and—"

"His sister! Oh my, you two must be getting serious." Ally's mother pulled two jars of tomato sauce out of a reusable grocery bag, then started to fold the bag. "Does everybody know? What did Kaity have to say? How is she, by the way? Your father and I are worried sick. I was thinking about giving her a call."

Ally smiled. "She'd like that, Mom. Just… don't ask her about the divorce. She's sensitive."

"I know, I know. I'm not clueless! But tell me about Ted, and his sister! Do you like her? More importantly, does she like you? Because, for a man who's as close to his family as this Ted seems to be, the two of you not getting along could really put a strain on your relationship…"

"Relax, Ma. Belle is great. She's not like Ted, though. She's much more opinionated—pretty feisty."

Her mother raised one plucked brow. "Hmmph. Sounds like someone I know."

Ally laughed. "Anyway, the point is, Friendsgiving was a success." Ally thought about the kiss she and Ted had shared in the kitchen, as they were cleaning up. More than the kiss, the agreement they'd come to, about taking their relationship to the next level. Friendsgiving had been more than a success…

"You're thinking about him, aren't you?"

"What?" Ally snapped out of it.

Her mother laughed. "You had this dreamy look on your face, I've never seen it before. I assume that's Ted's doing."

Ally shrugged, suddenly self-conscious.

"Embrace it, sweetie. Having a boyfriend isn't a bad thing. You don't need to hold yourself back to be safe. Just be honest, with yourself and with him."

Ally didn't say anything. She was too busy thinking about what these new labels would mean, for herself, for Ted, for their relationship. Because she'd meant what she'd said, about being ready for more. And she was being honest with herself, and with him!

She just…

All that didn't mean…

She wasn't in *love* with him. Was she?

Ted was in love with Ally.

And he had been for a while now.

It was all he could think about—and apparently his panicked musings on the subject were not so subtle.

"Earth to Ted," one of his coworkers called out from across the table. "Are you still with us?"

Ally was off visiting her parents and Belle and Kait had returned to Boston on the same train, so he had the morning free. In an attempt to build up some friendships, as well as to distract himself from the tumult of feelings he had for Ally, he'd invited a few of the guys from his team at work out for brunch.

"Yeah, sorry." He flashed a repentant smile at the other man.

Jordan waved a hand. "No worries. You just look like you've got a lot on your mind, man."

Sam cocked his head curiously. "What's up, Lewis? You can talk to us."

Kent, who was on the quieter side, said nothing, but he leaned in to listen.

Ted sighed. "I was just thinking about my girlfriend."

Sam's eyes narrowed. "Oh, so you *do* have a girlfriend now?"

Jordan's eyebrows knit. "Since when?"

A ghost of a smile curved Kent's lips. "Allegra Bryant," he murmured.

Ted did a double take. "How did *you* know? I mean, I had mentioned it to Sam, but..."

"I notice things." Kent's air of mystery increased tenfold.

"Well, I don't. I had no idea you two were together, so I guess that makes me the odd man out." Jordan frowned. "Last I checked, I thought she hated you."

Ted huffed a laugh. "She did."

"So, why'd she agree to be your girlfriend?"

Ted shrugged. "She asked me, actually. Thursday night."

Sam chuckled. "Thanksgiving is kind of a weird anniversary, dude."

Jordan knocked his shoulder into Sam's. "It's cool, man. My anniversary with Alicia is Valentine's Day."

"So?" Sam looked skeptical.

"All I'm saying is, it could be worse. Anyway, what's going on with Ally? She still hate you or something?"

"No!" Ted shook his head. "I just..." He looked around. These were his friends. New friends, admittedly. But he'd been working with them for over a month now, having lunch together and texting in a group chat, and they all seemed like stellar guys—not the ghosts of lax bros past.

Ted strengthened his resolve. These were his friends, his real friends, and he could trust them. "I worry I like her more than she likes me." At Jordan's raised eyebrows, he held up his hands. "She doesn't hate me. She just... Even though she was the one who asked me if we could start using labels, I prompted the conversation. Repeatedly. And I worry about whether or not she's really ready. Or at least, if she's as ready as I am. Because I'm ready. For everything. But I'm also...

scared. That I'm just too much for her. That my feelings for her are too strong, too soon."

Silence fell over their table for a few seconds as Ted's new friends processed his confession. He was worried he'd said too much, been too open—scared them off the way he was afraid he'd scare Ally away, if he told her even one tenth of the truth of the extent of his feelings for her—but then Kent put a hand on his shoulder.

"You're in love with her."

Ted jerked away. "I didn't say—"

"You didn't have to, man." This time it was Sam, smiling wryly.

Jordan nodded. "Yeah, and even if you hadn't basically said it, it's obvious in the way you light up whenever she walks into the room." They all hummed their agreement.

Ted narrowed his eyes. "I thought you didn't know about me and Ally."

"I didn't, but in retrospect..." Jordan shrugged. "Stuff makes sense, now."

"What stuff?" Ted demanded.

"The way you run for the elevator when she's in it. How you take the long way round to the conference room, so you can walk past her desk."

Ted blushed, feeling more than a little exposed.

"Don't freak out, dude. It's not just you."

Kent nodded sagely. "She's changed, the past couple weeks. Less angry, but still on edge."

"On a different kind of edge," Sam interjected.

"How do you guys even know this? Do you know her?"

Sam shrugged. "A little, we've worked together in the past."

"I'm friends with Vanessa," Jordan offered. "So, like, through osmosis..."

Kent shook his head. "I just notice things, like I said." He paused. "It's okay to be in love with her."

Ted let his head fall into his hands. For a moment, he just sat there, his eyes closed tight. Then, he lifted his head a little. "What if she's not in love with me?"

San smiled again. "Don't rush her. Just go with the flow. Eventually, you'll know."

"Know what?"

"Whether she loves you, too."

Jordan jumped in. "But in the meantime, maybe keep it on the down low?" He grimaced. "Chicks don't always dig big declarations."

Kent nodded again. "Allegra Bryant, especially."

He was right. They were right. Ted would just have to keep it all in. Loving her wasn't worth losing her. He couldn't afford to scare her off, not when she'd just taken their relationship to the next level. It would be hell, and it might hurt, but he wasn't risking anything. Not when he was finally, officially hers.

"Thanks, guys. I really appreciate it."

Jordan grinned. "It's cool, dude. We love gossip."

"And helping out friends," Sam added, pointedly.

Ted smiled, genuinely. Friends. He had friends. Real and decent friends. Finally.

As her train pulled into Penn Station and Ally was forced to navigate the unnecessarily complicated layout of the terminal, as well as the crowds of finance bros who had deigned to travel to and from their weekend homes in the Hamptons via the Long Island Rail Road, her thoughts drifted to Ted (decidedly *not* a bro). Well, they'd been drawn in his direction as if by some psychological undertow for practically her whole journey home.

Squeezing onto the crowded subway, Ally decided it wasn't worth fighting. Even if she was a little scared of where her mind would take her. Because, the thing was, Ally was not in love. The thought had occurred to her, in her parents' kitchen, but just because a thought occurred didn't mean it was correct.

Ally wasn't in love with Ted, and she knew this because she'd been in love before. With Everett. And that had felt completely different.

She didn't have, with Ted, the desire to completely subsume her own identity in service of his. She didn't have, with Ted, the constant need to impress him, born of an insecurity that needled and pricked. She didn't have, with Ted, the looming guilt that she wasn't good enough and they both knew it. All these things, these awful things, had been the hallmarks of her love for Everett. And they were all absent from her feelings for, her relationship with Ted.

With Ted, she felt confident in her own identity. She didn't need to alter her personality to better fit with his. With Ted, she could put herself first, attend to her own needs, and not feel like she was betraying him. With Ted, she wasn't worried about whether or not he was impressed with her; she felt secure in his affections, confident in his commitment. With Ted, the guilt was gone, as was the dread, as was the fear. With Ted, she felt calm not crazed, and reality wasn't going away.

So, Ally came to the conclusion that she wasn't in love with Ted. Because it wasn't like it had been, before.

As for her heightened emotions, her elevated feelings? The way her words wobbled whenever he walked in the room, the pale fire that lit up her limbs at the thought of him, the magma, molten at her core, that had come to replace her belly's butterflies...

Well, she was attracted to him. Very, very attracted to him. And not just sexually. Emotionally. She wanted to hear about his day, sit on the edge of the bed while she watched him put his laundry away. She wanted to bring him home to Syosset, and show him where she'd scraped her knee when, as a kid, she'd tried and failed to win a roller-skate race.

But all of that, intense and all-consuming as it was, wasn't love. It was just… hormones, or something. Pheromones, too. All the -ones, really, assuming there were others she didn't know about because she had taken exactly one science course in college and it was on the chemistry of colors, not lovers.

Ally shook herself as she walked up the steps from the station. Lovers had been the wrong word. She and Ted weren't lovers. Lovers *loved* each other. She and Ted were in a relationship. They were dating. He was her boyfriend and she was his girlfriend. And yes, that was amazing. And yes, she felt like she'd shot the moon or been dealt a full house. But it wasn't *love*. And that was a good thing, because love was one label, one word, for which she was not ready.

Ally fumbled with her keys then took the stairs two at a time because she had so much pent up energy. Panting slightly, she pushed open the door to her apartment. Heathcliff was waiting for her on the counter.

"Hey, Heathie! Did you miss me—" Ally stopped talking as she heard a crunch of crushed paper. Confused, she glanced at the floor, where an envelope was caught beneath her foot. *Huh*. It seemed to have been slid under her door.

Ally bent to pick it up. It had to have been hand delivered, the lack of a stamp or a full address confirmed. All it said was TENANT: ALLEGRA BRYANT in all-caps, a messy scrawl. Confused, and increasingly concerned, Ally tore open the envelope along the top seam. As she pulled out the typed letter, her stomach dropped, like she was on a roller coaster that had just gone over the peak. And, for some reason, she wasn't strapped to her seat like she should have been.

The letter, which was dated that day, had been signed by her landlord. It was brief and to the point. He'd performed an inspection, unannounced—something to do with replacing the stove. And what he'd found had violated the terms of the lease.

Ally knew what he'd found. He'd found Heathcliff. Her secret, her stowaway, her sweetheart. Ally's landlord didn't allow pets. And that hadn't been a problem previously, because Heathie was so quiet. So unobtrusive. So… innocent, and undeserving of all this.

He's just a cat, for fuck's sake! Ally wanted to scream.

Instead, she set the letter down on the counter and scratched Heathcliff behind the ears, thinking all the while of the last line. The sentence that informed her of the fact that she had two weeks to vacate.

All the good feelings from before had dissipated like dust met with an industrial vacuum. Ally was so totally, utterly fucked.

CHAPTER 19
PENALTY KILL

ALLY STORMED into the locker room on Saturday night, filled with fury. Her earlier anguish had been replaced by anger, the more she thought about her situation. Did her landlord have any idea how hard it was to find a safe apartment in New York City that wasn't the size of a closet, on her budget?

"Look what the cat dragged in." Wren's words, which only served to unwittingly remind Ally of the situation she was in, made Ally flinch. "You okay, Bryant?"

"I'm fine." She kept her head down.

"Well, while you sort your shit out, I'll be chatting with the officials." Wren turned to the rest of the locker room, which was full of her half-dressed teammates. "Hurry up, Monsters. I want you on the ice in five." Then she strode across the locker room, leaving the door to bang behind her.

Ally dumped her bag unceremoniously on the bench beside Ted. Ted, who was watching her with wide, worried eyes.

"Ally?" He said her name quietly, as if he didn't want to startle her. "You ignored my texts earlier. What's wrong?"

Ally was acutely aware of her teammates listening in. "Nothing." She stripped down to her underwear and started strapping pads to her limbs.

"Are you sure?"

Ally tugged her thick socks on over her shin pads. "Yes," she hissed. Then she wriggled into her bulky pants.

"Allegra, talk to me. Please."

She sighed. There was a tendril of hurt in his voice, and she couldn't ignore it. He was her boyfriend, and she might have been out of practice with that kind of thing, but... she cared about him. No matter how mad she was. "Fine." Her voice was thick and her throat felt sore. Tears pricked at her eyes but she refused to let them fall. "I'm being evicted."

She could practically hear Ted's eyebrows fly up his forehead. "What?!"

Ally nodded, the misery of her situation flooding her mind. "My landlord found out about my cat."

He nodded. "Heathcliff."

Of course he knew the name of her cat. He was attentive, a good listener. And he'd spent plenty of nights at her apartment. "Yes, Heathcliff. And the lease says pets aren't allowed. So. Yeah."

Ted was silent for a moment. "I'm so sorry, sweetheart."

Ally noticed, out of the corner of her eye, two of her teammates exchanging glances at the endearment.

"That's colossally unfair. How much time do you have to find a new place?"

"Two weeks. But it's impossible to find a place in Manhattan in two weeks that isn't infested with rats or out of my budget!" She stared at him, feeling the worst kind of hopeless. "I don't know what to do, Ted." Her voice broke on his name. "I just... I don't know what to do."

Ted was silent for a long moment. And then he looked her in the eye, and the locker room fell away. It was just the two of them. "Move in with me." It wasn't a question.

Ally stared at him like he was someone else entirely. "What?"

"Move in with me." He said it like it was the solution to all of her problems. And it was, in a way, except…

"*Why?*"

Ted spoke as though he was trying to soothe her. It had the opposite effect. "Well, we've been dating for a while…"

"A couple of weeks," she interjected, hotly.

"You're my girlfriend and I care about you deeply…" He continued, as if she hadn't spoken.

Ally huffed, feeling an old fear creep up on her. "That's not a reason to—"

"And you need a place to live because your landlord's a rat, like all landlords."

"Are you counting yourself in that estimation?" She demanded, unsure as to why she was fighting him so hard on this, except that she had to, she couldn't just… sit back and let him fix her problems for her. That would be akin to his controlling her life, the way Everett had always tried. Ally remembered how Everett had held their living situation over her, and she felt her throat close. "Because if I did move in with you, you'd basically be my landlord."

He appeared horrified by the suggestion. "What? No, Ally—"

"You'd own the apartment, and I'd live there. Would I pay rent?"

"Of course not," he said, simply, but it was clear his temper was rising. Ally felt her own mirroring his. "I figured maybe an even split on utilities and groceries, but… No, Ally. I wouldn't expect you to pay rent. You'd be my partner, not my tenant."

"I can't do that!" Panic seeped into her screech. She jumped to her feet.

"Why not?" He followed her, nearly tripping over his untied laces.

She wheeled around to face him and found herself forced to tilt her head back even farther than usual, because he was wearing skates and she wasn't. The difference in their heights enraged her. "Because I'm not sleeping with you just so I have a place to sleep!"

A hush fell over the locker room. Ted appeared aghast. "Ally, it's not like that—"

She shook her head, breathing erratically. "I have my pride, Ted."

"Your pride won't keep you from having to move back in with your parents. Christ, Ally, what is wrong with you? Why can't you just accept this offer at face value?"

"What's wrong with *you*?" She cried, picking her glove up off the bench and throwing it to the floor.

"What's wrong with *me*?" He asked, incredulously, following the path of the glove as it bounced half-heartedly.

Ally had a sudden inkling that she'd pushed him too far. Perhaps she should have accepted his generosity… But she couldn't. It was too much. She wasn't ready! And she wasn't accepting charity.

"What's wrong with *me*?" He repeated, even louder, and Ally knew she was in for it now. She'd never seen him angry, so she braced herself for the worst. "Ally, nothing is wrong with me! I mean, plenty of things are wrong with me," he said, his laughter anything but comedic, "but that's beside the point! I just want to help the woman I love—"

Ally could have heard a pin drop, if the floors hadn't been rubber. If her blood hadn't suddenly started rushing in her ears. "The woman you what?" Her question came out a whisper that everyone could hear.

Ted froze, a deer in headlights. He hadn't meant to tell her yet, the realization crashing over her like a wave. He'd been keeping his feelings a secret from her, because… because he'd been afraid of what she'd say, afraid of scaring her away.

"The woman I love," he repeated, his voice quiet yet strong—unyielding. His eyes, as blue as the summer sky, searched hers. He waited for a response, but she couldn't give him one.

Love? It was too much, too soon. She didn't know how she felt! Even if she did, she wasn't ready to admit it—especially not in front of the entire team.

Ted didn't turn away. He didn't break eye-contact. Understanding dawned on his face. He wasn't ashamed. But he was hurt.

Ally felt her own eyes fill. "Ted—"

Wren, oblivious to the two-person show they were putting on in her locker room, reentered. "Alright, team. Let's go."

The woman Ted loved was currently causing a scene in the crease.

"Ally, get out of there!" Ted heard Madison call to her from behind him.

At least one of his wings was in working order tonight. Clearly, his one-sided confession had upset Ally, because she had spent the better part of the first two periods riling up the other team.

What right did she have, to be this upset? Surely he was the injured party. He'd told her he loved her, he'd offered her a place to live, and she'd responded by what, shouting at him in the locker room and then giving him the silent treatment?

The whole game, she'd been ignoring him. Wren had kept Ally on the same shift as Ted, for some godforsaken reason. Maybe she thought they would work their issues out on the ice. Well, they couldn't. Because she wasn't speaking to him. She wouldn't even pass the puck to him. For that, she had Madison.

Honestly, Madison was a life-saver, mediating for the two of them without letting up in the corners. Right now, though, she sounded like she was at the end of her rope. And Ted couldn't blame her. He was fairly close to losing it, himself. A part of him just wanted to throw down his stick and skate off the ice. But then he'd be faced with the locker room, and he didn't think he could bear revisiting it quite yet.

"Ally, for god's sake, get *out* of there!" Madison skated past him, toward the crease. The ref had blown the whistle ten seconds earlier, but Ally was still battling one of the opposing team's defensemen: their sticks locked, their heads butting. Ted watched as Ally bent her knees, using her awkward angle to shove the opposing player up and away from her. Ted sighed heavily; he knew what was coming next—

The ref blew the whistle again, awarding Ally a two minute penalty for roughing.

Ted shook his head, catching Madison's eye. Usually a calm player, content to let Ally get herself into trouble, she looked pissed.

"Come on, Ted." She started down the ice, toward the face off circle in their defensive end. "Let's waste some time."

She was right. They were a man down; the smart thing to do would be to kill the clock by getting and maintaining possession. No risky moves, no aggressive maneuvers. Ted could do that. He didn't have the heart to try and start something, besides.

Rather, he had the heart, it was beating in his chest, but he was starting to wonder whether it had been broken. Absently, he rubbed at his sternum through the thick pads that protected it.

"Ted!" Madison called to him impatiently.

With a start, Ted realized he was still standing in the opposing team's end zone.

"Come on."

Ted pushed off in the direction of the defensive end, tempted to switch courses and head for the bench, instead. He wasn't prepared for a penalty kill. His mind was a mess, his reflexes were a joke, and his heart—his heart *hurt*, in the rare seconds that he slipped up and let himself to feel something. It was easier to be numb, and if not numb then angry.

Ally had hurt him, badly. And he knew it was his fault, he knew he shouldn't have said it, knew that saying it had been pushing her outside of her comfort zone. But he was constantly outside of his comfort zone, for her. And it was glorious. It had been glorious, those couple of weeks of "label-less" dating. And then Friendsgiving, when he'd allowed himself to hope, to trust, to believe...

She'd said she was ready. Ready for the next step, so long as it wasn't a leap. Well, Ted supposed, his teeth grinding into his mouthguard, moving in together would have been a leap. Confessing his love for her, that had been a leap. Everything he'd done, everything he'd said—it was all his fault. For forcing her to take, or else turn away from, that leap.

The whistle blew, the puck dropped, and the other center violently wrested control of it away from Ted, passing it back to his own defenseman. From halfway across the ice, Ted could hear Ally banging on the glass wall of the penalty box, yelling curses. She'd been playing with fire the whole first period, and her temper didn't show any signs of cooling now that they were well into the second, regardless of the minute and a half remaining in her penalty.

Ted shook his head and tried to refocus. Tried to think of anything but Ally, and her face when he'd offered her... Everything, he'd offered her everything. And she'd been horrified. He'd seen it in her eyes.

Up by the blue line, the opposing defenseman held onto the puck for a few seconds, then slid it along said line to his partner, who was waiting at the point. Before Ted could blink, the second defenseman lifted his stick and brought it down hard on the still-moving puck in a perfectly executed slap-shot. Ted couldn't breath as he watched the puck sail through the air in the direction of the net. Matt, however, was ready, and deflected the shot into the far corner.

Madison gave chase, but the opposing wing snapped the puck up and sent it north again. The defenseman held onto it, this time, teasing Ted, who was stuck in box formation with his teammates, protecting the net. The player yelled something, some kind of verbal signal, then suddenly dumped the puck, which flew around the boards and behind the net. Ted, seeing an opportunity, darted towards it, his head low.

"Not so fast, fucker," Ted heard someone mutter, even as he extended his stick, reaching for the puck.

Then he looked up and saw the boards rushing up to meet him. He felt a weight, like a body, thrown against his back, propelling him forward.

Ted tried to turn, but there was no time, no space behind the net, no way for him to pull away or slow down or even brace himself. Everything happened in an instant. Ted saw the lights overhead, unnaturally bright, heard someone scream his name. And then the world went black.

"Ted!" Ally's scream was simultaneously amplified and contained by the glass walls of the penalty box. She fumbled with the handle on the door, forgetting the minute she had left. All she knew was she had to get to him, had to help him.

The whistle blew and play was suspended. One of the refs tried to tell her to stop, to get back to the box, but Ally was beyond listening.

"Oh my god." She screeched to a halt next to Ted's immobile body, spraying snow all over the back of his jersey. "Oh my g—Ted? Ted!" She couldn't breathe. She wasn't sure if she should touch him or leave him be. Surely, if she touched him, she would make it worse? Could it get any worse? "Wren!" She practically screamed her captain's name, never taking her eyes off Ted's unmoving form. He was curled up against the boards, his neck crooked, and he lay unnaturally still. But he was breathing.

"I'm here," Wren said, from somewhere over Ally's left shoulder. "Step aside, Bryant."

"But—"

"You're hysterical, Ally. You can't help him like this."

Ally realized vaguely that she was crying, her whole body shaking. "But—"

"Nikki called an ambulance. The paramedics will be here in a minute. Madison," she addressed Ally's fellow wing, who must have been standing behind her. "Get Bryant to the bench. She needs to sit down before her legs give out."

"I'm not leaving him," Ally protested, even as Madison put her hand on her shoulder. Wren knelt before Ted, assessing his injuries. "I'm not leaving him!" She cried, shaking off Madison's hand.

Wren sighed, not looking up from Ted. "Alright. You can stay. Just, chill. Madison, go get my bag from the locker room. It should have his family's contact information, in case of a medical emergency—"

"I have it."

Wren turned to look up at Ally. "What?"

"I have his sister's number."

Wren shook her head. "Not his sister. His parents. He marked them as his emergency contacts. We're not scaring the shit out of his kid sister over a concussion. And you're not calling them, I am. I'm his captain."

"A concussion? That's what you think this is?"

Ted let out a low groan, and Ally's attention turned immediately to him.

"Is he awake? Ted? Teddy, can you hear me?" Ally fell to her knees beside him, even as he started to straighten his spine.

"Don't move, Lewis." Ted moaned, and the sound was so

saturated with pain that Ally flinched. "Keep your distance, Bryant. He needs professional attention."

"Can't we remove his helmet, or something? Just to make him more comfortable while we wait?"

Wren's gloveless fingers wrapped around Ally's exposed wrist. "Don't touch him. The helmet stays on until he's been stabilized. Come on, Bryant, haven't you ever read the concussion protocol sheets I email out at the start of every season, before baseline testing?"

She had, but right now she had forgotten their contents. She'd forgotten everything, in her fear and guilt and frustration. Fear, because she didn't know if Ted was going to be alright. Guilt, because he was in pain and it was her fault. Frustration, because according to Wren there was nothing she could do. "Can I at least hold his hand?"

Wren nodded. "I don't suppose it could hurt. But gently, Bryant. And don't get carried away. He'll be okay."

Except Ally wasn't so sure about that. She'd seen the hit firsthand. Watched as the other player checked him from behind while he was on the chase. A move that would have been illegal even if they allowed checking in this league. Suddenly, Ally felt a surge of anger, of raw and reeling rage.

"Where is he?" She asked, wheeling around. She started to get up. Wren grabbed her shoulder.

"Don't even think about it, Bryant." She stared Ally down. "Your boyfriend needs you." Wren guided Ally's hand, which was clenched into a fist, toward Ted's.

Another wave of guilt washed over Ally. Oh god. Were they even still together, after what had passed between them, earlier? Had she ruined their relationship, with her paranoia and her pride? Would Ted ever forgive her? Would he even be able to?

Tears fell, hot and fat, from her eyes, some of them landing on Ted's glove. Blinking hard, Ally removed it, gently, from his hand. Then she curled her fingers around his longer ones, clutching at his warmth. At any sign of his vitality.

"Ted…" She whispered his name over and over, like a litany.

He groaned, and his eyes fluttered open. "Ally?"

She could have wept with relief. But she forced the tears back, and tried for a brave smile. "Hey, there. You're gonna be okay." *Please, god, please let him be okay.*

"My shoulder…" He moaned, trying to move his arm, which looked unnaturally long beneath the sleeve of his jersey and lay at an awkward angle.

Wren's tone was firm but gentle. "Don't. You'll only make it worse."

Ted winced and nodded, but his voice was thick with confusion. "Who're you?"

"You don't remember me?" Wren asked, but she sounded calm.

Ally didn't know how she did it; *she* was starting to truly panic. At least Ted had remembered her. Ally squeezed his hand.

"I'm your captain, Wren. You've hit your head. Amnesia is a common symptom of concussions. The medics are on there way." She spoke in short, digestible sentences. Ally admired her ability to stay calm and in control. There was a reason why Wren was their captain, and it wasn't just because she could score goals.

"Got your bag, cap." Madison handed it to Wren.

She sighed and said, "Just the form would've been sufficient." Then she dug through the black canvas duffle, producing after some seconds a sheet of paper. "Just in time, too," she muttered, turning to watch the paramedics carefully cross the ice.

Wren got to her feet, taking her bag with her. Ally continued to kneel by Ted's side.

"Ally, give the medics some space." It was a command,

one Ally found herself reluctantly obeying. She watched as one paramedic knelt beside Ted, while two others brought a stretcher over. After performing some basic tests, and asking him some simple questions, they stabilized his neck and shoulder and lifted him onto the stretcher, strapping him down.

Watching them work on him, knowing that he was in capable hands, Ally started to breathe again.

"Anyone coming in the ambulance?" One of the paramedics asked.

Wren pulled Ally aside. "Think you can manage this?"

Ally nodded. "Just give me thirty seconds to take my skates off."

CHAPTER 20
BASELINE

IT WAS WELL PAST MIDNIGHT.

The lights were too bright. The noises were too loud. Everything hurt, and nothing made sense.

Ally sat by his side, holding his right hand. His left arm hung loose at his side, and every time he breathed his shoulder throbbed in protest.

"The doctor'll see you any second now, I promise. Just don't fall asleep, okay?"

Ally wasn't in any position to be making such promises, but Ted was too tired to point that out. Exhaustion aside, he wasn't in any danger of falling asleep. The paramedics hadn't given him any painkillers, so he had the stretching, stabbing pain in and around his shoulder to keep him awake. Not that it mattered. "That's outdated," he mumbled on an exhale.

"What?" She turned to face him, her eyes puffy, little smudges of mascara on her cheeks. Ted wished his arm worked, so he could wipe them away for her. Then, through the fog, he remembered their fight. What he'd said, what she hadn't said.

"You're allowed to sleep even if you have a concussion." He winced. "The rules aren't what they were when—when we were kids."

"Oh."

Trying not to shift his weight, Ted extracted his hand from hers.

She resisted, at first and then seemed to remember herself. Ally folded her hands in her lap and looked like she might start to cry again.

Shit.

"Sorry," she whispered, looking straight ahead and blinking rapidly. "How does it feel?"

"Which?"

Her eyes were on a kid, asleep in his father's lap. They sat in the waiting area, not far from Ted's curtained alcove. They'd been here when the ambulance had brought Ted and Ally, and he could only assume the reason they hadn't taken priority over Ted had to do with the urgency, or lack thereof, of the child's injury. Without looking away, Ally clarified. "Your head, I mean. But your shoulder, too. How do they feel?"

Ted opened his mouth to respond, but at that moment a nurse appeared, smiling grimly.

"Theodore Lewis?" He was holding a clipboard.

Ted nodded, then winced. "That's me. Ted."

Ally stood, awkwardly shifting in her gear. The emergency responders had long since cut Ted out of his, to better access his shoulder. "And I'm Ally, his—friend."

Ted winced again.

"Right." The nurse looked down at his clipboard. "Your intake suggests a dislocated shoulder and a concussion. We'll want to test for the concussion first, assuming you've previously completed a baseline, because the painkillers we're going to give you before we reset your shoulder will pretty much knock you out. Think you can handle leaving your shoulder like that a little longer? You're right-handed?"

Ted confirmed this monosyllabically, without moving his head or arm. "How long before I can have the painkillers?"

He was trying not to sound desperate or drug-seeking or whatever. But it hurt. His shoulder felt like it had been torn in two. Which, he supposed, it had, in a way. Christ, he felt nauseous.

"We'll administer an IV in about twenty minutes. Have you ever taken the SCAT 5 baseline?"

"What?" Through the fog in his head, Ted couldn't remember what the acronym meant.

Mercifully, Ally jumped in. "The Sports Concussion Assessment Tool, 5th Edition? Yes, I have his baseline results here." Her hand slightly shaky, she held out a wrinkled sheet of paper. "Our captain made us all take them, prior to play."

"Glad to hear it," the nurse replied, scanning the sheet she'd handed him. "I'll be back in a moment with a tablet on which you, Ted, can take the assessment again for comparison. There will be some physical tests, too, but it's important to get an immediate read on your symptoms so we can assess the severity of your concussion and treat and monitor accordingly. I'll bring Dr. Sheffield with me, when I return, so that she can oversee your testing."

"Right. Thanks." The nurse seemed to waver in front of him, like a mirage in an empty desert, and suddenly Ted swayed. Ally caught him, however, supporting him on his good side.

"Try not to move. If you need to vomit, there's a pan under the bed. And tell me if you do."

"Do what?" Ted rubbed his temple with his free hand, taking practiced breaths.

"Vomit. It's a red flag symptom. We're watching for bleeds."

Wren arrived forty-five minutes after Ted and Ally had been ushered in, not long after the doctor had finished testing him for a concussion. Ally texted her their location: down the hall, to the right, in another curtained area. They'd moved Ted again, to allow for greater privacy and fewer disturbances.

Here, Wren texted back,

"I'll just be a minute," Ally told the nurse from earlier, who nodded even as he monitored Ted. "Our friend is dropping something off."

Ally stepped into the brightly lit hallway and immediately doubled over as it all hit her again. The way Ted's shoulder, then head, had crunched into the boards. The fact that it had been her fault. *She* felt sick.

"Bryant."

Ally straightened as her captain and friend walked down the hall, a small duffel slung over her shoulder. "Wren," she breathed in relief.

"Is Ted asleep?" She handed Ally the bag, presumably containing a change of clothes. She was still wearing the sweaty shorts and t-shirt she'd worn under her gear, which was in a pile by Ted's bed.

"No, he's just resting. I don't think he can sleep, with the pain that he's in. Although, they did just give him some kind of twilight opiate, so he'll probably be in and out of it."

"For his shoulder?"

"Yeah, they're gonna reset it, soon. They just—it's a busy night. And he's stable, so there's no real rush, I guess."

"They test him for a concussion yet?"

Ally nodded, swallowing. "I don't remember exactly what the nurse said, but they had him redo the test and apparently he's two standard deviations different or something like that. I'm not sure what it means, specifically, it kind of went over my head, but basically he has a bad concussion." She bit her lip. "Not as bad as it could have been though. I described the hit for the doctor, and she said that his shoulder hitting the boards probably saved him from a serious spinal injury—she said it absorbed some of the force of the impact, so it wasn't all on his head and neck."

Wren nodded. "Good." She paused, taking a moment to assess her. Ally was sure she looked a fright. Her hair was dirty and she probably smelled too. "I heard about what happened in the locker room."

Ally, who had been watching a nurse switch a saline drip, turned her wide, miserable eyes on Wren. "He loves me, Wren." She paused before adding, "Except, how can he? After…"

"What happened to Lewis is not your fault," Wren said firmly. Her tone brooked no disagreement. "You were riling up the other team's players, sure, but the choice to make that hit? That's on the other guy, not you. You couldn't have stopped him, just as you didn't force his hand."

"Wren, you don't understand…"

"You think I don't get it, Ally? You think I've never nearly lost a teammate—a friend—on the ice? In all my years playing? Hockey is a dangerous sport. We all know the risks. But that doesn't make it any easier to accept when an accident happens."

"That was no accident," Ally ground out. "And Ted isn't just my teammate, or my friend."

Wren eyed her appraisingly. "So, you love him, too?"

Ally shrugged hopelessly. "I don't know. I think maybe I've loved him for a while. He's so… good. Fundamentally. And he makes me feel alive, again. After everything, I…"

Wren was silent for a moment and Ally began to fall back into her fear. Then her captain spoke. "Don't tell him yet. Wait, until you're sure."

Ally opened her mouth to argue. "But I am—"

"Because if you're not sure, if it's just grief and fear and guilt speaking, and you mislead him…" Wren sighed. "All I'm saying is, he's a good man. Like you said. He doesn't deserve to be toyed with."

"I would never!" Ally protested.

Wren watched her. "I know. But you might not mean to." She clapped a hand on Ally's shoulder. "C'mon, get changed. I can't stay long but I'll look in on Lewis while you're freshening up. And I'll be back with the rest of the team in the morning."

Ally nodded, then made her way to the nearest bathroom. The hospital was a bit of a maze, and she had to ask for directions twice, but eventually she found herself in a large, sterile room, lined with sinks on one side and stalls on the other. As she performed her ablutions, she thought back to what Wren had said.

She was wrong, of course. Ally needed to tell Ted how she felt. If she didn't tell him now, how would he ever know? What if she didn't tell him, and then she never got another chance? What if he cut her out of his life completely? She wouldn't blame him. She'd brought him nothing but suffering.

Having washed her face and underarms until she smelled like hospital soap and not cold sweat, she pulled a comb out of the bag and brushed her hair. The rat's nest reduced, she picked a stall at random and started shedding her sweat-drenched clothes for clean garments. It was all Wren's stuff, so it didn't fit exactly, but it was comfortable—a NWHL t-shirt, a Team USA sweatshirt, and plain black leggings. And fresh socks, a size too big.

When Ally emerged from the bathroom and made her way back to Ted's room, Wren was waiting for her outside, having gathered up Ally's hockey gear.

Ally hadn't been sure, when they were taking Ted away, whether or not she had time to change completely, so she'd gone to the hospital in full gear, looking like a fool. Ally didn't care. She had just needed to be there. For herself, but mostly for Ted. To make sure he was taken care of. To make sure he wasn't alone. To make sure he was okay. Or at least, that the damage wasn't irreversible. The damage she'd done to him.

Ally leaned against the grey wall, heaving a hard breath. It hurt, this love. That was how she knew it *was* love. Not even guilt could cause such nausea. Which wasn't to say that the guilt wasn't overpowering.

"Hey." Wren once again put a hand on Ally's shoulder. The weight of it was comforting. "Don't do that."

Ally straightened, after a second. "Do what?"

"Don't get inside your own head. If you can't stay the night, I'm sure—"

Ally glared at her friend. "I can and I will. Ted needs me."

Wren watched her thoughtfully. "It might be the other way around, too." Before Ally had a chance to respond to a statement she was admittedly sure was true, Wren smiled kindly. "Then I won't linger, Bryant. Hospital's full enough as is. Call if you need me—I'll be back with the others in the AM."

"We may not be here." The thought had occurred to her in the bathroom, as she'd changed, thanks to something the nurse had said earlier.

Wren's brows pulled together. "What do you mean? Won't they want to keep him overnight, to monitor him?"

"The nurse—he told me that they may not have enough beds to keep Ted. Apparently, Saturday nights are busy in Manhattan ERs," she added, dryly. "Plus, his concussion isn't all that bad. I mean, it isn't good but the nurse is confident there isn't a bleed or else he'd be... Well, he'd be in worse shape than he is now."

"Text me when you have updates," Wren replied, after a long moment. "If they kick him to the curb, take him back to his place and we'll all visit him there. You found his keys?"

Ally nodded, feeling entirely too awake and yet exhausted all the same. "Yep. They were in his coat pocket."

"Take care of yourself, Ally." It wasn't a command; it was a plea.

Out beyond the bounds of his bedroom, Ted heard the elevator door open. Ally jumped up as footsteps echoed in the foyer. "That'll be them."

Ted nodded, not sure who 'they' were, but past the point of caring. He was in his own bed, at long last, with a sling around his left arm and his favorite pillow under his head. Ally had spent half an hour adjusting it so it was just right. She hadn't left his side since three, and then only briefly.

A minute later, Ally reappeared, followed by their captain and assistant captain. Their friends.

"Well, well, well." Matt smiled down at him. "You look better than I thought you would."

Wren frowned. "He looks like shit. Check out the bruising on his shoulder." It was true, his bare upper arm was a mottled mix of blues and purples beneath the sling.

"Good morning to you, too." It was morning, wasn't it? Ted shook his head slightly, as if to clear it, and immediately regretted the movement. It jostled his brain and shoulder, both of which had had enough jostling for the foreseeable future.

Matt crossed the room to his side. "How do you feel, man?"

Ted shrugged, then winced. "It hurts. Not as bad as when they popped it back in, but…"

"I can tell." He turned to Ally. "When's his next dose?"

She walked around to the other side of the bed, where his discharge papers and meds schedule rested on his bedside table. "Not until ten."

Wren joined Ally and started flipping through the stapled sheets. "Huh. They've got you on the good stuff, Lewis."

"Not for long," he managed. Talking was tiring.

"The team's worried sick," Matt said, and Ted was reminded that the other man stood by his side. "They'll come 'round to check on you, Ted." His expression must have grown panicked, because Matt clarified, "Not all at once, don't worry."

Ted relaxed.

To his left, Ally yawned. "I'm going to go make a pot of coffee—assuming you brought some?"

Wren nodded, putting down the papers and pulling a bag of ground coffee and an aero-press out of her backpack. "Why am I not surprised that *Teddy* here only drinks tea?"

"It's better for you!" He protested weakly, as Ally left the room.

Matt chuckled. "Health nut."

He refocused on his friend, who was still standing by his bedside. "What happened with the game? Did we have to forfeit?"

Matt waved a hand in the air. "Nah, man, don't worry about that."

"Matt—"

"They've suspended the player who hit you. We've rescheduled the rest of the game; we're going to play the third period in a couple weeks, when we meet again. Personally, I think we'll do fine with the delay. The team needs some time, anyway, given how rattled everyone is."

Ted shut his eyes and sighed. "Sorry."

"Hey. Look at me." Ted opened his eyes again, reluctantly. "This is not your fault. You are not to blame. Capisce?"

He nodded, slowly so as not to worsen his headache.

"Now, that's probably enough small talk for you, for now. Get some rest. I'm gonna go get a cup of whatever Ally's brewing." He started for the door. "I'm taking over for her, by the way, so she can get some sleep."

That made sense. But he couldn't let Ally leave without

putting an end to the tension between them. It had only gotten worse, as the hours dragged on. She practically vibrated with nervous, guilty energy. "Hey, Matt? While you're in the kitchen, could you…"

Matt turned back at the foot of Ted's bed. "Yeah?"

"Could you send in Ally? I need to talk to her."

Matt's eyes softened. He'd been there, in the locker room. Heard Ally's reaction to his declaration. Her rejection of it—of him. "Of course. I'll round her up and send her in."

A minute later, Ally reentered his bedroom, glass in hand. There were circles like bruises under her eyes and she was chewing on her lip anxiously. She greeted Ted with a half-hearted wave.

"I started in on the unopened cold brew—couldn't wait for the water to boil." She smiled sheepishly, then her expression grew nervous again. "Matt said you wanted to talk to me?"

Needed. He needed to talk to her.

Ted turned to Wren, who was still perusing his discharge papers with a frown. "Can we have a minute?"

She nodded, replacing the packet on his bedside table, and made a swift exit. Not before exchanging a glance with Ally, whose eyes then flitted nervously back to Ted.

"What's going on, Ted? Is it your head? Do you want me to plump the pillow—"

No, it wasn't his head. It was his heart. She'd cleaved it clean in two. "No, I'm fine." He wasn't, really. Everything hurt, and the daylight, though dimmed by the curtains, was too bright. He felt nauseous and weak and his shoulder ached like a son of a bitch, despite the painkillers, which themselves were muddying his already muddled mind. "I just… About what I said, in the locker room."

Her eyes went wide. "Ted, I—"

"No, don't." He took a centering breath and shifted slightly against the pillows. He had to say this. "I love you.

But you don't love me." Her eyes widened still, and she looked like she was about to protest but, instead of letting her lie in a misguided attempt to spare him from inevitable hurt, Ted continued. "You don't love me back. And that's…"

It wasn't okay, it wasn't fine, it wasn't anything but awful. But Ted had to communicate, had to be clear, through the throbbing of his shoulder and the fog in his knocked-about brain. "It is what it is. And I'm not angry with you."

"Not even for… Ted, it was my fault!" Her voice was a little too loud, and when he winced she flinched. But that didn't stop her from continuing, in a furious whisper. "If I hadn't been so focused on riling up the other team, that *asshole* would have never—"

"I'm not angry with you," he repeated, and it was true. "I'm just… tired." Waves of exhaustion started to roll over him, like a cosmic ocean lulling him to sleep. "And I need you to know that I don't want to hear it."

"Hear what?"

He sighed, rubbing his temple with his good hand. "If you've got some speech, some protest, some… declaration… Just, don't. I can't. It's guilt, Ally. It's not love."

"Ted, you don't know—"

He held her gaze, determined. "I know you stayed the night. I know you came in the ambulance with me. I know you held my hand, even when I… I couldn't hold yours back. But it's not love, Ally, that compelled you. It's guilt."

She stared at him, her jaw slack. Her voice was a whisper, when she found it. "Please, don't do this…"

"I rushed you. And I'm sorry for that. But you… you don't want me. You never have, not really." The words, the thoughts required to form them, were sapping his strength, and Ted could feel sleep tugging on his eyelids. He slurred, slightly, as the world seemed to tilt on its axis, and Ally with it. "I'm letting you go, Ally. Matt will take care of me. Get some sleep. Go. Please."

And don't come back.

A tear slipped from the corner of his eye, even as he heard Ally sniff once, twice. It was painful, but the pain she felt wouldn't break her. Soon enough, she'd be fine.

He was the one who'd been driven out of his mind by love, by loss, by the stricken look in her eyes when he'd let slip the truth about the extent of his feelings for her. He didn't know how he would ever recover. But Ally? She'd be fine. It wasn't love. And he didn't want to hear her lie.

CHAPTER 21
SNOWDROP

"Christ on a bike, you really haven't slept."

"Thanks, V." Ally's tone was as dry as the deserts of Arizona. Not that she'd ever been, but a girl could dream. A girl could dream about a lot of things. "I had some bad nightmares."

"About Ted?"

She'd told Vanessa about the accident, if you could call it that. She'd texted her from the hospital. And later, from the subway on the way back to her apartment, the messages struggling to send from the underground tunnels. But she hadn't called. She wasn't sure, then, that she could trust herself not to cry. As it turned out, she'd been right. After Ted had told her to go, as soon as she was home with Heathcliff, she'd come undone.

"Yeah." Ally scratched the back of her neck. It would be a while before Ted could do the same without pain, with his shoulder the way it was... "I dreamed that..." She'd dreamed that it had been worse. She'd dreamed that Ted had died. She'd dreamed that she'd been the one to hit him, to send him sprawling out on the ice. Her guilt, her anger, her anguish, it had all bled through. She'd dreamed that he'd broken up with her—oh, wait. That one was the truth. "Anyway, it's over now."

"Your nightmare? I hope so."

"No, I mean…" She took a deep breath. "Ted and me. He…"

"Oh, Ally…" Vanessa pushed her rolling chair away from her desk, swiveling it so that she sat closer to Ally. She took her hand. "Do you want to talk about it?"

Ally shook her head.

"Okay." Vanessa wove their fingers together. "But I'm here for you, babe."

They stayed like that, for a few minutes. Ally's breathing slowed and her tear-ducts eventually ceased their production. She felt the warmth of her friend's fingers, safe harbor in the storm of her emotions. But all good things came to an end, and eventually Harold spotted them.

"This isn't social hour, Ms. Bryant. Have you finished that email blast, Ms. Chen?"

Vanessa sighed. "No, sir. I'll get back to it."

Reluctantly, Ally relinquished her friend's hand. An idea occurred to her, then. "Excuse me, I just have to check with the Green Team about that copy they wanted me to draft. For the new product they're pitching." It was absolute bullshit, but Harold didn't need to know that.

"I wasn't aware that you were working with Mr. Lewis' team. You do know, he's out sick?"

She knew. She was the very reason he was 'out sick.' "Yes, sir. It'll only take me a moment. And I can consult one of the other team members."

"Very well. But be quick." Harold turned on his heel and headed back to his office.

Vanessa rolled her immaculately lined eyes, whispering, "He's the worst, truly."

But Ally was already on her feet. "I'll be right back, V."

A minute later, she stood before Sam Lyons, the actual

copywriter for Ted's team. They'd trained together, in the early days. He looked up at her, surprise flitting across his features. "Ally, to what do I owe the pleasure?"

"I need to talk to you. About Ted."

Sam nodded. "I heard he got in an accident, at the rink."

Ally shook her head. "It wasn't an accident, but that's beside the point."

"O-kay. What is the point?"

"I need you and the rest of your team to visit Ted."

Sam's eyebrows shot up. "In the hospital?"

"No, at his apartment. He went home. They didn't have the beds to keep him and his concussion isn't as bad as—" She paused. "He's alone, most of the day." Even between the many members of the team, they couldn't pull together a full-time nursing schedule. Besides, Ted had insisted that he was fine, so long as he had a supply of smoothies and access to all the audiobooks Jeremy Irons had ever narrated.

Sam's brows lowered, then knit. "Why aren't you with him? Don't you have any PTO?"

Shame rolled like thunder through Ally. She blinked back the accompanying rain. "He—he doesn't want me there." Her voice shook embarrassingly.

"Dude..." Sam looked up at her pityingly. "What happened?"

Ally hooked a nearby chair and rolled it over. She slid into it, feeling somewhat like a slinky. All tension, no self-control. "I think we broke up." Just saying it, she felt nauseous. "I mean, he told me he loved me and I—"

"Ohhh..." Understanding dawned on Sam, relaxing his features. "He told you too soon, didn't he?"

"What?" Her head whipped up.

Sam grimaced sympathetically. "Ted told us—me, Jordan, Kent, no one else—that he was in love with you."

Ally stared at him. "When?"

"I dunno. Saturday? Whenever you went home to wherever."

"Syosset."

"Right. Well, Ted called, and said he wanted to hang out because his girlfriend was out of town and he needed company. I think he's been making an effort to make friends. Good dude. Anyway, we all got together and it was good. But we had a bit of guy talk. And Ted told us some stuff. Namely, that he was in love with you, but you weren't in love with him."

"I—"

"Don't sweat it," Sam said, kindly. "Love comes slowly to some and all at once for others. Just because he fell first doesn't mean you won't fall at all. It isn't a race. Don't let the pressure get to you, dude." He stretched his neck and back— something Ted couldn't do without stabbing pain, Ally thought bitterly. "Ted isn't the one applying it, anyway. That's all in your head."

"Thanks, Sam," she replied, dryly. She loved being told that she was the problem. Like she didn't already know it. "I just wish…" That he'd told her in private? That he hadn't brought it up right before a game? Right after she learned she was getting evicted?

Shit, she was getting evicted!

"Whoa, what's wrong?" Sam held up his hands in alarm. "You just got that panicked look that I only ever see when you miss a typo and only realize it after the page is live."

Ally bit her lip. "Do you know anyone looking for a room-mate, Sam?"

"I can ask around. I assume you're asking for you?"

"Yeah. Thanks. Thanks for… everything." He'd given her a lot to think about. "I'd better go before Harold yells at me. But would you—and maybe Kent and Jordan, too—would you go visit Ted? I'm worried he's bored, and lonely, and generally in a lot of pain. He dislocated his shoulder, you know, in the—when he got hit. On top of the concussion."

"Damn, that's gotta be a bitch."

Ally huffed a humorless laugh. "Something like that."

"Sure, Ally. Text me his address?"

"Will do." She bit her lip. "Just… don't say I sent you. And don't let him look at screens!"

"Tell me again why we can't just video chat, Belle?"

His little sister huffed. "See? Your concussion is messing with your memory *and* your common sense." Then, in a practiced, more patient tone of voice, "You shouldn't be looking at screens because they're really taxing. Your brain is trying to heal, and your shoulder, and the light from the screens, plus all the excess information they offer, will exhaust you and probably make you dizzy and possibly slow your healing and certainly interfere with your sleep. So, no video chats and no movies."

Ted sighed and turned the volume down on his phone. "Alright. Then tell me something good, Bluebell." He needed to hear something good, something great, something that would erase the memory of Ally's stricken face when he'd sent her away.

"I got a perfect score on my Chemistry exam! And my Poli-Sci professor liked my paper, even though it was, according to him, 'mildly hyperbolic.' Which is ridiculous because the Reagan administration really did ruin everything for all time."

He smiled, for the first time in days. "That's amazing. I'm so proud of you." She really was the smartest in the family. "Have you told the parents?"

"That Ronald Reagan was the worst? Yes, I tell them every

day. That is, I would, if I spoke to them every day. Speaking of, when was the last time you talked to Mom and Dad?"

"This morning. Mom called to check in." She'd called Sunday and Monday, too. "She insisted that I send her pictures of my discharge papers for one of her doctor friends to look over. No word back yet but she didn't like that they didn't keep me overnight to monitor me. Something about Natasha Richardson." Honestly, it was hard to remember his conversation with his mother. He'd been so groggy, in part due to the brain injury, in part, the painkillers.

"Oh, yeah. That was tragic. You know, she really looked like Princess Di."

"Are you sure it wasn't just the hair?"

He could practically hear Belle frown, in thought. "Maybe. I'd tell you to look up pictures but remember—"

"No screens." Ted shook his head, then winced, regretting it. "Yeah, yeah. I know. But audio's okay, right?"

"Sure, as long as it's not too loud."

"Then maybe I shouldn't be talking to you…" Ted teased, feeling a bit more like himself.

Belle gasped. "I am not loud!" More quietly, she continued, "Well, not right now. I'm practically whispering so as not to give you brain damage. And also because my roommate is asleep. Hangovers, man."

Ted's phone beeped, signaling a second call. "As much as I would love to interrogate you about your weekday drinking habits, I've gotta let you go. I'm getting another call."

Belle sighed dramatically. "Okay, Monsieur Popular. Just try to squeeze some sleep into that social calendar of yours."

"Bye, Belle."

"Goodnight, sweet prince."

He'd have rolled his eyes, but it would have hurt too much. "Oh, shove off, I'm not *dying*."

She laughed and muttered, "Thank god," then hung up.

The other call was coming from inside the building. Ted took a breath and picked up on the final ring. "Hello?"

It was Albert. "Hello, Mr. Lewis. How is your head?"

"Not so bad as yesterday, thanks." It was kind of his doorman to care. "What's up?"

"You have visitors."

"Oh?"

"A Jordan, a Sam, and a Kent. Should I send them up?"

"Please do. Thank you, Albert."

A few minutes later, the elevator door opened on Ted's floor. "I'm in here," he called out, a little weakly. "And take off your shoes, please."

"Alright, alright. One sec." Sam's voice carried down the hall. In a minute, the man himself appeared at Ted's bedroom door, followed by Jordan and Kent.

"Sweet digs," Jordan said, taking in the massive king-sized bed—and Ted lying immobile in it. "Oh shit—your shoulder!"

Ted grimaced. "It... It feels about as bad as it looks." Ally had held up a mirror for him, before she left, so he could see the damage for himself. Ally...

Ted felt his face sort of crumple, felt tears well and threaten to spill over. But he was determined not to dwell on her. Which was easier said than done, given the fact that her face, shocked and bewildered, kept materializing whenever he closed his eyes. "How—how did you get my address?"

"A little birdie told me," Sam said, cheerfully. "She didn't want you to be alone."

Ted huffed. She had no right, no reason to interfere. It was presumptuous. It was her guilt speaking. "I'm not alone. I was on a call with my sister when you arrived."

Sam nodded. "She didn't want you staring at screens, either."

"I wasn't!"

Jordan raised his hands in a peace-keeping gesture. "Hey,

man. I know your head hurts, and your shoulder hurts, and, well, your heart hurts, too. But we're your friends. You can talk to us."

Kent crossed the room to Ted's bedside, his eyes skipping over Ted's shoulder to find his face. "Sam says you told her too soon."

Sam nodded from the foot of the bed. "Far as I can tell, she got spooked."

Ted frowned. "My girl—my *ex*-girlfriend is not a horse, Sam."

"And you're certain she's your ex-girlfriend? Because the way she's been coordinating your care—"

"I broke up with her." Well, technically he'd never told her it was over, but... She'd gotten the message. He'd seen it in her wide eyes, brown as the coffee she'd neglected to brew. And maybe he'd hurt her, but she'd hurt him first. And his hurt, he knew, was worse. "She doesn't love me. She wasn't ready. It wasn't going to work."

Still, the fact that she'd sent his new friends... No, Ted couldn't think about what that meant. She just felt guilty, probably pitied him.

"Are you sure she doesn't—"

"She doesn't, Sam." His tone was unyielding, if tired.

Kent's expression was pensive. "And you, Ted? Do you still love her, after all that she's done and you've said?"

"She hasn't *done* anything. It wasn't her fault that I got hit. I don't blame her for that." His head ached, but not as much as his heart. Why oh why were his friends making him discuss this? Honesty, however, compelled him to continue, to answer Kent's question. Possibly, the painkillers loosened his lips. "But... yes, I still love her. Sometimes I think I'll always love her." And there it was, that rush of love, that surge of unsuppressable emotion. "But I can't—I have to let her go."

Kent took his good hand and gave it a squeeze. Ted was surprised, he hadn't pegged him for a particularly physically affectionate guy. But it was a comforting gesture, one Ted appreciated.

"Alright, that's enough interrogation for now. You can tell us all about what happened later." Jordan strode over to the bedside table and starting thumbing through the papers there. "According to this, it's time for another smoothie."

"Ally." Dr. Boyd opened the door to her office and ushered Ally inside. "Welcome. Do come in." The steady familiarity of the greeting soothed her, as did the faint lavender scent of Linda's air freshener, enveloping Ally in calm as she entered the large office and made her way to the blue velvet couch. "It's been some time since we last spoke."

Ally settled herself on the couch and turned her phone to silent. "Right, well, there was Friendsgiving."

"Ah, yes. You spent it with Ted, didn't you? And how is he?"

Ally flinched.

"Ally? Are you alright? The last time we spoke, you seemed quite happy." They'd had a long and fruitful conversation about labels and relationships and the like.

"I was." Ally closed her eyes. "But… A lot's happened."

"In the two weeks since our last appointment?"

Ally nodded. "I—" She sighed and opened her eyes to find Linda watching her, carefully. "I suppose I'd better catch you up to speed."

"That might help us make sense of things, yes."

"Well, Friendsgiving was a success." She tried to smile, but it came out more of a grimace. "I met his sister, and he met Kait. And we—" Ally bit her lip at the memory, briefly sweet, now bitter. "We made things official. He didn't push me," she assured Linda, although the doctor had offered no objection. "I was the one who… Whatever. The point is, he was my boyfriend. And I was his girlfriend. He was mine and I was his."

Linda frowned, slightly, but her tone was without judgment. "Was?"

Tears welled behind Ally's eyes but she valiantly blinked them back. "It's complicated. I mean, it isn't, really. I—I fucked it up." She couldn't bear to look at Linda, so her eyes fell instead upon her therapist's collection of books. As if their silent pages could offer solace.

Gently, Linda inquired, "What happened, Ally?"

The words came out in a rush, accompanied by a torrent of tears. "He told me he loved me! In front of everyone and I —I didn't say it back."

Linda was silent for a moment. "Because you don't love him?"

"No!" Ally glared at her therapist. "Because I was—Oh, christ. I was *scared*, Linda. And overwhelmed! And it was so soon—I wasn't ready for love, I was barely ready for a relationship, but—"

"But you do love him?"

"Yes! And it's not just guilt talking, which is what *he* thinks—I really do love him, Linda! And I'm ready. I know I just said I wasn't, but I am. I'm ready. And I would have told him that, too, but, he told me in the *locker room*. In front of everyone. And I was reminded of Everett, his constant controlling PDA—and Ted offered to let me live with him, because I'm being evicted—yes, we can talk about that, just, in a minute—and anyway that made me think about Everett even more because that was, like, his ultimate move—and I just started to panic. And now... It's too late. I told you, I fucked it up."

Linda frowned. "We'll circle back to the eviction later, but first... How did you 'fuck it up?'"

"Because he got hurt. And it's my fault."

"I can imagine that a public rejection would hurt him, yes, but—"

"No!" Ally shook her head wildly, tears streaming. "No, I mean he's hurt, physically. He has a concussion and a—a dislocated shoulder, and he'll be in bed, in pain and bored out of his mind, all week—all because of me! I was the one riling up the other team. I was the one who should have taken the hit. Not him. Never him."

Her sobs subsided slightly, and she looked up to find Linda watching her sympathetically. "I never wanted to hurt him," she whispered. "I—I love him."

Linda nodded pensively. "And how does he feel about what happened?"

Ally almost laughed. "He calls it an accident. Which is only further proof of his brain's being addled by—"

"Ally." Linda's tone was firm. "Allow Ted some agency."

Ally sighed, nodding reluctantly. "I just… I don't know what to do. It's not guilt!"

"Oh?"

"If it were guilt… I already felt this way, before he said he loved me. I just didn't want to admit it to myself, much less to him, since I didn't know yet that he—he *loved* me. And I am ready! I never would have fallen for him if I weren't. I never would have *let* myself love him, if I had doubts about him. About us."

Linda nodded slowly, uncrossing and recrossing her ankles. "You said he loved you. Past tense."

Ally felt fresh tears welling. "Yes. How can he still—after everything that happened… And the way he looks at me now, I—" Abruptly, she fell silent, at a loss for words.

"Have you told Ted you love him? Has he said he no longer loves you, in so many words?"

Ally shook her head, sniffing. "We… He told me—the morning after, he told me to leave. He said it was just guilt keeping me. He told me he was letting me go." She took a steadying breath, the memory like a knife, twisting in her chest. "But he never gave me the chance to tell him how I feel."

Linda frowned. "I think, now that he's had a chance to heal somewhat—he was injured this weekend, yes?"

Ally nodded.

"I think it's time you told him the truth. About your feelings for him, about whether or not you're ready for this."

"There is no *this*!" Ally protested. "He put an end to this. *I* put an end to this, like the fucking fool that I am—"

"Ally."

"What, Linda?" Her tone was acid. "What? Are you going to pretend this bed isn't of my own making?"

"No," the therapist replied, simply. "Are you going to pretend you don't have the power to make things right, to set the record straight? Are you going to play the victim, while insisting you're some kind of villain?"

Ally recoiled. It was the harshest her therapist had ever been with her. Harsh, but fair. After a moment's silence, Ally answered her. "No, I—I suppose not."

"Because if this is love, you have the opportunity to fight for it. And even if it's over between you and Ted, Ted deserves the truth. He deserves to know how you feel. Beyond guilt, beyond shame, beyond fear. Love doesn't come around every year."

Ted was excruciatingly bored. The guys had wanted to come over and hang with him, but he couldn't deprive them of their Friday night. He was pretty sure Kent had a date. So, he turned on an audiobook—*Brideshead Revisited,* not for the first time—and pulled a plate of lasagna from the fridge. As he set about cutting himself a piece, his phone pinged.

It wasn't a typical notification sound; it was specific to an app. To Flutter, the 'dating app of the future,' as one of his new friends had referred to it. To be honest, he wasn't sure why he hadn't deleted it when he'd been dating Ally. He supposed he'd just been so wrapped up in her, he'd forgotten all about it. And now...

Well, he might as well get rid of it. Ted wasn't ready to date again so soon. And, a little voice nagged in the back of his head, he wasn't even sure where things stood with Ally. So, Ted unlocked his phone and opened the app, intending to take down his profile. But what he saw on that screen stopped him.

A match.

He'd matched with someone.

Someone had prioritized him, according to the app's rules of engagement. And not just anyone, but Ally.

Ted hesitated but, after a moment, he clicked to open it.

I'm sorry, Ted. And that's not all I want to say to you, but the rest... I'd prefer to say it in person. So, call me. Please.

Short and bittersweet.

He wondered why she hadn't just texted him. Or called. Not calling him, he supposed, was her way of putting the ball in his court, of giving him control. But not texting him...

Was this—could it be—a romantic gesture? A sign, a signal, something more than an apology? Hope blossomed in Ted's heart, like a single snowdrop at winter's end.

CHAPTER 22
CRAZY

Ted realized, belatedly, that he'd left Ally on read. He realized because he'd spent all of Saturday reading and rereading her message, and all of Sunday morning, too. Sunday afternoon, it occurred to him that his read receipts might be on. Up until then, he hadn't given it any thought.

Shit.

He hadn't called her. He had no intention of calling her, of listening to her talk from a distance of seventy blocks. It wasn't because he didn't want to hear her voice. Sometimes, he thought the only cure for his near constant headache these days would be the sound of her: sweet, when she wasn't irate —and even then, there was a warmth about her.

But he didn't want it filtered through 5G and nervous uncertainty. So, instead of calling her, he was going to watch her play some hockey. And then, after the game, they'd talk. Not in the locker room, in front of everyone, but someplace private. Where she could say whatever it was she wanted to say. Whatever was left to say.

Ted didn't know what Ally wanted to talk about. He hoped—but he wasn't going to get his hopes up. She probably just wanted to let him know that she didn't love him, couldn't love him, after everything. It had been guilt speaking, and grief, when she'd tried to tell him that she loved him, in the hospital. She hadn't been thinking straight. It was too much, too soon. Ted was too much, with his cavernous loneliness, his cravings for her and her alone.

And maybe Ted wasn't thinking straight, coming to this game. Maybe he was being too much, once more. He was, without a doubt, setting himself up for heartbreak. But he owed it to Ally to hear her out, to let her say her piece. Maybe then, when the snow settled, Ted would know peace. He doubted it, but he needed closure as badly as he needed her. And he was determined to get the former, if not the girl.

Woman, he reminded himself, with a faint smile. But it faded as he stepped off the subway.

It felt strange, to arrive at this rink without a stick in hand. But the doctors had been clear: he couldn't play. Not until after the holidays. Inhaling, and immediately regretting it as he caught a whiff of urine and trash, he made his way up the stairs, out of the subway station. It was a short walk to the rink. Once inside, he took a right, instead of his usual left, and strode in the direction of the stands.

"Ted!" Hardit smiled warmly at him, rising to greet him. "How's your head?"

They shook hands. "It's better, thanks."

"You gave us quite a scare," a woman in a faux fur coat said, from her seat beside Hardit. "I'm Nikki's mother, but you can call me Carol. Would you like a seat warmer?"

Ted smiled, and reached past Hardit to shake Carol's hand. He accepted the cushion with some confusion, never having used one before. "Do I just… sit on it?"

Carol, Hardit, and the rest of the Monsters fans laughed. "I'm glad to see your brain is still working, after that hit," Carol said in reply. "Go on, sit."

Ted did as he was told.

"By the way, I'm Matt's girlfriend, Shanae," another woman said, offering him her manicured hand.

A tall man with a salt-and-pepper mane waved. "I'm Jim. Karl's boyfriend." Karl was a quiet man in his late thirties who played defense. Ted waved back, then turned to look out at the ice.

Warm ups were over, and the game was about to start. They'd adjusted the line up to accommodate Ted's absence, putting Wren back in as starting center with Madison and Ally as wings. Ally was on the far side, her front facing the stands. Her opponent jostled her, but for once she didn't retaliate. Just kept her stick under his, her knees bent. For all that Ted was in her line of vision, she seemed too intent on the puck drop to note his presence.

He was here. In the stands. He was watching her. He had been ever since the puck drop.

After leaving her on read all weekend—which had been a special kind of torture, devised by the devil just for her—he was *here.*

Ally struggled to rein in her spiraling mind, which was coming up with all sorts of circumstances and scenarios, good and bad, which explained his presence. The best was that he was here to accept her apology. The worst was that he wasn't even here for her at all.

"Ally!" Madison whooshed past her with the puck, hissing, "Head out of the clouds!"

Ally jumped to attention, forcing herself to look at her friend and not her ex-boyfriend. Christ. Ex-boyfriend. It hurt even to think it. So, she wouldn't think about it. She would continue to do what she'd done all game, which was to focus on the play at hand and not the pain in her heart—and certainly not the person in the stands.

The second period went smoothly, no goals scored on either side—same as the first. After a brief intermission, in which Ally refused to let herself so much as glance in his direction, they took back to the ice. So far, Ally hadn't racked up a single penalty. And she didn't intend to start now. She would play this game clean—to prove to Wren that she could, so that Ted would see that she'd changed, and above all for herself. She needed a clean game almost as much as, possibly even more than, she needed a win. She was better than she'd been.

"Bryant, where's that head at?"

Ally swiveled to face her captain. "Doesn't matter. What's the play?"

The ref was approaching, a puck in his hand. Wren, Madison, and Ally were huddled near the opposing blue line, waiting for the whistle, while the defense—Nikki and Skye—settled into their starting stances.

Wren spoke in a hushed voice, wary of giving away their plans to the other team. "I'll send the puck back to Skye, they'll pass it to Nikki, she'll dump it around, and then I want you to engage with their wing on the boards. Send it back to point if you get possession, or over to Madison, who'll be waiting by the crease."

Ally nodded, but Wren wasn't done.

"Keep it clean on the boards, Ally." A warning, but not without a degree of understanding. The pressure was on.

To Ally's surprise, the face off played out pretty much exactly as Wren had intended, and Ally was able to recover the puck after Nikki wrapped it around the boards. Madison was unable to get free of the defenseman's stick, however, and Ally couldn't drop the puck back to point because Skye wasn't in position, for some reason. An abundance of caution, perhaps.

So, Ally took a deep breath and let loose her wristshot—the one Wren had once called "wobbly" but which she'd been practicing with Ted for weeks until it improved. The puck flew through the air—past Wren, who was locked in combat with the other team's center, past Madison, whose stick was tangled between the defenseman's legs, and past the goalie's glove, which closed around empty air.

As soon as the puck hit the back of the net, Ally's arms went straight into the air. Cheers broke out on the bench, and her teammates who were on the ice skated over, clobbering Ally with bear hugs. She'd put the Manhattan Monsters on the scoreboard. And not a second too soon.

The rest of the game, the remaining ten minutes, was tense as the Monsters were forced to defend their one point lead against an onslaught of complex offensive plays. Somehow, no doubt due in part to the fact that they didn't have to kill a single penalty, the Monsters succeeded.

After shaking hands with their opponents, they took to the locker room. It was a raucous affair, as Matt had brought beer, and the energy was as high as the rink's domed ceiling. But Ally couldn't quite bring herself to celebrate. Not when she herself was a still a bundle of nerves over Ted's surprise appearance. Was he still there, in the stands? Would he be waiting for her when she undressed?

Ally tore off her pads, shoving them haphazardly in her bag, determined not to let him disappear without first— what? Talking to him? Begging for his forgiveness? Apologizing for everything? Ally may have been the one to ask him to talk to her, but his lack of a response meant she hadn't actually planned anything yet beyond the vague outline of an apology.

"See you later, guys!" Ally slipped out the door without waiting for a goodbye. She would stop in the bathroom, on the way to the stands, to brush her hair and splash the sweat off her skin. She would—

"Ally."

She stopped short, her bag nearly knocking her over. "Ted!" She was breathless, and an octave higher than her normal pitch. "What are you doing here?" Why was he in the hallway? He was supposed to be in the stands! This wasn't what she'd planned. Lord, she definitely smelled—and probably looked a mess. But he'd seen her worse, hadn't he?

"I was waiting for you," he replied, simply. His left arm was still in a sling. "You said you wanted to talk."

Ally nodded. "I, uh…" She laughed, nervously. "I'm sorry, I really wasn't expecting to see you—"

"Ally, look. You don't have to apologize. It's not your fault I got hit. I don't blame you. So you don't need to feel guilty." He sounded so grave, so glum. But resolute.

"Ted, that's not what I wanted to apologize for. I mean, I still blame myself for that hit. But that's not why I reached out." She took a deep breath, even as her heart seemed to jump up into her throat. "I'm sorry for reacting the way I did, to your… declaration. I know you didn't want to rush me, and I know I reacted about as badly as humanly possible, given that you were just telling me you loved me." There it was, the L word. "And there's no shame in loving someone. Regardless of whether or not it's requited."

"Ally, if you're trying to tell me that you don't love me, I don't need to hear it, okay?" Ted laughed without humor. "Trust me, I've got the message." He started to turn away.

"No! Ted. Ted, look at me."

Sighing, he turned back to face her. "What?"

It was now or never. She had to tell him. She *wanted* to tell him. Not just him, everyone. The whole world! But Ted first. "I love you, Ted." She grinned. It felt so good to say it. "I love you."

His blue eyes were wary, bruised. "Ally, we've been over this. Trust me, I don't—"

"No, Ted!" She let her bag fall to the ground, punctuating her outburst. "*You* have to trust *me* when I tell you that I know the truth. That I know myself well enough now to know what I do and don't feel. Do you trust me? *Can* you trust me?"

He paused for a long minute. Several of their teammates filed out of the locker room, beers and bags in hand, but they went the other direction down the hall. Ted's eyes were wide and watery. He seemed torn, until Ally reached out and took his good hand, willing him to give in to the truth, to give up his doubts.

At last, staring down at their interlocked fingers, his answer was breathless, a whispered, "Yes."

"Then trust me when I tell you this: Theodore Lewis, I love you."

He tried to sweep her into his arms but the bruising on his shoulder must have made itself known because he winced, and even his good arm fell.

Ally stepped into what would have been the circle of his arms, and cupped his cheek in her hand. "I can hold you as well as you can hold me."

Gently, she snaked her arms around him, pulling him close. Ted buried his face in her loose, sweat-tinged hair, inhaling deeply. Ally burrowed against his jawline, pressing kisses to the curve of his neck. They stood like that, tangled in each other, for a long minute, swaying slightly. Then Ally pulled back and said the rest of her piece. "I love you, Ted, but I'm not ready to move in with you."

His eyes found hers and they were warm, and filled with understanding. "That's okay," he said, a little gruffly. He cleared his throat. "I should never have pressured you—"

"You didn't, not really." Ally smiled ruefully. "I overreacted because… Well, I can explain more later, but basically because I used to live with my abusive ex-boyfriend, Everett. And he held it over me, constantly. Moving in with him was supposed to make my life easier, happier, better—but in the end it turned out to be just another form of abuse. Your offer —your kind, thoughtful, considerate offer—it turned out to be a bit of a trigger for me. I'm sorry. And I'm working on it in therapy."

"Hey, don't be sorry. I didn't know, but I still shouldn't have rushed you. I can't imagine how scary it must have been, to be transported back to that time in your life."

"Thanks, Ted." Ally sniffed, but smiled through the swell of tears. "I really appreciate the fact that you always try to understand, even though you don't know what it's like first-hand." She paused, taking a breath. "Anyway, that doesn't mean that living together is forever off the table. I just need a little time to sort myself out, first."

He smiled back, sweetly. "Sounds good to me. And when —or if—you ever do move in with me... I wasn't kidding about the second bedroom. It's yours, if you want it." His eyes sparkled with mischief. "I wouldn't dream of depriving you of your independence."

She stood on her tiptoes and knocked noses with him playfully. "A smart, sweet, sexy boyfriend *and* a room of my own? Woolf wouldn't know what to say."

She could feel her first orgasm fizzing at the edges of her consciousness. Her first, tonight, because he'd promised her many, many more. It swelled like the notes of symphony, like the wind up to a slapshot. And then his fingers dipped inside of her, teasing and toying and touching her. Deeper and deeper he delved, hooking his index and middle within her until she was caught, until she cried out—he stroked and she squirmed and Ally could feel a single tear roll down her temple and suddenly, suddenly she was free.

Ally let the vibrator roll away, loose, until it landed with a soft thud against the sheets and continued to buzz. She heaved a breath, certain that she looked a mess—she wasn't like the porn stars, who looked sexy when they came. Her face scrunched up and she screwed her eyes closed and she held the air in her lungs until it was done. But it didn't matter, because he'd seen her come before. Opening her eyes on an exhale, she saw Ted sucking on his fingers, the fingers that he'd just pulled out of her. When he saw her watching, he winked. Then he reached up to stroke her cheek.

"Did you—"

She huffed a laugh, blissed out and breathless. "Do you even have to ask?"

He blushed. "I just wanted to be sure." He paused, picking up the toy and turning it off. "The vibrator worked." They had stopped at her apartment on the way to his place, to pick it up. A brilliant forethought, on his part.

"It usually does." She smirked, remembering the first time they'd used it together. "Give it here."

"I hope you're not planning on putting it away."

Ally shook her head, inordinately pleased by his enthusiasm. "God, no. I just think, if you're open to it, it might be your turn." She twisted the bullet's base until it rumbled back to life.

Ted's eyes lit up. "I've never…"

Ally sat up. "I know. But it could be fun?"

"I can only imagine—but first…" He smiled, his hand straying to the waistband of his boxers, where his cock was straining against the fabric. "I want to do that again. I want you to come, and I want to be inside of you when you do. So I can feel you."

"I'm pretty sure you just did," she said, with an amused glance at his free hand. The other was still immobilized by the sling.

Ted rolled his eyes, but there was a certain heat to his stare. "Don't make me spell it out for you."

Ally grinned. "Spell it out for me, Harvard. Put that poor education to use."

Her boyfriend sighed, shifting closer so that he could whisper in her ear. "I want to feel you, your… cunt. Tight and wet and hot."

Ally's breathing hitched.

"I want to feel you around me, enveloping me, encompassing me entirely." Ted pulled away to meet her gaze, his blue eyes a little wry. He started to explain, "I'm a bit rusty, when it comes to talking dirty…"

Ally placed her hand against his sternum, silencing him. His heartbeat steadied her, a rhythm that soothed her soul. "I want to feel you, too. Hard and heavy. Deep inside of me. I never want you to leave—"

He caught the words from her lips in a fervent kiss, whispering, "Then I never will."

And then he was easing her down again, onto her back. And her hands were tugging the waistband of his boxers down, her thumb finding the head of his cock, seeping anticipation, her fingers wrapping around his velvety girth. She opened her legs again, her cunt ready and aching for him—only him, always him.

He propped himself up with his free hand and angled his body so that it aligned with hers, allowing her to do the work of guiding him to her entrance. When she nodded, he began to push—shallow thrusts, at first, to acclimate their bodies, but quickly sliding deeper as he discovered how wet, how relaxed, how ready that orgasm had left her.

In an instant that felt like an eternity—or, perhaps, an eternity that felt like an instant—he was buried to the hilt. Ally couldn't help, didn't try to stop, the sound that escaped her lips. The squeak of pleasure, the sigh of satisfaction. Ted's eyes met hers, wide and wondrous, and she felt she could happily drown in their twin depths.

"How do you feel?" He was breathing heavily.

She thought about this. Then she smiled up at him. "Pleasantly full."

He captured her mouth in a carnivorous kiss, mumbling against her lips, "Fuck 'pleasantly.'" And then he sort of snapped his hips, and just like that he brought her world down around her, like reality was just a house of cards.

She gasped his name and he groaned hers. Then he kept it up, thrust after powerful thrust. Putting that ass of his to good use.

Keeping one hand on the back of Ted's neck, Ally fumbled blindly with the other for the vibrator she'd set aside. Having found it, she flicked it on with expert fingers, then brought it to the place where their bodies met. Ted moaned as the vibrations travelled through her and into him, setting the two of them ablaze. His thrusts became erratic as he struggled to maintain a rhythm in the face of overpowering pleasure. Ally's own movements—the twist of her hips, the arching of her back—faded to frenzy as she felt herself start to fall apart.

It was so fast, so intense, but there was no shame in the speed of their mutual release, aided by this little, versatile machine.

"Are you—"

"I'm—"

"Ted!" She hardly recognized her own voice, high and keening.

Ted's eyes, for some time screwed shut, opened wide with wild abandon, disbelieving desperation. "Allegra—"

His breath caught even as she held hers; a great shudder rolled like thunder through him while her hips jerked up to meet his, her legs shaking uncontrollably as though she'd been struck by lightning; and together they fell from a great height down into an unprecedented pleasure.

In the calm that followed the crash, Ally closed her eyes and listened for the sound of her boyfriend's breathing, raw and ragged above the vibrator's steady buzz. With an unsteady hand, she switched the toy off. Ted slumped, falling on his good side, to the bed beside her.

Together, they'd drawn down the very stars from the sky to twinkle against the shut lids of her eyes.

A couple minutes later, Ted huffed a laugh. "I don't know if I can do that every time."

Ally opened her eyes, feeling dazed and confused. "What do you mean?"

"It's just that, orgasms like that... The recovery lasts longer than the sex itself." He turned his head to smile blearily at her. "We both finished in what—three minutes? I hardly had time to think."

Ally laughed. "It's sex, Ted. You don't have to think." Then she feigned a thoughtful face. "But I know what you mean. Still, I'd have thought a D1 athlete would have had a bit more stamina."

Ted nipped at her earlobe. "I'm surprised someone who only ever played club was able to keep up."

"I only came because you did!" Ally started to sit up, prepared to protest her own performance.

"Bullshit, baby." Ted grinned up at her. "I just drive you crazy."

Ally clambered over him, careful not to nudge his bad shoulder. Her loose waves fell like a curtain, framing his handsome face. "That, Harvard, has always been—and will always be—true."

CHAPTER 23
STARLIGHT

TED COOKED dinner with Ally's help, and they ate it in front of *Bringing Up Baby*, which Ted didn't mind rewatching so soon because Ally was in the mood.

He'd do anything for her, he'd realized, whether that meant ceding control of the remote (they had similar taste), bringing toys into the bedroom (awesome, not a problem), or learning to live with her faint snore (she'd never admit it, but he'd heard it). He loved her. So he'd adapt to her. He already had, during those weeks they'd dated without the luxury of labels.

The one thing he wouldn't put up with, however, was Ally putting herself down. Which was why, at the end of *Baby*, when she turned to him with wide eyes and asked him in a voice so small it hurt Ted to hear it, "Why do you love me?" He swiftly stepped in.

"I mean, I can understand why Grant's character falls in love with Hepburn's. She's charming, if chaotic. But me? I'm messy, I'm rude, I'm irritable—and if my earlier question is any evidence, I'm clearly insecure. I can't cook for shit and I drink too much. I eat grapefruit, even though my psychiatrist tells me not to. I never make my bed, as you've already learned. I—"

But Ted refused to listen to this litany of self-deprecation any longer. "You're uncompromising. You've got more integrity in your pinky than most people have in their whole bodies. You call it like you see it, even when no one else will. You've been hurt before, badly, and yet you're still willing to take a chance on me. On us.

"You're smart, funny, strong. You're creative and feisty and fierce. You're a warrior. You keep me on my toes, on and off the ice. You know about art and literature, and you're an excellent copywriter—ask any of our coworkers. And you love your family. *And* you're sweet to my sister."

Her stare had softened, but Ted kept on. He'd keep on until she was so thoroughly convinced, she never doubted herself or her place in his heart again. "You make me smile, Allegra, and most of all you make me want to work hard to make you smile. Because I love you. And you're worth hard work."

She smiled at him then, shyly at first but then beaming so brightly, it was like she had gathered all the sun's rays in one expression. "I love you, too, Harvard."

He rolled his eyes. "You have got to stop making fun of me for that, I can't help that I got in and you didn't!"

She swatted at him playfully, then stuck her nose in the air. "I'll have you know, I didn't even apply—"

He bundled her into his arms, at least as well as the sling would permit. "I don't give a shit." And then he kissed her so thoroughly, she seemed to forget all about their one-sided rivalry.

"I'm not staying overnight again tonight," Ally warned Ted, as she swept the sleep from her eyes.

Ted nodded and rolled over onto his good shoulder in his

king-sized bed to press a kiss to her forehead. "I have no intention of bullying you into submission, baby."

She glanced up at him, one arm snaking around his neck, her smile coy. "Keep calling me 'baby' and you won't have to bully me. I'll be all too ready to comply…"

Ted's eyebrows shot up. He hadn't taken Ally for someone who would be into D/s dynamics. Certainly, she'd never expressed any interest. Had he?

"Relax, Teddy-bear." She grinned lazily. "I'm teasing. Although…"

Although, indeed…

Ted cleared his throat and made to extricate himself from her embrace. "Let's table that, for another time. I *need* to hit the shower."

Ally refused to relinquish him quite yet. "Mmm, take me with you?" When he paused, deliberating, she continued, "I've been in your shower. It's big enough for two. Three, if we were feeling frisky…"

Ted shook his head resolutely. "You're the only girl for me."

"Woman, please." But her words were a throwback, a tease. "Come on, I'll even let you blast me with cold water, once we've washed all relevant body parts."

"It closes the pores! Besides, how did you know I—"

She smirked. "You have a little sister, one to whom you actually listen. An icy rinse is a really common part of a young woman's skin-care routine. *Teen Vogue* was all over it, a couple years ago."

Ted frowned as he pushed himself out of bed. "I wasn't aware Belle read *Vogue*."

"Teen *Vogue*. And they're actually quite progressive, politically. Possibly some of the best journalism out there for young feminists." She tumbled out of bed. "Race you to the bathroom?"

"You are not allowed to slip on the hardwood. Another ER visit is the last thing we need!"

Ally sobered briefly, nodding. Then a smile snuck back into her expression, lighting up her face with mischief. "Alright, alright. But we both know I'd beat you."

Ted sighed, but his answer wasn't the least bit indulgent. It was honest. "On and off the ice. Hey, ignore the non-sequitur, but have you checked out SpareRoom yet?"

Ally paused in the doorway, mid-shimmy out of his t-shirt. Ted swallowed, his gaze immediately flicking to the taut curve of the underside of her breasts. The skin there was soft and pale, unseen by the sun...

"Eyes up here, you lech." Ally grinned. "And no, I haven't had time to check, what with all the wild sex." She pulled the t-shirt up and over her head, then tossed it on the bed.

Standing naked on the threshold, illuminated by the morning light like some kind of late goddess or early saint, she let him look at her for a long moment. Then she broke the ethereal spell with a mundane question, "Do you think I'll find something on there? Vanessa also mentioned it."

Ted swallowed, shaking his head to clear it of all the things he wanted to do—to her, with her, for her. "I, uh, I've heard good things. Sam was saying that it's a lot of people who are stuck in a lease, so often the listings are for only a few months."

"So, theoretically, I could get my feet back under me, living-situation-wise, and give this—our new and improved relation-ship—a go for a few months, and then, assuming everything's just fine and dandy, move in with you once my sublease is up?"

Ted nodded, not quite put-together enough to speak.

Ally put her hands on her hips, cocking her head. "It does sound... ideal. I'll look into it today at work. When I've finished that fucking email blast that's had Harold up my ass."

He snorted. "I didn't realize you were into that, either."

She smiled, elusively. "You'll just have to wait and see..." Her eyes met his, smoldering and full of erotic promise. Ted was tempted to drag her back to bed, GreenLight be damned.

But they were on a schedule, and the next alarm would go off while they were still showering, which meant the *next* alarm would go off before they'd finished breakfast, and then in turn the *next* alarm would ring before they'd gotten dressed—even with Ted's twenty minute allowance for clothing, knowing Ally there would be yet more tomfoolery—more delays, which he couldn't begin to begrudge but still, by habit, was bound to at least *try* to mitigate.

Forty minutes, one sensual shower, two green smoothies and a plate of eggs, and several outfits later, they stood in the foyer, admiring the chandelier.

"Is it a replica?" Ally inquired, a question which he suspected she'd been wanting to ask for a while now.

Ted nodded. "My aunt loved the opera, and every time she went she wanted to take a piece of the Lincoln Center home with her. Something more substantial, more sturdy than a program."

Ally frowned. "It doesn't look sturdy," she said, gesturing to the elegant explosion of gold spikes and clear crystals.

"It survived more than one fall, when first installed, with only cosmetic repairs." He took a deep breath. "It... it reminds me of you."

Ally spun around to face him, her eyes wide. "What?"

"It's intimidating. All sharp edges and cut crystal. But breathtakingly beautiful—elemental, even—like a star bursting into light."

"I remind you of a dying star?" Her tone was dry, but a suppressed smile twisted the line of her lips.

Ted huffed a laugh. "It sounded more romantic in my head. Something about beauty, and power—the power you have over me, I mean—and obstinance, of course." He smirked. "Like your hair that night at the hospital, you're positively unruly."

She swatted his good shoulder. "Hey! I was distraught!"

He caught her wrist and pulled her in for a slow, thoroughly possessive kiss. And when it was, lamentably, finished, he murmured against her lush lips, "You were brilliant. You always are."

Ally sighed contentedly, nudging his nose playfully. "You know, we don't *have* to go to work."

Ted barked a laugh. "If I miss any more time, I'll be fine. I can extend my medical leave. You, on the other hand, my delinquent darling... Harold's got his evil eye on you."

Ally grumbled something unintelligible.

"Besides, it's about time we told HR. Especially considering the fact that I'm technically your superior..."

Ally's jaw dropped. "In your dreams, Harvard. We work in different departments!"

Ignoring her second point, which may or may not have been valid, he bent to nuzzle said jaw. "Mmm, in my dreams indeed."

A week and several late nights later, Ally's apartment was packed into moving boxes. Just in time, too, as her landlord was evicting her in the morning. Luckily, she'd found a three-month listing on SpareRoom, a two bedroom in the Village with a person who didn't *seem* like a serial killer. Actually, they appeared to be quite nice. They'd offered to help her move tomorrow. Which was good because Vanessa was in New Jersey visiting her folks and Ted was still recovering from his shoulder dislocation—Ally wasn't about to let him risk a repeat.

"I couldn't have done this without you, Ted." She cupped his chiseled jaw—now peppered with dark stubble. He hadn't shaved that morning as he'd stayed the night and Ally's apartment was devoid of razors. That was another nice thing about Ted, she realized; he didn't mind her leg hair. No, he loved her just as she was. "Thank you."

Ted bent his head, brushing his lips once, twice, across hers. "Anything for you. Besides," he said, perking up as he pulled back, "packing up your apartment has taught me so much about you."

Ally started to roll her eyes.

"Who knew, for example, that you don't possess a splatter guard? That you have three copies of *The Tenant of Wildfell Hall*, one of them bound with duct-tape? That half of your underwear is decorated with mythical creatures—actually, scratch that, how could I *forget* after that first, memorable night, with the unicorns…"

Ally found herself giggling. "Ted, can we *please* not talk about my underwear? I told you, I bought it on sale!"

"And who am I to begrudge you a good bargain? And an even better array of patterns?" He grinned.

Ally shook her head, failing to smother a wide smile. "You are impossible, Theodore Lewis."

"Mmm, but not as impossible as you, Allegra Bryant."

Ally stuck up her nose—primly, but also so as to be in the best position to receive a kiss. "And yet you love me, despite my impossible-ness."

He fulfilled her unspoken wish, capturing her mouth with his. Then he growled, low in his throat, "I love you *for* it." And continued the kiss.

Heathcliff wound his way around and between Ally's legs, which were wobbly under the weight of her arousal and almost gave way. Ted's good hand quickly snaked around her waist, steadying her. And not just physically, either. In his arms—even just the one—she felt secure. Like no harm could come to her. Or at least, no lasting harm. Nothing she couldn't handle, with Ted by her side.

This was love. It was simple, even when it wasn't. It was always—and would always be—enough.

Always. That was a word Ally once would have balked at using, at even thinking. But tonight, in her boyfriend's still-limited-by-injury embrace, she didn't mind thinking it. She didn't mind using it.

Ally broke the kiss, but did not pull away. "I love you, Ted," she whispered. And then she added, because she could, because she forever would, "Always."

HAPPILY EVER AFTER

THREE MONTHS LATER, the Manhattan Monsters found themselves short another player, despite Ted's having returned to the ice (to much fanfare). Wren had a stomach bug —something she'd caught at work, no doubt, managing a bar downtown. Kait happened to be in town, so Ally suggested a substitution. Their opponents, a co-ed club from way out in Westchester, reluctantly agreed to the swap on the condition that the Monsters paid for the post-game beers.

After the first period, Ally skated over to Kait, who had long-since lost her initial skeptical look. She seemed excited, enlivened by the play. Her cheeks were an adorable pink, flushed with exertion and energy. "Got your fill yet?" Ally teased.

Kait answered breathlessly, even though she wasn't the one who had just played a three minute shift. "No... Never." She seemed surprised by the enthusiasm of her own answer.

"You ain't seen nothing yet," Ally warned, laughing. "Our star center is home sick today. She's a real firecracker."

"Is she going to be okay?" Kait's concern was genuine, as was her anxiety. "You know I can't stay..." Kait was considering moving to New York, once she'd finalized her divorce, but this trip was supposed to be short and sweet.

Ally nodded. "Just a stomach bug. I'll tell her you were asking after her, though."

Kait blushed. "Please don't."

"I'm only kidding!" Ally frowned thoughtfully. "Although, you are her type…"

Ted, who had been chatting with the refs about god knew what, skated over. "What are we talking about?"

"Nothing!"

Kait glared at Ally, who grinned.

"What were you talking to the refs about?"

"My girlfriend's pugilistic tendencies," he replied with a smirk. "Ally, baby, just because our captain isn't here to rein you in doesn't mean I won't."

Ally barked a laugh. "I'd like to see you try."

"My roof, my rules." He was referring to the fact that earlier that morning, with Kait's help, and Albert's assistance, Ally had moved eighty blocks uptown. She'd enjoyed her time in the Village with the roommate she'd found on Spare-Room, but that lease was up and, besides, she was ready—ready for the next chapter of her life to begin.

Ally's gloved hands found her padded hips. "I'd like to see you try to enforce that, Teddy-bear."

"Trouble in paradise already?" Madison had skated over to join them. "Poor Kait, forced to listen to you two squabble." She turned to Kait, whom she'd met that day. "You're welcome to crash on my futon," she offered the other woman, "if Ted's guest bedroom isn't far enough away from their fighting. Although, I suppose, it's better when they're fighting."

Kait cocked her head to one side, her eyes wide behind her borrowed helmet's grill. "What do you mean?"

Madison laughed. "They're annoying when they argue, to be sure, but when they get sappy and start quoting classic literature at each other?" She feigned gagging. "English majors, man."

"Hey, I studied art history!" Ted protested, but Madison was already gliding away.

Kait sighed, a bittersweet sound.

Ally's head whipped around. "You okay, Kait?"

"Yeah, I'm really happy for you. I just… I wish I had that, too."

Ted placed a large, gloved hand on Kait's shoulder. They'd become fast friends, in the months since Friendsgiving, to Ally's eternal delight. "You'll have it again, Kaitlin, I promise. We'll find you someone new."

Ally nodded. "Let's just finish this game—win it, naturally —then get wasted on Natty Light in the locker room. It'll be like college all over again."

"Or boarding school," Ted offered.

"Oh, shut up. There's no way they let you drink in the locker rooms at Essex." Ally rolled her eyes.

"Actually," Kait interjected, "There was a fair amount of illicit drug use in the locker rooms at St. Katherine's…"

Ally stared at her friend. "I forgot, you went to prep school, too. Jesus, what is the world coming to?"

Ted laughed, throwing his arm around Ally.

She leaned into him, then immediately regretted it. "Oh god. You *need* to get your gear cleaned. You smell like feet *and* floor."

Ted knocked helmets with Ally, gently. "Yeah, but you love me."

She sighed, gazing up at him. "Yeah, I do."

They stood like that, swaying slightly, for a long minute. Until the buzzer went off, reminding them that they still had a game to play. And Ally was determined not to rack up any penalties.

ACKNOWLEDGMENTS

Pride and the Penalty Box actually predates, in its earliest forms, my set of novellas, which I published first. But it needed a little more nurturing than they did.

My first draft was a fair bit shorter and went by a different name. On the advice of my editor, I lengthened it into a full novel. Not wanting to tempt a certain university to litigation, I changed its title. Of course, there's no pleasing everyone. And if I am to please anyone, I would like it be you, my lovely reader.

I owe many people a lot of thanks for their assistance in getting this novel off the proverbial bench and onto the ice. Some of them had no idea that they were helping me to write a novel, like my father, who used to get up at four in the morning on weekends to drive me to hockey tournaments in neighboring states; like my childhood teammates, who took me in despite my then being truly terrible at the sport; like my former coach, who pulled me aside one day after practice to work on my slapshot until it was, well, formidable. Until *I* was formidable. If he hadn't believed in me, I would not have believed in myself. If he hadn't shown me how to love hockey, I would never have loved it so dearly myself.

Some of those who lended their kindness and expertise to this novel's creation *did* know what they were getting themselves into. *Pride and the Penalty Box* benefitted greatly from the intellectual contributions of my brother, who picked up the phone whenever I called to ask about drills or plays (or, inexplicably, quantum physics); of my friend Paul, who shared their vast medical knowledge with me and my long-suffering characters; and of Peter and Conor, who sussed out Syosset for me one exhilarating afternoon on the Heineken Terrace.

If I have a team now, one of its key players is surely my editor, Jen. She never fails to be brilliant, and this book needed her especially. Another teammate is Grace, my copy-editor, who keeps me from committing *egregious* comma crimes and is honest with me about when my characters are acting like serial killers. I'd also like to thank Lara, my illustrator, who created this book's beautiful cover.

Finally, I'd like to ask my analyst to take a bow. Our work together continues to make all the difference.

ABOUT THE AUTHOR

Phebe Powers cut her teeth on lithium carbonate tablets and historical romance novels. An avid romance reader as well as a firm believer in Happily Ever Afters, she's happiest when tucked away in the basement stacks of her local library, writing her own book or reading someone else's.

ALSO BY PHEBE POWERS

If you enjoyed *Pride and the Penalty Box*, check out Phebe's other books:

Après-Ski: A Romance Novella is a whirlwind winter romance in which a romance novelist falls madly in love with her ski instructor. If you like love at first sight, hot chocolate, and men with mustaches, you'll love *Après-Ski*. Read on for an excerpt.

The Best Crew: A Romance Novella is a summer fling-to-forever that's far from smooth-sailing, as a grumpy skipper tries and fails not to fall in love with her sunshine-y crew. If you like lobster and champagne and small islands in Maine, you'll love *The Best Crew*.

APRÈS-SKI: A ROMANCE NOVELLA: CHAPTER ONE

"Seventeen bucks for a sandwich?" Estie stared at the sticker in disbelief.

"This *is* an airport," her younger brother pointed out, unhelpfully. "Didn't you get Mom's text last night?"

"Which text? There were rather more than several."

"The one where she told everyone in the family group chat to bring something to eat."

Estie eyed him skeptically. "Don't tell me *you* packed a meal."

Freddy shrugged. "No, but Ben made me breakfast before we left his apartment."

"At five in the morning?" She was impressed. Why didn't she have a boyfriend like that? Probably because she bolted at the first sign of commitment, typically.

Her brother smiled smugly, reading her mind. "Get your own soulmate. Or find a job that actually pays." As Estie struggled, due to the early hour and her lack of sleep, to come up with a suitably snarky response, Freddy picked out a bag of chips, two waters, and some spearmint gum. "See you at the gate!"

Estie sighed as her brother walked away. She loved writing, she really did. But... it was hard. Self-publishing took a lot of time and effort, the actual drafting and editing of her romance novels aside. And, as her brother had so kindly pointed out, it didn't quite pay the bills. Not fully. Thank god her parents were willing and able to cover a large part of the rent on her studio. Admittedly, the little apartment was a luxury, but she needed to be alone to write. Estie had tried and failed to have both a career and roommates. Then again, maybe she just had yet to find the right person to live with. Someone who'd inspire her to add to her backlist, not stall her creative process.

"Estie!"

She whipped her head around. "Oh! Hey, Miles." Her older sister's fiancé approached, wallet in hand. "Did you and Flo forget to eat breakfast, too?"

He shook his head. "Nah, but you know how she gets if she doesn't have two cups of coffee, and we only had time for one because the taxi arrived early."

"And they couldn't wait?"

"We were lucky to get a car at all. And I wouldn't put the love of my life through an early morning ride on the Red Line." Miles laughed, ever upbeat. "Anyway, do you want me to get that for you?"

Estie shook her head rapidly. "No, no. I mean, thank you. But no. I can afford a sandwich." A brazen lie, given the sandwich in question's price, but she had her pride.

"Fair enough." Miles knew better than to argue with her, especially at an early hour. "Besides, you'll be buying all of us sandwiches, when your next book becomes a bestseller!"

Oh, Miles. He really was sweet. "Sure thing." She smiled at him blearily. Maybe she needed a coffee, too... What time even was it? Estie checked her phone. A few minutes before eight, which meant it was almost time for her to take her meds. "Actually, Miles?"

He turned back to her. "Yeah?"

"Could you get me a coffee, too? Just a bit of milk, no sugar."

Miles nodded. "Whole or skim?"

"Whole." Estie believed in living fully, and that meant not settling for white water that called itself milk. "Thanks, M!"

"No worries." He smiled again, an absolute golden retriever of a man. "I'll bring it to the gate."

Estie grabbed the sandwich, budget be damned, and made her way to the self-checkout. There, she impulse-bought some dark chocolate, too. She'd save the sandwich for the plane—her thyroid medication required an empty stomach, she reasoned—but she could munch on the chocolate bar while waiting to board.

After a brisk walk back to the gate, Estie was greeted by her entire family, minus Miles: her mother, anxiously checking the delicate wristwatch that had once belonged to Estie's grandmother; her father, belatedly engrossed in Estie's second-to-most-recent release; her sister, snoring softly in her seat; and her brother and his boyfriend, who were engaged in a very public display of affection.

Estie felt nauseated—and lonely, as per usual. She averted her eyes, a touch dramatically. "Freddy, can you stop tonguing your boyfriend's tonsils for five seconds and move your bag off that otherwise open chair?"

Her brother disentangled himself from Ben in order to glare at her. "Find your own seat."

"There's nowhere else to sit!" She gestured around the waiting area. "They're all taken."

Grumbling, Freddy moved his bag. "Fine, but you're ruining the mood."

"I'm not sure there can be much of a 'mood' given that we're in an airport and it's eight in the morning."

Ben laughed. "Estie, you write romance novels. Surely you know that airports as a setting are romantic to the point of being a cliché?"

"Only if you're running through them, Ben."

"Whatever, Estie." Freddy rolled his eyes. "Consider any and all moods ruined by you, regardless."

Estie sighed. "Blame it on my *mood* disorder." Ben shifted uncomfortably, but Freddy was unfazed. He opened his mouth to argue, but Estie held up a staying hand as she slumped into the newly vacated seat. She was too tired to hear or herself summon a smart rejoinder. Where was Miles with her coffee?

"I'm going to try and get some writing done," she announced to everyone and no one. Then she pulled her laptop from its pink, padded sleeve. Prying it apart, she found that her word processor was already open, the waiting document as menacing as Moby Dick himself in its wordless whiteness.

When it came to writing, and life, too, Estie was a pantser, through and through. But for whatever reason, in the past month, the requisite words had refused to come. She was increasingly concerned—to the extent that she'd even considered going against the grain, throwing her lack of caution to the wind, and plotting out her next novel in advance of actually writing it. Like some kind of organized, methodical, sane writer. But the only two things Estie planned meticulously were falling in love and refilling her medications—which was why, her older sister had commented, a little unkindly, she did the latter monthly and the former never.

Estie sighed and started to type, trying to wrangle her muse as well as her mood. Method wasn't the reason for her block, but a lack of inspiration. And somehow she doubted she'd find any on this family ski holiday—the first in a decade, and her recently retired parents' treat... No, for her the slopes held only terror, and not romance.

While her siblings had significant experience on mountains all across America, as well as in Canada and even (in her sister's case) the French Alps, Estie hadn't skied since she was a kid. And that had been… an experience. Not only was she undoubtedly terrible now, at twenty-five she was old enough and wise enough to be terrified.

Still, Flo had promised Estie that she'd have fun in Blue Sky, the mountain town in Montana that lent its name to the nearby ski resort, that she would find things to do if skiing didn't work out, that she wouldn't be lonely or bored—even though her whole family would be abandoning her to the mild humiliation of ski school while they shot the chutes and dared the triple black diamonds. Freddy had been raving about something called the Big Couloir, only accessible by the very exclusive (and apparently expensive) tram. Estie thought it sounded dangerous, and that anyone who went up there willingly was deranged. Her siblings included.

But, Estie had for some godforsaken reason promised her family that she would at least try. And trying meant enrolling in the aforementioned ski school. For a day. After that, she'd stay home at the house they were renting and, keyboard in hand, continue to plead her case with the mercurial inhabitants of her mind's Mount Parnassus.

"Flight 362 to Boseman is now boarding at Gate 18."

Estie perked up, even as her sister jerked awake.

"Are we boarding? Where's Miles? We can't forget him again—"

Chuckling, Miles appeared at his fiancée's side, balancing three cups of coffee between his triangulated fingers. "Relax, sweetheart. I'm here. But I'm afraid we all might have to chug."

Estie took her coffee gratefully even as her sister tore the lid off her own cup and muttered, "Sophomore year trained me for this…"

❄

"Alright, team. One more trip up the Magic Carpet, then I want to see your best pizza turns all the way down. Sound good?"

A chorus of small children cheered their approval. James had lucked out today—the kids were enthusiastic and quick learners, all of them. There had only been one tearful incident, and he'd quickly remedied that with a promise of hot chocolate and a sing-along when the day was done.

James didn't usually teach kids; he preferred working with adults. But his supervisor had given him a choice between work and no work, and he couldn't afford to take more than one day off a week, what with the pittance the resort paid him. Private lessons were the only real way to make a living on the slopes, and unfortunately James had yet to build up a substantial client list. Unlike his roommate, Drew, who had a list of thirty or so clients so loyal that they'd followed him north when he left Vail for Blue Sky.

Still, James managed to make ends meet, supplementing his instructor's income with the occasional gig at one of the two bars in town. The locals might get tired of his Randy Travis covers, but the out-of-towners loved a late night rendition of "Deeper Than The Holler," and they tipped fairly well, once they'd had a few.

"Mr. James?" Kayla—who had informed him, immediately upon their introduction, that her seventh birthday was next week—tugged on the sleeve of his blue regulation ski jacket.

"Yes, Kayla?"

She gestured to her boot, which had somehow come free of its trappings. "My ski popped off."

"Do you remember how to put it back on?" James held her mittened hand so she wouldn't fall over as she balanced on one ski. There was nothing so detrimental to a student's confidence, or sense of safety, as a bad fall. Luckily, kids were pretty good at bouncing back. Better, in fact, than adults, who felt the humiliation more keenly with their grown up sensibility. It also helped that kids were shorter, which meant closer to the ground, so when they hit it, it didn't hurt so much. "Toe in first, yep, just like that. And then the heel. Stomp on it, like you're trying to kill a spider."

Kayla did as she was told, but when her boot had clicked back into place, her ski sliding a little against the packed snow, she looked up at James with eyes that were wide behind her pink-tinted goggles. "But spiders are good bugs. I don't wanna kill any spiders."

James considered this. "You're right, Kayla. I'll find a new analogy." Her nose wrinkled in clear confusion, an expression he recognized from having grown up babysitting his little cousins in Vermont; James realized he'd forgotten to adjust his vocabulary to better suit a seven year old. If she was still curious, he'd explain later. "Now, how about we join the rest of the group up on top of the slope?"

They were skiing within the confines of the designated teaching area, accessible to students and instructors only. There wasn't much to it, other than a small half-pipe where the students who were new to skis practiced the basics, and a short, not very steep slope called Lazy River. The teaching area also boasted the so-called Magic Carpet, which was really just a conveyor belt that carried skiers young and old up the miniature slope. There was another, bigger conveyor outside of the teaching area that led part of the way up a green, but James' students weren't ready for wide open spaces—or heavily trafficked areas—just yet.

Kayla inched onto the Magic Carpet, which was already whisking her peers up the hill, keeping her knees bent like they'd practiced. A few seconds later, it was James' turn. He squinted up the slope, counting helmets to make sure he hadn't forgotten a student, then shuffled onto the conveyor belt himself when he was satisfied that no child had been left behind.

At the top, the kids had spread out, hiking sideways across the ledge at the top of Lazy River. "Everybody ready?" James called out, throwing his voice so the kids could hear him above the whistling wind. They all nodded, some more dubiously than others, but generally they were a pretty fearless group. "Mike, why don't you show us how it's done? I want to see three wide turns and a nice slow stop at the bottom. No collisions."

An eight year old at the far end of the ledge saluted him. "Yes, sir!"

James saluted him right back. He'd be lying if he said he didn't enjoy the kids' respect, and how seriously they took this—unlike most people, including the majority of his family back east, who saw his seasonal gigs as well as his songwriting and singing as a couple of childhood hobbies that he'd wasted himself on, rather than budding careers to which he'd devoted the whole of his adult life. But who cared what they thought? They were estranged, after all, with the majority of them having cut him out after he'd taken his mother's side in her divorce. James sighed. Then he forced himself to do a little meditative breathing as he put the thought of his extended family aside and returned to admiring his students' gravity.

Maybe he was rubbing off on them, after three hours of acquaintance. Drew, in amused agreement with pretty much all of the other instructors, did sometimes say James took himself and his job too seriously. But James wasn't a slacker, and skiing *was* serious business. It was dangerous, first of all, at every level. Second, and this was probably why he volunteered to teach Level One, bad habits were ingrained early. It was James' job to nip all that in the bud, and in its place to promote precision, proper techniques, and good practices—all leading to clean, crisp skiing. Safety first, and the skills would follow.

Mike took off, slowly at first, then picking up a bit of

speed. He was one of the best in the group, although he tended towards hairpin turns. James monitored his wedge—the shape his skis made, their tips turned together—which was stable, and kept an eye on his tails—the back ends of his skis—as he finished his final turn, coming to a slow stop at the bottom of the slope, near the line for the conveyor. Mike's final turn had been a bit fast, and he'd yanked his upper leg into position, rather than shifting his weight and letting his edges guide him through a slower turn, but there was no use in yelling this information down the slope, only to have the wind whisk it away. So, James mentioned it to the rest of the kids and made a mental note to talk to Mike about it later.

One by one, the rest of James' students made their way down the slope under his close supervision, only one of them careening out of control—and, even then, Alexis managed to recover her balance before falling. Just when James thought she'd end up running into the mesh fencing that closed off the training area, she jerked her skis together and sideways at the same time, stopping so suddenly she looked a bit wobbly. James sped down the slope toward her. When he stopped, using the same maneuver she'd performed, albeit more expertly, his long skis sprayed her short legs with snow.

"Sorry about that," he said, gesturing to the white powder that was now spread across her shins. And then, more gently, "Are you alright?"

She nodded, looking a bit pale. "What was that?"

"What you just did? That's called a hockey stop. It's pretty advanced stuff. You don't play ice hockey, by any chance, do you?"

Alexis nodded again, understanding dawning. "A little, with my big sister on the pond in our backyard."

As he'd suspected. "That means you acted on instinct. Hockey stops are important because they can help prevent collisions, but they can also be scary because they happen really fast."

"I'm not scared!" She protested, straightening in her blue and green onesie.

James nodded gravely. "I'm glad to hear it. And I'm proud of you, you handled that really well." She beamed. "Now, shall we all ski over to the lodge?" The other kids had gathered in a cluster by the fence. "If we take it slow, avoid other skiers, and remember to stay in pizza mode, we won't have to worry about hockey stops." When working with kids, the instructors tended to use food-inspired terminology. Pizza was the name for the wedge shape beginners made with their tips, which helped them control their speed. French fries meant the more advanced, parallel skiing.

"If I stay in pizza can I have hot chocolate?"

James nodded solemnly at Sarah. "Of course." He always kept his promises.

An hour later, James sat in the instructors' lounge, which was really just a fancy name for the basement of the same building that housed daycare and the ski school office. The kids had all been picked up by their parents, some of whom remembered to tip, after a long round of Disney sing-alongs and a pitcher full of instant hot chocolate made with water—because the resort wouldn't spring for milk.

"Hey, man." Drew shuffled in, his gait smooth despite his clunky boots. "You done for the day?"

"No, I've got another round with the kids this afternoon. How was Sergio?" Sergio was one of Drew's private clients, one of the many who'd followed him from Vail.

"Good! We went up the tram—the line was long but, man, the triple blacks were worth the wait." Only the most advanced skiers took the tram up to the top of the mountain, in pursuit of the triple black diamond trails and rocky chutes, as well as access to the Big Couloir.

"Was there enough snow?" Sometimes the resort had to close off access to the trickier trails, whose ski-ability depended on how much snow there was and the temperature at the top, as well as visibility. They generally wanted to avoid any rise in mortality rates, although the near-death nature of the experience didn't exactly deter the more fanatical thrill-seekers—quite the opposite. Adrenaline junkies, all of them. James understood that high, and the accompanying cravings, but he didn't seek it anymore. Not after his adolescence.

"Yeah, Thursday's storm replenished the snowpack. But I've been looking at the forecast and I'm not sure they won't have to close off some of the chutes, come midweek. It's going to be a scorcher. And you know what that means." Less snow, more rocks, ice in the morning and slush in the afternoon—typical spring skiing, made worse by climate change.

James frowned. "Still, spring break isn't over. The hordes continue to descend." He sighed. For a while there, after the winter holidays, there had been a lull in visitors to Blue Sky Resort. Weekends had remained busy, but the weeks themselves were fairly empty, leaving him plenty of time to write music and relax. The past couple of weeks, however, had seen the tranquil resort transformed into a zoo. It would be like this for the next few weeks, too. Until the end of the season, really, which was in April.

Spring break was the bane of James' existence as a ski instructor. It was worse than the winter holidays, in terms of visitors. Mostly because over Christmas and New Year's families found their way to the mountain, whereas spring break summoned not only families but packs of screaming college students who were more interested in the après, the after party, than in doing any actual skiing. They showed up in their "retro" onesies—garish recreations of '80s snow bunny styles—with their borrowed lift passes like fake IDs, not bothering with helmets and wearing ill-fitting rental skis. Little did they know, the Blue Sky après situation was mediocre at best, dire compared to exotic Courchevel or even the more local Jackson Hole.

James tried not to let his disdain for spring breakers get out of hand, but it was really frustrating when he was trying to take a group of beginners down a green only to find it clogged up by tipsy twenty-somethings. Personally, James didn't drink. He didn't do drugs at all, including caffeine— with the exception of a pot of perfectly brewed green tea, twice a day. Speaking of which…

"I'm making some tea, do you want any?"

Drew grimaced. "Not if it's that genmaicha stuff. Tastes like pond-water."

"To each his own." James bent to unbuckle his boots.

Drew sat and followed suit. "How were the kids?"

"Good, I had a good group." James eased one foot out of the tight fit, then the other, flexing his freed toes.

"You're back to adults tomorrow, right?"

James nodded, his mouth twisting into a line.

"You don't look too happy about it," Drew observed, taking in James' expression. "I thought you preferred working with adults."

"I do. I just worry."

"About?" Drew groaned as he got his left foot free, rolling out his ankle a few times.

"It's spring break. No one's going to take it seriously."

Drew laughed. "Dude, you've gotta lighten up. They pay you either way, so have some fun! You never know what's to come. Or who." He winked, and James rolled his eyes. Drew was convinced that James' latest dry spell was soon to end. James, on the other hand, had resigned himself to a lifetime of loneliness. At least, he thought, standing up, he had his music. And his tea.